WHERE THE LIGHT SHINES THROUGH

WHERE THE LIGHT SHINES THROUGH

An Olivia Penn Mystery

KATHLEEN BAILEY

First hardcover edition: November 2021
First paperback edition: November 2021

ISBN (hardcover): 978-1-956270-02-0
ISBN (paperback): 978-1-956270-01-3
ISBN (e-book): 978-1-956270-00-6
ISBN (audio): 978-1-956270-03-7

Editing by Serena Clarke at Free Bird Editing
Proofreading by LaVerne Clark at LaVerne Clark Editing
Cover design by Robin Vuchnich at My Custom Book Cover

Published by:
Rhino Publishing LLC
P.O. Box 295
Fairfax, VA 22038-0295

www.kathleenbaileyauthor.com

For my Dad

The poet lights the light and fades away.
But the light goes on and on.

— EMILY DICKINSON

CHAPTER 1

Olivia Penn drove past Hamilton & Sons General Store, counting down the final fifteen minutes to her hometown of Apple Station for a last visit with her father before her move to New York the following week. She had delayed leaving her condo in Georgetown until after the Monday morning commuter rush, ensuring her escape from the city progressed unimpeded by slowdowns, breakdowns, or shutdowns. The remaining scenic stretch of the two-and-a-half-hour trip west to her hometown carved a serpentine trail through Virginia's horse country. The late May midmorning sun lit the spring sky and spread shadows across the rural road, mirroring the railed fence posts stretched along both shoulders of the undulating lanes.

She glanced at her workbag on the passenger seat of her Expedition. Two papers lay on top. Yesterday she had printed the e-mail her editor had sent her with the curated questions from her readers for her syndicated "Penn's Pals" advice column. Her phone chimed, signaling the top of the hour. The tolling of the West-minster Quarters warned her deadline loomed, and she was behind schedule.

Olivia smiled at the signature "Delighted Daddy" accompanying the first e-mail on the top sheet. Ever since she created her column for a mid-Atlantic publisher of local presses, her father had sent in a weekly question, asserting he was simply doing his part to ensure she would never lack a following. Even after one of the largest media companies in Washington, D.C. had admired her skill and lured her from the regional market, offering national syndication if she swapped her small town for city living, her father wrote without fail. Every year, around his birthday, she would answer his question in her Sunday edition, much to his amusement.

"Delighted Daddy" had asked this week about the etiquette of converting his daughter's childhood bedroom into a gym now that she planned to move far away for good. She grinned, sweeping her hair behind her ears. "Gym, really, Dad?" Her efforts through the years at encouraging him to exercise, in any form, at any level, had been as successful as nailing Jell-O to a tree. To outwit his obstinacy, she schemed, resorting to the tried-and-true strategy adopted by adult children who, like her, were at a loss for what else to do: she bought him a dog to walk. Buddy, a beagle puppy, was twelve weeks old when she bundled him in a baby-blue blanket and wicker basket, bringing him home on a surprise weekend visit this past December. Within two months, her father had countered the Trojan horse by training Buddy to open the refrigerator, fetch the paper, and retrieve the remote control.

Her visit this week was the last scheduled until at least October. Her promotion to the corporate office promised to extend her column's reach through wider distribution, and her editor in Washington had confirmed whispers from New York colleagues that her novel had received a favorable reception by a major publishing house. Though the relocation would take her farther from family, she had accepted the position, believing she soon would be engaged to Daniel after they celebrated their two-year anniversary in December. Now that their plans for a shared future were no more, she doubted her decision. In going alone, she had no close connections in the city.

Her phone buzzed and rattled in the dash console cubby, and she pulled over onto the shoulder of the road and stopped. She stretched forward, grabbing the cell and swiping the screen to read the text: "Column?" She started a reply and then backspaced, deleting all she had written. A tractor trailer zoomed by, recklessly surpassing the speed limit on the two-lane country road. She looked up and stared through the windshield, estimating how long it would take her to finish her copy. Twenty yards ahead, a raccoon staggered from the side of the road into the left lane. It paused for a moment and then walked in circles. *Rabies.*

The theme from *The Great British Baking Show* played, and she glanced at the screen, tapped the speaker icon, and answered the call from her boss. "Angela, I was going to call you when I got settled."

"Did you get my text? I need your copy by two. How long are you staying? Don't forget the online Q&A on Thursday, and what about the conference call with New York on Friday?"

"I'm here through Sunday. I blocked the meeting time on my calendar. And the Q&A … you realize I'm technically on a vacation. You know these live online chats are not my forte. Remind me again why you insist we do them."

"Because your readers want engagement. Every week the number of participants has gone up. Ms. Penn in the hot seat. Now that's entertainment."

Olivia sighed. "It's not entertaining for Ms. Penn."

"Come on, Olivia. It's only an hour. Speaking of good times, I'm texting you a picture from Jasper's birthday party last night."

Olivia's phone buzzed. "Jasper? Your cat?" She opened the message and enlarged the photo. A black cat sat on a sofa wearing a gold party hat and a matching bow tie.

"Fur baby, Olivia. I have a small gathering every year. I thought of inviting you as a twofer celebration for your send-off, but I figured you'd be busy packing."

"Good call on that. One hardly knows what to get kitties these days anyhow."

"You need a Jasper in your life, Olivia. New York winters can be long and lonely. Are you sure you won't take my sister's Siamese? She wants to find him a home before the baby arrives, and you could really use company in your new condo now that you're a single." She paused. "Sorry, too soon?"

Olivia set her cell on the passenger seat in front of her workbag. "Thanks again for the cat offer, but I'm good. Let me get back on the road. I'm about ten minutes from my dad's house, but I need to stop in town first. I'm almost done with the column. I have a couple more replies to do, and then I'll send you my copy. You e-mailed me over twenty questions, but you didn't mark any with an asterisk this week. I've been working under the assumption that it's my choice. Is that right?"

"Yes, but don't let the freedom go to your head," Angela said. "Any of them will do. Two o'clock. Don't make me hunt you down."

Olivia smiled. "You're the best. Bye, Angela."

They ended the call. After checking her mirrors for oncoming traffic, Olivia got back on the road. The sickly raccoon, though, had wandered into her lane. She slowed to a crawl, giving it time to stumble safely out of the way. But it sat instead, close to the side but not fully off the road. She stopped and glanced in her rearview mirror, seeing no one approaching from behind. A drainage ditch next to her lane's soft shoulder made that work-around a no-go.

The left lane was clear, though she was near the peak

of a blind hill. She reversed several feet and then maneuvered partially into the oncoming lane, peering over her hood to ensure the raccoon was safe from her tires. Frantic blaring from a vehicle's horn snapped her sight to a car that had crested the hill and now was aimed straight at her. She jammed on the brakes, clamping her eyes shut, and braced for impact.

She held her breath, waiting ... waiting ... waiting. All was quiet and still. She softened her shoulders and eased her grip on the wheel, peeking through narrowed eyes at a white Fiesta six feet from her bumper. She slowly exhaled, cut the engine, and freed the floored brake pedal. The subcompact's door sprung open, and a petite, irate driver with long ginger curls stormed between the slim separation. "What are you doing? Stay in your lane!"

Olivia flicked her hazard lights on and then opened the door. She turned in her seat, resting her feet on the running board until her knees steadied. "I'm so sorry. I didn't see—Cassandra?"

Her former schoolmate eyed her with swift recognition, colored by a complicated history. The sweet smell from a cluster of shaded, roadside Virginia bluebells drifted by as a vintage poppy-red pickup approached and moseyed around the stopped vehicles. The senior driver perched his bronzed forearm on the windowsill, inspecting for evidence of a crash. Apparently satisfied that all was well, without fatalities, he tipped his trucker hat and drove on toward town.

"Look who we have here," Cassandra said. "Dear Ms. Penn graces us with a visit. Do you realize you're on the wrong side of the road?"

Olivia posed with her politest customer service smile, summoning her best telephone tone. "Good to see you, Cassandra. Yes, I do. I'm really sorry. Completely my fault. A raccoon was in my lane." She looked in both directions for oncoming traffic and then walked cautiously around the front of her Expedition, seeing no sign of the sketchy critter.

"So, you come into my lane and almost cause an accident? Where did you learn to drive? Double yellow lines mean you can't cross. You'll fit right in, driving on the streets of New York."

Olivia turned back toward her. "Again, I apologize. We should get out of the road."

"If the book deal falls through, I suppose you could provide ridesharing or invest in a taxi medallion."

Olivia paused before countering. Cassandra's knowledge of both her relocation and potential publishing contract piqued her curiosity, but she had no desire to further pursue this while in the middle of the road. "This is dangerous to be stopped here. I'm sure you're busy, chasing down a story. I'll get out of your way."

Cassandra ripped her aviators off like a fighter pilot after a successful sortie. "You know, I'm the featured columnist for the paper now. I cover the council, crime, business—all of it. How's that thing you write for the lovelorn?"

Olivia bristled at the sucker punch that contorted her apology into confrontational fodder. Her attempt to assuage Cassandra's irritation quickly lost the influence of her cooler head. She checked up and down the road again. "We need to move our cars now. And I write whatever my readers ask about—what they need help with. What about you? Get much action on that crime beat around town?"

"Plenty." She hung her glasses on her collar. "What are you even doing here? Besides almost causing accidents, that is."

Olivia took a deep breath to compose herself and deescalate her tone. She slowly paced backward the few feet to her door, swiveling her head and looking for traffic. "I came home to visit my dad. We're planting our summer garden, and I'm sticking around for the festival on Saturday."

Cassandra shifted her weight, looking back and forth between the bumpers. "It's a fine end to May then. A celebrity and a celebration. I'll include a warning in Wednesday's edition for everyone to be on alert for meandering drivers roaming around town. Do us a favor, stay in your lane." She turned, walked to her car, and got back inside.

Olivia did likewise while checking the road in both directions. She fastened her seatbelt, pressed the push-button start, and turned her hazard lights off. As she steered back into her lane, Cassandra pulled alongside of her, stopped, and lowered her window. Olivia glanced in her rearview mirror and then pushed her window's automatic down switch.

"See ya around, Ms. Penn," Cassandra yelled across the road. "Thanks for dropping by."

She shook her head as Cassandra pulled away. A Bronco crested the hill and barreled down the oncoming lane, and she breathed a sigh of relief, grateful for her guardian angels. She checked the time display on the dashboard touchscreen and then continued along her way. She was about a mile from Apple Station, and she had planned a few quick stops in town before heading to her father's house. First up, Grossman's Construction. This day can only get better.

CHAPTER 2

Olivia cruised into the heart of Apple Station five minutes after her run-in with Cassandra and parallel parked several storefronts down from the entrance to Grossman's Construction. The town square looked much the same as when she moved away for college. The gazebo, swing set, benches, and expanse of manicured lawn all appeared as if eternally embraced within the cozy capture of a Norman Rockwell painting. She lingered behind the wheel, recalling the countless summer afternoons playing here when she was a child, and then when grown, eating lunch at Jillian's Cafe with her mother. A meandering breeze wafted through her window and blew a wisp of hair across her face. She pulled out an elastic tie from her pocket and fashioned a ponytail. The gentle warmth of the midmorning sun had not yet ceded to the heat and humidity typical of the late spring. For now, all was pleasant.

She entered the contractor's office, tripping a motion sensor and triggering a double chime. "Mr. Grossman, hi!"

Frank's eyes sparked as he swept her off her feet with a bear hug. "Welcome home! What a sight you are for these old eyes. When did you arrive?"

"Just now, I'm straight from the city. Haven't even been out to my dad's yet. I wanted to drop by, say hi to everyone, and pick up the tiller. We're planting the garden tomorrow."

He released his hold, stepping back, and winked. "I've got it ready to go, tuned up and fueled. I sharpened the tines yesterday, so you'll have no problem breaking through the surface. Only the best for my favorite goddaughter."

"I'm your only goddaughter."

"Still, always my favorite. Your dad told me about you moving to New York. We couldn't be prouder of you. Big-time publishing. I'll be reading your column every day."

The encouragement bolstered her. Frank was her father's best friend, dating back to their days in the National Guard. He was an imposing figure—a hand over six feet tall. His stature earned him the nickname "Frank the Tank" as a linebacker in high school, which remained apropos given his present girth. He opened his general contracting business in his early thirties and had been the go-to company for minor construction projects for locals ever since.

Olivia peeked around his shoulder at a lanky male her age leaning into the corner of the back wall with his thumbs hooked in the pockets of his carpenter jeans. The tilt of his chin slanted his scowl.

"Junior." She offered a tepid half-wave, officially checking the box for her obligatory hello and goodbye to him for the week.

He completed the turn of the do-si-do countering with a cursory head nod. "Hey."

She knew Francis Grossman, Jr. well. Family dinners and outings had frequently intertwined during their childhoods, but a dreadful venture into dating while they were seniors in high school resulted in permanent tension. She had attempted to make amends through the years, but over time, she accepted his icy reception as their relational norm.

The last of the assembled trio stepped around Frank, tenderly wrapped his arms around her, and brushed her cheek with a soft kiss. "Liv, welcome home."

"A.J., I've missed you. You're coming to my dad's for dinner tomorrow, right?"

He squeezed tight and released her, immediately corralling her back for a quick half-hug. "Wouldn't miss it. I can't wait to hear all about the book contract and that new condo of yours. I bet that sets you back a fortune."

"Potential contract. Nothing's for sure. And I haven't signed the paperwork yet for the condo."

"Say what you want. I believe in you. Expect me to frequent your posh digs whenever I can—whether invited or not. Daniel will just have to deal with it."

She smiled, glancing at the floor. "You're always welcome to come."

"I've prepped some self-defense moves I wanna teach you before you hightail it north. I'll show you them tomorrow after dinner." He posed à la Bruce Lee with fists of fury, frightening off a pair of flies edging along his desk.

A.J. had been protective of Olivia since the days of their shared carefree childhood. He lived with his adoptive mother Martha Matthews in a Cape Cod next door to Olivia's family until she passed when he was twenty-eight. He had no siblings, and as Martha was a widow when he came into her life, he lacked any other close family ties. Olivia's father provided paternal guidance when needed, and her mother had always helped Martha ensure he kept well-mannered, well-tempered, and well-fed. Frank apprenticed him at eighteen as a carpenter and then hired him full time when he turned twenty-one. He now split supervisor duties with Junior across job sites. When Martha died, he sold her house to an elderly couple to help pay off debt. After a series of short-term rentals and on-again, off-again couch surfing with Olivia's family, he arranged a discounted, semi-permanent stay at the historic Apple Station Inn in exchange for occasional handyman help.

Frank fetched Junior's desk chair, inviting her to sit, but banging on the suite's window suspended Olivia in mid-stance as they all swiveled toward the commotion.

"Liv!" Paige Warner bolted through the entrance and captured Olivia in a rocking embrace. "A.J. told me you were coming today. I saw your Expedition parked out in front of the clinic when I left the office. Congrats on your column. When will you need an assistant? I can pack and be ready in an hour."

"Great to see you too," Olivia said as her long-time friend finally released her. "I wanted to surprise you, but it seems secrets stand no chance when you're on the case. Don't quit the day job just yet, I'll be lucky if they'll still want me up there after a month."

They both laughed as Paige waved to dispel the notion and then extended her hand toward Frank, offering a formal business greeting. "Mr. Grossman." She acknowledged and dismissed Junior in a blink. A.J. caught her glance, and she composed her stance and tone. Paige smiled and then turned back to Olivia. "So, word on the street has it you encountered my esteemed colleague on the way into town. Unconfirmed rumor reports wandering drivers have infested Apple Station, threatening the health and well-being of our fair denizens. By chance, Liv, do you know anyone like that?"

"Guilty as charged. Cassandra, gracious as always. Maybe she's right to warn others about me—you know us city folks, never quite staying in our lanes." All but

Junior joined in the jest. He stood stationary in his propped pose like a defeated boar affixed to the wall.

Paige checked her watch. "She convinced Cooper's mother to include a blurb in Wednesday's edition about all the visitors we'd be seeing this weekend who may be, shall we say, 'strangers' to our streets."

"I thought Mrs. McCarthy retired." Olivia tried to recall the last late-night catch-up session she shared with Paige. When she first moved to Washington, they had chatted by phone or video at least once a week. Over the past year, though, they spoke about every other month. She blamed herself. The preparations for her move with Daniel had monopolized her free time, and much had kept her busy at work.

"No. Not yet. She's still the head honcho for a few months. There's a ton to bring you up to speed on, but I can't talk now. I'm working on something special for the paper, and there's an absolute, can't extend, better not miss deadline involved."

"A.J.'s coming for dinner tomorrow at my dad's place. Why don't you guys come together?"

Paige hesitated, peeking his way. "That sounds great."

A.J. swiped his cell and sunglasses from his desk. "Do you need a lift somewhere? I was heading out, so if you—"

"No, I'm good. Thanks, though. I'm running out to Grove Manor. Just finishing up an article on the auction."

Frank unclipped a carabiner of keys from a belt loop on his khakis. "It's a shame, that property. No one has lived there for years. The land's been unkempt, the manor completely neglected. Be careful. I worked there in the past when the owner was alive, but inspectors say now the building needs to be torn down."

"I'm just gathering a picture or two before the sale. Liv, tomorrow. Can't wait." Paige enclosed Olivia in her arms one last time and departed in the same whirlwind fashion as when she arrived.

"I'm sure you wanna be on your way to your dad's. Let's load that tiller for you." Frank tossed Junior the key ring. "Go get it. Put it in her car."

A.J. started toward the back. "I'll do it."

"No. Junior, go."

A.J. stopped in mid-stride, slipping Olivia a sly smile. Junior wrapped the key ring around his index finger, whistling as he twirled it, scuffing his way to the shop's rear bay. After imparting her goodbyes, she waited ten minutes by her Expedition before he emerged hauling the tiller. He loaded his cargo without a word and brushed by her, reeking of smoke and cheap cologne. He stepped onto the sidewalk but lingered for a moment before turning and pacing backward.

"Good to see you, Liv. We should catch up sometime too."

She tightened her ponytail while holding her breath, not wanting to intake any of his noxious throw. Then she checked the time and closed the liftgate, envisioning no reasons their paths would need to cross again during the coming week. Her deadline was creeping closer, but it would have to wait as Big Ben chimed, warning she was late for her scheduled stop at the clinic.

CHAPTER 3

Maria Cortés Macías was working at a rustic rectangular table in the foyer of her daughter's physical therapy clinic when Olivia arrived, a laptop, math workbook, and papers spread in front of her. The retired teacher regularly tutored children from the local elementary school, and as the summer break was nearing, Olivia guessed she was planning lessons for anxious students needing help with final exams. Maria's mother, Josefina, sat with perfect posture on a high-back sofa across from the entrance, thumbing through the same powder-blue three-ring binder of her go-to baking recipes she had used to teach Olivia to make breads, cakes, and pies.

"Olivia, mija! My dear, come." Maria approached with grace, embracing her as if she were her own daughter. "How lovely to see you! Sophia told me you were coming today."

"I'm so glad to be home. You have no idea how much

I've been looking forward to this week. I'm on my way to my dad's, but I wanted to stop in and say hi. Is Soph busy?"

"She's finishing now. I'll let her know you're here." Maria walked to the hallway off the foyer and poked her head into the first doorway, alerting her daughter to the arrival. Sophia's grandmother stood, setting her assembly of sweet family secrets aside, and greeted Olivia, taking hold of her hands and squeezing them with warmth and strength.

"Abuela, I missed you."

Josefina nodded, not needing to say a word for Olivia to understand the affection was mutual. "You should eat. Lunch is almost ready." The matriarch of the family walked past Maria and through the corridor that led to the kitchen before Olivia could politely decline.

The remodeled bakery served as a perfect hybrid office for Sophia's clinical practice. A.J. had spearheaded the renovations, converting the pastry shop into a suite fronted by the ample foyer. A hallway extended to the rear of the building, where a commercial-size kitchen once churned out doughnuts, cookies, and pastries by the dozens. He reconfigured the back baking bay, keeping intact the appliances Josefina deemed indispensable, while adding a dining area that seated twelve if all relinquished a smidgen of personal space.

Olivia peeked through the open doorway into the play gym her best friend had designed as an adventure zone for children with special needs. A platform swing, climbing wall, and mini-trampoline awaited tyke-size daredevils with courageous spirits and heroic hearts. Rainbows and teddy bears danced along the walls under soft lighting that filtered through tranquil blue covers stretched across the fluorescent fixtures.

Sophia knelt on a foam mat, helping a toddler sit balanced on a stability ball. His feet were flat on the floor, and she steadied him at his hips. "One, two, three—stand up." She provided a subtle uplift and released his right hand. He maintained weight-bearing for ten seconds before his legs collapsed under him. He laughed, and Sophia clapped. "Nice standing. Let's do it again." She picked the child up and placed him back on the ball. The sequence repeated twice more before the boy grabbed Sophia's thumb, pointing toward Olivia in the entrance. She flashed a welcoming grin and stood once she secured the youngster on the ground.

"I'm sorry. I didn't mean to interrupt your session. I got delayed coming into town, and I had to stop at A.J.'s office."

"No, you're fine. Don't worry about it. We're done here. This superstar stood for seven seconds by himself today." Sophia squatted, holding up her hand for the toddler to reciprocate with a high-five. "Hey, Mommy, can you work on this tonight? Have Tyler sit on a low step, hold his hands, and then cue him to stand, like I did."

Victoria Wellington stepped off the mini-trampoline and swooped her son up in her arms. "I'll give it a go, but he'll pitch a fit with me. He's such a show-off for you, but at home, this tater tot ignores his momster on the regular."

"Tori, hi!"

"Liv Penn, what are you doing here?" She grasped Olivia's ring finger, searching for a sparkle. "That's a shame. Hey, baby boy. Looky, it's Auntie—unadorned as ever. I didn't know you were coming to town this week. Thanks for the memo." The chubby-cheeked, high-spirited toddler pointed and pursed his lips, blowing raspberries at her. "Excuse me. Tyler has loads to share with you, apparently." She lifted her son's wrist and helped him wave at Olivia, who mirrored the greeting. "You haven't seen Ty-Ty for a while."

Olivia tickled his toes. "No, but he gets more adorable each time I do. Does he have an honorary uncle as well?"

"As soon as Daniel pops the question, he will. And you're right. Though my tiny Ty was an early arrival, he came packed full of charm." She kissed her son with three quick pecks on his nose, eliciting giggles from all. "How long are you staying? Is Daniel with you?"

Sophia glanced at Olivia, raising her eyebrows.

"Through the weekend," Olivia said. "I'm alone. He didn't come."

"I see. I sense a conspiracy between you two. Keeping secrets? It's written all over your face, Liv." Tori prided herself in possessing an unassailable intuition she credited to meditation and daily unblocking of her chakras.

"I told you. I knew it. You're too good for him." Josefina entered the room, halting the reunion, and waved for all to follow her to the kitchen. "That's my cue to leave. Soph, thanks. Ty's making so much progress. He'll be running me ragged before I know it."

Tyler grabbed a fistful of Olivia's hair. Sophia unwrapped his clenched fingers one by one. "Seems he already is. I'll see you tomorrow. And do his exercises with him tonight."

Olivia and Sophia joined Maria in the kitchen, where Josefina had prepared a bountiful midday spread served on Talavera tableware, spanning sunglow linens. Olivia slipped her phone halfway out of her pocket and texted Angela: "Need extension. Will send by five." The phone buzzed in reply—an angry face emoji.

Sophia pulled out a chair for her. "Everything okay?"

"It's someone from work. I'll handle it later."

"You must try Abuela's churros before you go. She's been testing recipes since last week to defend her title at the festival's baking competition on Saturday. We're all up a few pounds—but it's for a good cause."

"I've won the past three years."

"You're the best, Mamá." Maria settled next to her daughter, unfolding her napkin and placing it in her lap.

Josefina sat beside Olivia and passed her a plate of crumbled queso fresco while dropping a handful of tortilla strips into her soup bowl. "You need to get married. Have children."

"Mamá, let her alone. I'm sure she'll share news when she's ready."

Josefina eyed her granddaughter. "You too. You both should start families of your own. I won't leave this earth until I see your grandchildren. Bisabuela."

Sophia filled a ladle of soup from a tureen on the table. "Great-grandmother? You go first, Liv. Or, we both could stay single forever, so you'll always be with us, Abuela." Sophia, Olivia, and Maria laughed as Josefina made the sign of the cross and raised her arms in a prayerful pose, offering supplications in Spanish to both St. Joseph and St. Priscilla.

Olivia breathed in the scene as the three generations of women mused on matters debated only when men were not around. She missed being among those who loved her like family. Though not truly related, Sophia's family had treated her as if she were ever since her mother died when she was in her early twenties. Without Maria's maternal support and guidance, Olivia would not have become who she was now. She would miss these trips. New York would be a solitary life for the foreseeable future. Though not the scenario she had planned, she wanted the promotion, and the prospect of publishing. Moving was progress—career building with the promise of opportunity.

Sophia tossed her napkin on Olivia's lap. "Liv, space cadet."

"Sorry, you were saying?"

"Do you want food to take home for your dad?"

"That would be great. He'll love it." Maria loaded a generous plate and packed it in a tote bag for her to carry. "I should go. I have a column to write, and I've skirted one deadline already."

"Okay, mija. Say hello to your father. You'll visit before you leave, right?"

Olivia understood the question was nonnegotiable. "Of course. I want to soak up as much as I can before I go." She pushed back from the table, hugged Maria and Josefina, and walked with Sophia out toward the foyer.

"Liv, call me tomorrow," Sophia said. "I'm working in the morning, but I'll be free in the afternoon. Maybe we can talk about what happened between you and Daniel. Are you sure you're all right?"

"I'm fine. It was mutual. I'll deep dive that rabbit hole with you later."

"Okay. Say hi to your dad for me."

Olivia waved and left the clinic. Her phone buzzed, and she shook her head, not even needing confirmation. *It's coming.* She anticipated a slew of lightning bolts, frogs, flies, and cows warning her Angela stood ready to unleash the plagues. Instead, she received emojis of zombies and clowns—the apocalypse was at hand. She started a reply, pivoting abruptly toward her Expedition, and immediately collided dead-on with a broad-shouldered, middle-aged man who mistimed his bid to counter her spin. She stumbled and fell to the ground, spilling the contents of the canvas bag on the sidewalk.

The flustered stranger quickly regained his balance

and paced backward. "Hey, watch it, lady. Look where you're walking."

He turned, pressing on as she directed a healthy dose of silent, colorful karmic wishes at the back of his black T-shirt and work-worn jeans. She picked herself up, rued the ruined food, and gathered the remnants. *Unbelievable.* She took two deep breaths and brushed off her pants. Her phone alerted her to a message, but she did not bother to check it. She only wanted to get home, relax, and enjoy the rest of the week without the slightest hint of any further trouble.

CHAPTER 4

Olivia turned her Expedition into the gravel driveway of her childhood home, gently rubbing the abrasion that reddened her palm. Debris had embedded in the scraped skin, promising her a bit of a bite when the time came to wash away the dirt and blood. William Penn stood on the full-length covered porch of the Colonial-style house, leaning against the side railing, soaking up his customary daily dose of vitamin D. A three-seat glider bench and an Amish rocker on the left side of the porch balanced a petite patio table, a Windsor rocker, and a bistro chair on the right. Prussian blue shutters atop white vinyl siding flanked the sides of the second-story windows, while the ground-level double-pane bay window afforded the living room a bounty of morning light. The long, linear drive skewed lateral to the right of the residence and stretched lengthwise to allow for five cars parked bumper-to-bumper, though normally only her father's ruby-red compact SUV occupied the space.

Olivia rolled to a stop behind the Escape, sliding her hands to the bottom of the wheel. She could paint the endearing scene by memory with confident brushstrokes. Her father waved as she hopped down from her Expedition and returned his greeting, closing her door with a gentle nudge. She bounded the four steps to the porch and encircled him in her arms with an enthusiasm as if it had been years, and not mere months, since they last visited.

"Honey, you had me worried. I thought you'd be here sooner. You didn't have car trouble, did you?"

She grinned, releasing her hold while keeping an arm around his shoulders. From the day she turned sixteen and received her driver's license, any delay to her expected arrival time led to inquiries about her car's well-being. When did she last change the oil? Rotate and balance the tires? Fill the windshield wiper fluid? She never grew tired of his expressed concerns, and she always kept a spreadsheet of her service records up to date to satisfy him. "No, the Expedition's in tip-top shape. I stopped in town and picked up the tiller for tomorrow. I intended a quick flyby the clinic to say hi to Soph, but you know her grandmother. She made lunch for everyone. Maria sent along a plate of leftovers for you, but I took a spill when I was leaving and ruined the food. Don't ask."

"I had an egg, bacon, and cheese sandwich for breakfast. I'll be good until dinner."

"You need more protein, more calories, Dad."

"I'm out of sausage."

"Not quite what I had in mind."

"I have a gallon of fudge ripple in the freezer I've been meaning to open—now that you mention it."

"Still not what I was thinking."

"Well, I'm sure you'll force-feed me vegetables this week, so there. I'm just glad you're here, sweetie. It's getting stuffy. Let's cool off inside." He laid his daily paper and reading glasses on the round-top table. "You all packed up? Get all your gear secured in the storage unit? You can still bring it here. I have space, and I'd charge you a lot less."

"Gee thanks, with an offer like that. Besides, you'll have to find some place to store all my old furniture once that new exercise equipment of yours arrives."

"I'm still waiting for advice about that situation, so until I hear back, the room is all yours." His smile faded as he slowly sighed. "Guess you won't have much of a chance to come visit for a while."

"I'll need a few months to settle in, but I'll be back before you have time to miss me."

He pulled the screen door open but released it almost immediately and turned toward her, slipping his hands into the pockets of his Bermuda shorts. "Sweetie, are you sure about this? Living up there on your own? I wasn't Daniel's biggest fan, but at least when it was the two of you, I felt better you'd have someone there. I worry about you—I don't want you to be alone. There, of all places. What will you do if your car breaks down? Who will you eat dinner with? Talk to after a long day?"

His candid unease offset her balance. Though she shared similar concerns about moving on her own since her recent split, she had dismissed her doubts for the sake of the opportunity. "It'll be fine. I'll be fine, Dad." She followed the flight path of a helicopter passing over the house, allowing the glaze in her eyes to dissipate. As the years went by, she knew she needed him as much as he relied on her. "Last I checked, they have service stations in New York. So that's covered. If I need someone to talk to, I'll call you every night."

He pulled her close with a side hug. "Every night? Let's not go overboard. Come on in. I'll show you what I've taught Buddy."

She opened the door, and as they entered the living room, the beagle raced toward them from the kitchen with his collar tags jingling an exuberant greeting. He swiped at her shin and barked, wagging his tail with a spirited beat. "Hey there, little fella. Are you watching Daddy for me?" She squatted and playfully scratched along his neck and chin as he jumped, coaxing her to catch his front paws.

"Seems he missed you as much as I have."

Buddy barked twice more and bolted behind the television. He returned in a sprint with a crimson-colored ball secured in his mouth and dropped it at her feet.

"Sure thing, li'l Bud. Ready, set—go." She rolled the ball through the living room and into the kitchen. The puppy scampered after it like a first responder on a search and rescue mission. In no time, he returned to her side, ball clenched in his jaws, ready for another round.

William straightened his arm, pointing toward the sofa. "Watch this. Buddy, snacks." At the command, the pup hightailed it to the end table by the recliner and returned with a clipped bag of kettle-cooked potato chips.

"Dad, you're unbelievable." Her muted phone buzzed, and she retrieved it from her pocket. Angela's ID was displayed on the screen, under a photo of her dressed as an angel at last year's office Halloween party.

"You need to get that?"

"I should. It's my editor. I have a deadline, and I've already extended it once. Do you mind if I finish my column? I'll be free the rest of the day."

"You can use my desk or go out to your mother's office. We'll have plenty of time to talk later. You do what you need to do."

She glanced into the library off the living room, where her father had his desk. "Here's fine." After she retrieved her work bag from her Expedition, she settled in his chair, turned on her laptop, and randomly picked a question from the printouts.

Dear Ms. Penn,
I recently graduated from college, and I'm starting law

school in the fall. My dad is an attorney, as was his father.
I'm expected to follow in the family footsteps. I'm not sure
that's what I want. Should I give it a go or take a stand? I
don't want to disappoint them. — Loathe Lawyer-to-Be.

She stared at the blinking cursor for a minute and
then started typing her response. She stopped and
deleted what she had written and thought for a minute
more.

Hey Loathe Lawyer-to-Be,
Navigating family expectations to follow a road you're
unsure you want to travel is never straightforward. We all
need to explore various paths before we have a sense of
what feels right for us. This may change throughout the
years. For a season, for a reason. Stay open to what piques
your curiosity. Follow your interests—these will guide your
choices. It's okay and normal to be anxious during times of
transition. We all learn as we go and grow. Point your feet
in the direction where your heart beats the loudest. Whether
your family agrees with your decision or expresses disap-
pointment has nothing to do with you. Opinions belong to
their owners alone.

Dear Ms. Penn,
I've been dating my boyfriend for two years. We've talked
about marriage, but now, when I bring it up, he changes
the subject or makes excuses. How long should I wait? —
Ticking Clock.

She leaned back in the chair. Two years. That was how long she had been with Daniel. Things happen. People change.

Hey Ticking Clock,

Time is up. What do you want from this relationship? Your frustration is apparent. You thought you were heading in the same direction, and then your partner changed course. When he has made excuses, have you discussed your concerns without issuing ultimatums? If he doesn't want to marry, are you okay with continuing the relationship given these terms? At what point does this become a deal-breaker for you? If you're spinning your wheels on the same patch of ice two months, six months, twelve months from now— are you good with that? Tell your partner what you're feeling. Then tell him what you've decided. Don't wait for him to make your decision for you. Be prepared to ditch the car and walk.

Olivia checked the time. With five minutes to spare, she e-mailed the file to Angela. An immediate text reply lit her cell's screen: "Thanks." Then another: "Tomorrow, please, earlier. Here's another picture from Jasper's party."

She smiled, thinking Angela may be right about her adopting her sister's Siamese. A dog would need more room to roam, but a quiet cat—she was coming around to the idea. Buddy had been lying by her feet as she worked on her laptop, but her tidying prompted him to retrieve his ball from the hallway. He coordinated his front paws and nose, rolling his toy in as straight a line as he could toward her. Her phone rang, and she answered with certainty.

"I promise tomorrow I'll get it to you sooner."

"Ah, Liv? It's Soph."

"Oh. I'm sorry. I didn't even look. I thought you were someone else. Can I call you back in a second?" She switched to speaker, starting a text to Angela.

"Liv … I have, ah … I've got some … um …"

"Soph, are you there? You okay?" A photo of a cat posed in front of a gift box with a black ribbon bow popped up on her screen. "Something up? Hello?"

"I'm here, but … I'm sorry, I have awful news."

CHAPTER 5

Silence separated the connection between Olivia and her friend. "Liv, Paige is dead."

Olivia closed Jasper's photo, rewinding the words. "What?"

"It's Paige. The police found her at Grove Manor."

"What? Paige Warner? As in Paige, our friend from the paper? No, I saw her this morning."

"Liv—"

"I think I misheard you."

"It's Paige. I just spoke with my dad a few minutes ago. The police were checking on the property ahead of the sale and found her there unconscious. The chief called for an ambulance, but the first unit blew a tire en route. He contacted my dad in the ER, and he followed the second unit that left from the fire station across from the hospital. By the time he got there—"

"Paige? No, no. Not Paige."

"I'm so sorry, Liv."

"I can't believe this. Oh, Soph, no …" She slumped in the seat, burying her face in her hands, nauseous and unable to speak. Buddy nudged his ball aside and lay his front paws on her toes. She stared at the floor and then at the framed Bodie Island Lighthouse sketch on the wall until the stripes blurred and the black and white blended.

"I'm leaving to see my dad now. He's still on site with the police. I thought maybe you would want … will you go with me?"

"I don't understand. How could this happen? I just saw her. We had plans—we were meeting tomorrow. I don't … I can't believe this. Yes, of course. Come over. I'll be waiting."

"Thanks, Liv. Be there in a few."

Olivia sat motionless for minutes. The impact of Paige's loss stunned her like the failure of a backup parachute. Her friend—a confidant she had known since they worked together at the high school paper—was dead. The first story they covered was the homecoming game the year the seniors stole rival Valley High's bulldog mascot and dressed it in a tutu and tiara. They shared the byline and a celebratory dinner, toasting the launch of their journalistic careers. Their summer vacation to Cape Hatteras the year after their graduation coincided with a category five hurricane that cut them off from the mainland when Pamlico Sound washed over Highway 12 all the way to the Atlantic. They sheltered in a rented two-bedroom cottage without power for three days until a Coast Guard crew arrived, checking if they needed aid. Paige complained of sudden, mysterious symptoms she insisted required a thorough examination by the group's unwed doctor. He left her with a passing grade and his phone number. She and Olivia attended *Mamma Mia* whenever the tour traveled to the National Theater. They danced in the aisles and sang each song of the encore montage as if auditioning for the company's cast. Before this morning, they last met three months ago for lunch at Jillian's and speculated on when Daniel may propose. Olivia rued she had not cemented their brief visit today in her memory. Paige had embraced her with affection for a friendship neither time nor distance diminished. *Why didn't I tell her how much I missed her?*

William knocked on the open door. "Are you finished? I wanted to see if—honey, what's wrong? Why are you crying?"

"You remember Paige Warner?"

"Of course. You played varsity softball together."

"Dad, Paige is dead. I don't know what happened."

"What? Paige? How can that be? No, no. Come here, sweetie." He held her, steadying her as tears dampened his shirt sleeve.

She plucked a palmful of tissues from a box on the printer stand. "Soph is coming over. She asked me to ride out with her to Grove Manor. That's where they found Paige. Dr. Reyes is there now. I'm going with her."

"Okay. Yes, go. Is it safe?"

"The paramedics and police are there. The chief is the one who called for the ambulance."

"Payne?"

She nodded, turning toward the hall, alerted to Sophia's arrival by three light taps on the porch's screen door. William walked with her to where Sophia waited, and the best friends hugged, each comforting the other in their shared sorrow.

He retrieved his keys from his pocket. "I can drive you two out there. Sophia, did your father say what happened?"

"No. He didn't give me any details."

"No, Dad. You stay here. Sophia and I will be okay. We won't be long, I promise."

Olivia and Sophia departed, taking a shortcut along the back roads in stunned silence. Grove Manor's history had been well documented in the newspaper over the past few years as local interest grew in what would become of the dilapidated property. Whenever Paige had posted an article about it on the paper's website, Olivia always left a comment and shared a link to it across her social media feeds.

Grove Manor was last owned by Jeremiah Jackson—a wealthy man whose grandfather operated the train depot that shared the town's moniker. His grandfather's holdings included most of the buildings in the borough that lined what was, back then, little more than a two-lane main street. Jeremiah, who inherited everything, sold the properties one by one until only the manor remained. He was a widower from the day of his lone child's birth. Anna, his beloved daughter, died when she was only thirty-three. He suffered inconsolable grief from her tragic passing. With Jeremiah now long gone, and with no known heirs, the bank had scheduled an auction of the property on Friday to satisfy a tax lien.

"There's my dad's car." Sophia maneuvered onto the grass and aligned her car behind his Explorer.

A county fire engine blocked entry to the drive beyond where they had parked, and two ambulances were stationed in the roundabout in front of the house with their rear doors open. Duffel bags and polypropylene hard-shell cases lay piled up. The crews circled a patch of lawn an arm's length from the driveway, four of the responders kneeling and three others next to a lowered stretcher. Chief of Police Raymond Payne was speaking to a pair of his deputies, Cole Lee and Bert Branch, several feet from the paramedics.

Olivia had a soft spot in her heart for Cole and Bert. Two winters ago, they had helped to free her car from a snowbank she had slid into while trying to avoid a truck that had spun out in front of her on an icy patch of road near Hamilton's general store. They had been off duty at the time and on their way to a family Christmas party, as they were cousins to each other, related through their mothers. They had worked for over an hour, digging out her car, and for that, she was forever grateful.

Sophia's father waved his daughter over as he spoke with a detective by the fire truck's cab. The stranger sported a faded black denim shirt and blue jeans with a badge clipped to his belt. A banded ivory Stetson sat in perfect alignment, with the brim dipped on his brow.

"Papá."

"You two shouldn't be here. The poor girl." He hugged Sophia as the detective waited, respecting the tender moment before taking his leave.

"Dr. Reyes, thank you for your cooperation."

"Please call me Ernesto, detective. I'll do whatever I can to help."

"Yes, sir. I'll contact you if we need any further information. Ladies." He tipped his hat and joined Payne further up the driveway, watching the responders complete their grim duties.

"What happened, Papá?"

"It's awful. There was nothing I could do. Your friend —she had already passed when I arrived. Dana up there, she's the medical examiner, believes her injuries are consistent with blunt trauma."

Sophia put her hand to her mouth. "You mean someone hit her?"

"More like something. The deputies located a suspect truck around the back of the manor."

Olivia gasped. "But, Dr. Reyes, this place—it's deserted. Who was out here? Why? Who would do this to her?"

"I don't know, Olivia. This is a police matter now."

The paramedics guided the covered stretcher to the waiting ambulance and lifted it inside. Silent tears streamed down Olivia's cheeks. She wiped them with the back of her hand, but the remnants diverted, running a trail along a vein in her arm. The early evening's waning light revealed the moon rising in the vacant sky. The dilapidated dwelling, pitched against the densely forested backdrop, imparted an eerie aura, reminding her of a TV show she DVR'd in October on haunted estates of the Deep South.

Payne spoke with the detective as an EMT shut the back doors of the transport, punctuating the scene's finality. As Ernesto gestured for his daughter and Olivia to follow him to their cars, the deputies emerged from the trees around the right rear of the manor, hollering for help. The chief and the detective raced toward the commotion, enticing Olivia and Sophia to inch closer to the house for a better view.

The night's stillness amplified the steely voice of one of the four pursuers in the backwoods. "Down on the ground. Hands where I can see them. Quit your fighting. I said stop fighting."

Sophia and Olivia glanced at each other, sharing an unspoken thought. *We should get back.* But neither budged. They remained rooted, awaiting the unveiling of the apprehended. The detective led the group, prodding the cuffed man forward and lifting him in coordination with Payne whenever the suspect slowed the procession by dragging his feet. With the entourage moving closer, Olivia and Sophia abandoned any hesitation and backpedaled toward their vehicle.

"I didn't do it!" The captive dropped to his knees, but the detective grabbed him with one arm, yanked him upright, and pushed him forward.

The panicked voice froze Olivia in place. *No.* She shook her head, reversing course, and headed toward the approaching formation.

Sophia stopped, but she did not follow. "Liv, where are you going? Stop. Come back."

She kept to her route. The four officers and the detained man marched like Marines, drilling in double time. A laceration over the suspect's left brow leaked a narrow band of blood above his blackened, swollen eye.

"Liv, I-I, it, it wasn't me!"

The detective spoke without breaking stride. "Ma'am, step away." She persisted, following the group to a police cruiser parked near the ambulance, and reached out to touch the prisoner's arm while they waited for Bert to open the rear door. "Please, ma'am. You need to leave now. This is a crime scene, and you're verging on interfering. I will arrest you if I have to."

"Liv, I-I, please, you've gotta believe me. Please, help."

Her heart sank, but she dared not move an inch closer. "A.J., what did you do?"

CHAPTER 6

Bert shoved A.J. into the backseat of Cole's cruiser before he could say another word. Olivia pounded the window with her palm as he doubled over, tucking his chin to his chest. The detective interrupted his instructions to the deputies, staring at her from across the Defender's roof, waiting for her to step back. The ambulance carrying Paige from the scene slowly drove past them, departing the roundabout without sirens or flashing lights.

Olivia could see Sophia talking to her father by his Explorer. He hugged her and pointed in Olivia's direction. Cole removed his bulletproof vest and sandwiched his patrol bag between the first aid kit and his tactical shotgun scabbard in the trunk. The glow from the ambulance's taillights dissolved in the distance, and she looked again at A.J. a few feet from her, unable to think of a single thing she could do.

Sophia came over and ushered her away from the cruiser. "Liv, come on. Let's go."

"I don't understand what's happening. Why did they arrest him? He wouldn't harm her. He couldn't."

She gently turned Olivia's shoulders, steering her down the drive to where they had parked. "I don't know. Why would he be out here?"

Olivia slowed, glancing back to see Payne speaking with the detective a few feet from Cole's cruiser while waving over the medical examiner and dialing his cell. She strained to hear what he was saying, but could not decipher any more than a few random, inflected words. "We need to get him help."

Sophia continued nudging her forward. "What are you thinking?"

"He needs a lawyer before he says anything to the police."

Sophia opened the passenger side door, waiting until Olivia settled and secured her seatbelt. Cole's cruiser passed by them en route to the exit, shadowed by the detective in his black extended F-150. Sophia U-turned, swinging into the grass of the outbound lane, and followed behind the entourage.

"You have any contacts in D.C.? What about the guy you dated with that firm in Penn Quarter? Wasn't he a criminal attorney?"

Olivia pulled her phone from her pocket. "Justin. It's been a while since we spoke. He lives in Great Falls, though. A.J. needs help now, tonight. I think I have a better idea."

Sophia chased after the convoy, but the two lead vehicles quickly vanished from view. They caught up with them in town and parked on the square's corner across from the post office as the detective wrenched A.J. from the backseat of the cruiser. The chief and Bert appeared, and the four officers surrounded him and escorted him into police headquarters.

They sat in silence, staring at the idyllic streetscape that concealed the severity of the affairs transpiring within the station. After five minutes had passed, Sophia's phone lit with a text.

"That's my mom. She wants an update. You think Junior's dad got your message? I hope he knows a lawyer who can—" She stopped as Olivia slid open the lock switch on her side and kicked her door wide. "What are you doing? We can't go in there. Would you wait? Let's see if he shows."

"He may not even check his voice mail at this hour. I'm going in." She launched out of the sedan as Sophia unfastened her seatbelt, grumbling a few choice words under her breath.

The unoccupied reception desk ensured their intrusion went unnoticed. Olivia had never heard of a murder committed in Apple Station in her lifetime, but the detective and the two deputies dispatched in collaborating duties, appearing to follow protocols straight from a television crime drama. A three-foot high oak-wood gate with a center swing door separated the foyer from the station's business end. A.J. was hunched forward in a metal folding chair against a wall, with a file cabinet guarding his right. His head hung low, and cuffs restrained his hands behind his back. Cole stood as a sentry on his left, as if A.J. was ready to enact a scene from *The Fugitive*. Bert prompted him to his feet and penned him in a cell built into the corner of the workroom.

The detective glanced up from a file on his desk as Bert passed by and spotted Olivia and Sophia watching him from beside the pamphlet rack. His eyes narrowed until Cole stepped into his sight line, handing him a clipboard and asking for his signature on a set of forms.

The door behind Olivia flew open, and Frank barreled in, breathing as if he had just completed a four-minute mile. His eyes darted from her to Payne, then to A.J. and back to her. "What's going on? Why's A.J. in custody? I rushed over as soon as I got your voice mail."

"Thanks for coming," she said as he brushed off his dusty twill work shirt and comforted her with a quick half-hug. "I don't understand why they arrested him. He needs a lawyer. I thought you'd have some local connections because of your business. I know someone, but he's—"

"Don't worry. When I heard your message, I called Benjamin Billingsley right away. He's my attorney, he'll know what to do. We'll sort this out. You said you were out at Grove Manor? The police found somebody dead there?"

"Payne called Dr. Reyes to the scene, and Soph and I drove out. I don't understand what's happening. A.J. could never—"

"Let's get the facts first. I'll go talk to them and see what we're dealing with here." His phone rang. "Wait, that might be—yes, it's Ben. I'm going outside to take this. Don't worry. We'll get him help." He ripped the door open to its limits, slamming the knob against the wall and chipping off flecks of almond paint. His voice faded as he distanced himself from the station.

Payne barked orders at Bert, and Olivia turned toward the commotion, seeing the detective's radar locked on her. He shoved his file into Cole's chest and strode to where she and Sophia stood in the foyer, emphatically kicking the swing gate with the toe of his boot.

"Can I help you with something?" His comportment imparted more civility than courtesy.

Olivia mirrored his glare. "Why did you arrest A.J.?"

"Excuse me, but I didn't catch your name. Strange, you both show up at Grove Manor, and now, here you are. Do you have business with the department?"

Sophia grabbed Olivia's arm, holding her back. "My dad is the doctor you spoke with at the scene."

He shifted his eyes back and forth between them. "You have any pertinent information to share?"

Olivia inched forward. "Paige was our friend. So is A.J."

"I see. I'm sorry about Ms. Warner. As for your other friend, he's in a heap of trouble. Ladies." He tipped his Stetson and retraced his steps.

Payne leaned on the detective's desk, engaged in a phone conversation in which he did most of the listening. Olivia caught "body," "charges," and "judge." Cole and Bert buzzed about like worker drones, collating, stacking, and filing forms. Few words were exchanged between them, and they maneuvered with precision and urgency. Solemnity infused the air.

"I'm Olivia Penn." At her words, the detective stopped short of the partition. "My name is Olivia Penn."

He turned and faced her. "Preston Hills." Then he pushed the swing gate inward and returned to the business at hand on the other side of the divide.

A light breeze blew behind Olivia as the station's door slowly opened, and she turned to see a woman in her late sixties wearing a navy twill hooded jacket. One of the two straps from June Warner's purse had fallen from her shoulder, and the remaining support slid closer to joining the plummet to her elbow with each step. She clutched a wad of tissues as her tears formed twin streams, running down her cheeks.

Olivia embraced Paige's mother. "I'm so, so sorry." The three of them sat on a bench to the right of the reception desk, exchanging condolences and comforting one another.

June struggled to suppress her sobbing. "The police chief asked me to come and answer questions. Did they make an arrest?"

Olivia stared toward the cell, barely registering either the surface she sat on or June's hand that gripped hers. The deputies appeared as if in slow motion, with their movements out of sync with their speech. Sophia held tight to June, conveying the only fact they knew. "A.J.'s in custody."

"He would not harm my daughter."

Olivia looked down at the knots of the heart pine flooring between her feet. The lines of the wavy grains blurred, and she wiped her tears. Then she turned to June. "How do you know him?"

"He would never hurt Paige." She searched her pockets and then her purse for more tissues. "Olivia, you know that's true. Help him, for her. Find out who did this."

Olivia's eyes widened as shock drove her sorrow headlong into a brick wall. "Me? Mrs. Warner, no, I'm not—the police will, they'll find who did this. I don't know what's happening. I just got into town this morning."

"You're a journalist. You must have connections in Washington—investigators, state police, FBI."

Her mind went blank. She felt as if she had been asked to recite the first hundred digits of pi. She never referred to herself as a journalist—doing so would make her feel like an imposter. "Mrs. Warner, I'm not an investigative reporter. I write an advice column. I don't have those types of connections. And the local authorities have jurisdiction. I'm sorry. I wish I could—"

"There must be someone you can contact. Paige admired you so much. She told me about you moving to New York. She wanted to work with you there." June's eyes moistened again, and Sophia put her arm around her shoulders and handed her another tissue.

Olivia leaned forward, propping her forearms on her thighs. "I saw her when I arrived. She was coming to my dad's for dinner tomorrow."

Cole approached them and removed his campaign hat, placing it over his heart. "I'm sorry for your loss, Mrs. Warner. Detective Hills is ready to speak with you. May I escort you over to him?"

"Thank you, officer. Please give me a minute. I'll find my way."

"Yes, ma'am." He squared his broad-brimmed hat in solemn alignment with respect and sympathy. "Ms. Olivia, Ms. Sophia." He paced backward several steps and bumped into the reception desk before disappearing through the swing door.

June wiped her cheeks and rummaged to the bottom of her honey-brown handbag. She pulled out her leather clutch and unsnapped the closure, displaying the ID window. "This picture is from last month. The nineteenth was my birthday. Paige threw a surprise party for me at the inn." The momentary spark lighting her eyes faded along with her pained smile. "I had no clue. No idea at all. I better go speak with the detective. Thank you for being there for her." She stood, and Sophia and Olivia did the same. "Please, if there's anyone you can talk to, anything you can find out."

"Paige said this morning she was going to Grove Manor to take pictures for a story about the sale. Do you know anything about that?"

"She said she was working an angle that would change everything. I laughed. Paige always tells me—she always told me things like that. I was wrong. I should've asked her." She took a slow, deep breath to steady herself for the interview ahead.

Preston glanced at Olivia from behind his desk, and she turned away, wanting no further one-on-ones with him tonight, or on any night for that matter.

June clasped Olivia's hand, leaning in close. "Watch yourself. Don't trust any of them."

CHAPTER 7

Olivia lingered entangled in her sheets for five minutes after waking on Tuesday, groggy from her restless night. She yawned and rolled toward the wrong side of the bed, grasping at air instead of the water bottle she would have within arm's reach at home. She fluffed her pillow and watched the ceiling fan's motor wobble, making a mental note to clean the blades and tighten the screws before she left on Sunday. The sealed slats of the miniblinds blocked the morning light, leaving no clues as to the actual time. She swiped for her cell, but it slipped from her grip and bounced off the bedframe, landing with a thud. Last night's scenes flashed through her mind like a slide show: the covered stretcher, A.J. in handcuffs, the sorrow in June's eyes.

Olivia joined her father in the kitchen, discerning the signature aroma of the Kona coffee she had gifted him as a stocking stuffer last year for Christmas. She related all that had transpired at Grove Manor and the police station as he sat with his forearms on the table, slowly sliding his cup back and forth between his hands.

"Is there any way you can help him?" he asked.

She poured coffee into a stoneware mug left for her on the counter to a quarter-inch from the brim. "I wish there was, but I don't see what. I hadn't spoken much with Paige since February. I have friends from the paper who have connections, but their sources won't be of any use here."

"Do you think A.J. could be involved?"

"No way. Impossible. He's not capable of this."

Her father's silence lingered longer than she expected. He pushed back from the table, and placed his reading glasses by his wallet next to the convection oven. "Sometimes you think you know someone your whole life, and they end up surprising you. What's going through their head, their motives—you can't even try to make sense of it."

She cradled her mug, allowing the steamed fragrance of almond and honey to waken her senses. "Do you know Benjamin Billingsley?"

"Not personally. He has an office in town on the corner near the bank. He lives around Paris, a little west of Middleburg. In the fall, he hosted a gala at his estate to raise funds for the cancer center at the hospital. They're renovating the wing your mother was in. There were photos in the paper. He has stables and an arena for training—like those jumping events you see in the Olympics."

"Mr. Grossman called him last night."

"Frank will do whatever he can to help. A.J. is more of a son to him than Junior sometimes, it seems. We don't have to plant this morning, sweetie. It can wait until the weekend. You've got more important things on your plate."

"No, let's do it. I want to do it today. I'll go change. You go get your map."

Olivia and her father had cultivated a vegetable garden together for the past eighteen summers. As William aged, the physical demands of planting grew too strenuous, and he relinquished all the labor to her. His role now was to ensure the alignment of the annuals matched the map he drew on a single sheet of yellow legal-size paper. His chart served as the master record on which he tracked yields and growing characteristics of the harvest. This season's roster included tomatoes, cucumbers, butter lettuce, green beans, and sweet potatoes. Every year, they selected a novel crop as an experiment. The tradition began and nearly ended with habaneros. A four-pack of plants yielded over fifty of the fiery peppers, which proved too hot for either of them. He asserted that nitroglycerin patches from his medicine cabinet used as fertilizer induced both the volume and heat. She challenged the claim, but the narrative persisted. This season they planned for a trial of mini pumpkins. The Jack Be Littles were destined to grow to proper plumpness by October, if they survived the dual threats of summer storms and curious squirrels.

After getting changed, Olivia met her father at the side of the house, where he was waiting with his clipboard and a narrow dogwood tree branch in hand. After four overlapping passes with the borrowed tiller to loosen and aerate the ground, she gathered her materials and knelt on the softened earth. Her father used the pale gray limb he had salvaged from a pile of storm debris to direct her where to place each plant. She repeated the procedure for each seedling: excavate the soil, add potting mix, pour water in the well, insert the plant, cover the roots, and compact the base. With each hollow, he guided her forward, back, left, or right so that each row perfectly aligned. In the past, her father's persnickety placement had tried her patience. In recent years, though, she neither displayed nor admitted any annoyance with the micromanagement.

She worked with efficiency as she established a natural rhythm. The mechanical procedure provided a reprieve from the pressure that had been pounding in her head like a jackhammer since Sophia's call yesterday afternoon. After about an hour, she removed her gloves and wiped the sweat from the back of her neck.

"I hope Paige's mom remembers to pick up her cat. He's probably been waiting by the window for her to come home. Poor thing." William nodded but said nothing. She stared at her mother's office that bordered the rear of the property. The single-room, cornflower-blue outbuilding, trimmed with deep sapphire shutters, resembled a New England cottage in miniature. A screen guarded the winter-white front door, inviting the free flow of springtime breezes. An arched wooden trellis adorned with lavender clematis framed the portal. Two east-facing windows welcomed the day, forever embracing morning's first light.

She scooted forward to start the next row, but kept her gloves clutched in one hand. "Mrs. Warner will have a lot to take care of. So much left behind. She told me Paige wanted us to work together in New York."

Her father, now resting in a webbed lawn chair beside the border's brick edging, set his clipboard on the ground and leaned forward. She hoisted a tub of potting soil from her right to her left, fixating again past the end of the garden.

"Do you think Mom regretted not having her writing published?"

He removed his ball cap, swatting at a gnat. "Your mother wrote every day. Even on the weekends. Like clockwork, she'd go out there for an hour each morning, and then at ten, she'd come inside for a second cup of coffee. I always told her I would bring it to her, but she said the walk back and forth did her good."

"Last time in the hospital, she talked about publishing a poetry collection."

"Her wanting that—I'm sure it was more for you than for her. She regretted nothing in her life. Being published didn't matter to her." His eyes lit as he drifted along a placid sea of private memories that sparked a smile and softened his cheeks. "You, me, the family, meant everything to her."

She leaned back on her heels, resting her palms on her thighs. "Dad, I was considering—"

Her cell rang. With one touch, she silenced the tone without removing the phone from her pocket. A second call followed immediately, and she retrieved her phone, checking the ID. Her father tapped the screen with his stick. "You better answer that."

"Angela, I'll get you my copy by—"

"Hey, Olivia. You don't need to send me anything today. Sorry, but your column is being cut tomorrow."

"What? Why?"

"August St. James—you know, the lead singer for Cicero's Fate—and Ambrosia are getting married over the weekend. You're aware of that, aren't you?"

"Who and who?"

"Olivia, you need to get out more. Anyway. We're devoting an extended spread to cover it since we have exclusives on the pre-reception events. They're bringing in elephants. Imagine that. So, we adore you always, but you're bumped. Sorry, we need the real estate. Genuine elephants. Can you believe it?"

Olivia rubbed her forehead, feeling like she had been downed by a leg sweep. "Really? Preempted for pachyderms and pop singers."

"Don't be a hater. We're still on for the Q&A, right? Do you have Wi-Fi out there? Are you sure you'll connect when we stream? Maybe we should practice later. Wait, I can't. I'm attending Ambrosia's pre-bridal shower luncheon. Who knew that was a thing? Hey, gotta bolt. Go wild with your homecoming, city girl—I've got the bail money ready. I'll get back in touch before we go live on Thursday."

The call ended. Olivia glared at the ground in front of her, stabbing at the dirt with her trowel.

"Is there a problem? Do you need to write your column?"

"No. It's fine. Everything's fine. Is that last line of tomatoes straight?"

"They're perfect, honey. You did a fantastic job as always."

She continued working row by row until the plot matched the master design. When the last plant was in its summer home, she stood with a sore back and stiff knees. Her father watered the stocked garden, encouraging the tender roots to grow. She wanted to spend the rest of her day here, but she thought of A.J., she thought of Paige, she thought of New York. Though she still doubted how she could help, she went inside and cleaned up, changed clothes, and planned a return visit to where it all began.

CHAPTER 8

Olivia drove into town, passing Sophia's clinic, and parallel parked her Expedition in front of Grossman's Construction. Frosted air from the overworked AC chilled her as she entered the disheveled office suite. Nothing looked the same as yesterday. Now, files lay scattered all about, and trash was piled high next to overturned bins. Two distinct trails of scrapes on the ceramic flooring from the front to the rear hinted at a recent haul of a hefty load. Junior slouched in his seat, staring at his laptop screen. An array of invoices, blueprints, and folders overlapped across his desk, apparently of no priority to him.

"Is your father here?"

He unfolded one arm just enough to point at Frank's office. She discerned two voices, though she could not decipher the discussion through the closed door. "Do you mind if I wait?"

"Suit yourself." He clicked his mouse, leaning back in his chair.

The workflow seemed to stagnate without A.J. She surveyed his desk, noting all that was missing. Only a stapler and a mechanical pencil remained from the well-organized materials and equipment she had observed yesterday. A power strip plugged into the wall outlet held an orphaned cord that she guessed belonged to his tablet. "Did the police come this morning?"

"He'll get what he deserves."

"Why would you say that? He couldn't have hurt Paige."

Junior snapped his laptop shut, straightening in his seat. "The golden boy is innocent because you two have no secrets? You think he's a model citizen?"

She aimed to launch a defense but suspended her strike as Frank's door opened. He emerged accompanied by a stranger dressed in a black pinstripe suit, accessorized by a red paisley print tie. "Olivia, I didn't hear you come in. This is Ben Billingsley."

The attorney appeared younger than Frank by at least ten years. He coiffed his copious gray locks with fastidious precision and wore round gold-rimmed glasses reminiscent of business style savvy from 1920. He carried a saddle-brown leather briefcase in his left hand and flaunted a diamond-encrusted alumni ring on his right pinky.

"Ms. Penn, the pleasure is mine."

"Is there any news about A.J.? Have you spoken with him? Is he being charged?"

Frank nodded. "Go ahead, tell her."

"I saw Mr. Matthews this morning, but I can't disclose any information to you. As his legal representation, our discussions are privileged."

"Come on, Ben. This is Olivia. A.J.'s family." Frank's request was met with a staunch stare and silence. "Fine. I'm not bound by your rules. The commonwealth's attorney will bring charges against him. Ben plans to see her this afternoon and get details."

Billingsley settled his attaché case on A.J.'s desk, tapping his ring on the brass buckle in a rhythm intelligible only to those familiar with Morse code. He removed his glasses and thrust them into his shirt pocket.

"What evidence is there?" Olivia asked. "Did he confess to anything?"

Frank hesitated, avoiding her eyes, and sighed as one does before having to share unimaginable, horrific news. "The police found his truck behind Grove Manor. I'm sorry, Olivia. I'll spare you the details, but seems there's enough to connect it to Paige's death. Payne believes—"

"Guilty." Junior propped his feet on the desk, punctuating his ruling with a heavy thump from his work boots. Mud freed from the treads soiled the files and papers underneath.

Frank scowled. "Get your shoes off there. Sorry, Olivia. I don't mean to yell. I'm just upset."

"Me too. We're both worried." She turned toward

Billingsley. "Did he explain why he was there? What he was doing?"

"Ms. Penn, I realize he's your friend. The facts are what they are, though." He slid his briefcase from the desk and dangled it by his side. "The police found him hiding in the backwoods. His truck bears evidence that it was used against Ms. Warner. Mr. Matthews is not talking—not talking at all. Frank, I need to go. I'll call you tomorrow morning."

As the attorney left, Frank skimmed his hand over the thin veil of hair he kept swept from right to left. Coal-hued crescents below his eyes contrasted with his ashen skin, aging him overnight.

"Mr. Grossman, why don't you sit?" Olivia suggested. "Let me get you something to drink."

"Thanks, Olivia. I didn't sleep well. All of this happening—it's a nightmare."

She filled a plastic cup from the water cooler as he sat in A.J.'s chair. She handed him the cup and then sat next to him. The office's front door swung open, funneling a draft of cooled air into the disquieted suite. Cassandra strode in, her layered curls bouncing in sync with each accented step. "How predictable, finding you here. You're a harbinger for heartache. The ravens roost wherever you go, Livvy."

Olivia's spine stiffened. Cassandra was goading her with the grating nickname, referencing their elementary school days when Olivia was the shorter of the two. "Itsy-bitsy, little Livvy" was a daily taunt during second grade. Though decades separated those children from the adults they were now, Olivia recalled her seven-year-old self, bullied into silence and angered by the attacks. She stood to counter the aggression.

Frank rubbed his weary eyes. "Ms. Collins, what can I do for you?"

"As the lead journalist for the crime column of the *Apple Station Times*, I've come for a statement. Reaction to having your employee arrested for murder."

Olivia gave Cassandra nominal credit for investigative prowess, but her inquiry suggested either presumption or insider information.

"I'm sorry, Ms. Collins," Frank said. "You'll get no comment from me."

She clicked her pen twice and closed her reporter's pad. She did not ask a follow-up question, confirming Olivia's surmise that the interrogation was a fishing expedition.

Cassandra peered around Olivia, waving at Junior. "You ready?"

"Yep." He shot up, jamming his keys into his pocket. "Going to lunch. I'll be back in an hour."

Olivia did not see that coming. *The oddest couple ever.* She reached for Frank's empty cup as the pair left, holding hands. "Can I get you some more water?"

"No. Thank you, though. Getting off my feet for a few minutes has helped."

She steadied her chair as she sat back down. "Did you see Mrs. Warner last night at the station?"

"No. I was on the phone with Ben for a while."

"I spoke with her. She asked me if I could make some inquiries, reach out to contacts. Find out anything I could. She doesn't believe A.J. did this."

"I agree with her. You know anyone who can help?"

"Not really. She thought I may have connections from my work at the paper. I came here to ask you what your lawyer learned last night, but it seems there's not much to go on." She stared at the empty spot where Paige had hugged her yesterday, recreating and cementing the memory. "A.J. couldn't hurt anyone, but I'm lost. I can't make sense of this."

Frank crossed his arms high on his chest. "You and me both, Olivia. To think he could do something like this? No. I can't—won't accept that."

She scooted to the edge of her chair, rehearsing how best to word what she wanted to ask. "A.J. has worked here a long time. It must be, what—over fifteen years? He and Junior must make a good team. There are some people in my office I can't imagine working with for that long."

He unfolded his arms and leaned forward, bracing his hands on the top of his knees. "They're not drinking buddies, but they work well enough together here and on project sites."

She let the silence settle. "Junior seems to think A.J.'s involved."

Frank stood with a half-smile, knuckle-tapping the desk. "Don't mind Junior. He's just angry that I gave him two bid packets A.J. had been working on. Now that we are a man down, he needs to pick up the slack. I've been pushing him, but he's not like you. Your dad's so proud of you. I am too. Everything you've accomplished—this new job of yours, the places you're going. Sky's the limit for you. Junior doesn't have an ounce of ambition." He helped her to her feet. "Sorry, you don't wanna hear about my business. We need to focus on A.J."

"Thanks for what you said. It means a lot to me."

He wrapped an arm around her shoulders, pulling her close with a heartfelt hug. "I think of you as a daughter. You and Junior practically grew up together. I have to admit, I thought if he could ever get his act straight, that you two could—well, believe me, I know he's no prize. I should let you go or else I'll just keep rambling on, and neither of us wants that. Let's see what Ben comes up with, and if you think of anything, anything at all, let me know how I can help."

CHAPTER 9

Sophia cringed, sitting on the armrest of the sofa in the clinic's foyer. "They left together, holding hands? I'm sorry, Liv, I know there're some things that can't be unseen."

Olivia bobbed her head blankly, bewildered by the mysteries of attraction. "Are they a thing?"

"Not that I'm aware of. Unless, by thing, you mean like hemlock."

Tori sauntered out of the treatment room. "Ladies, are we planning to poison someone? Count me in on that."

Sophia peeked around Tori. "Is Ty okay in there?"

Tori glanced at her son, who was sitting on the mat as he tossed his shoes and socks in opposite directions. He stacked three blocks and knocked them over, punctuating the takedown with an emphatic "pow" and an infectious giggle. "Oh yeah, he'll do that for hours. We all should be so easily entertained. So, Liv, dear, talk to me—Daniel."

Olivia tugged at her shirt's shoulder seam and tucked her hair behind her ears. "Not much to tell. It didn't work out."

"But you were moving to New York with him."

"That was the plan, but—"

"He cheated on you—that scum."

"No. Why would you think he cheated?"

Sophia looked through the open doorway, checking in on Tyler. Then she turned back to Olivia. "You two were a minute away from getting engaged."

Olivia relaxed her stance, resting her hands on her lower back. "He received—and accepted—a job offer in Los Angeles."

Tori sniffed as if a half-dead skunk skulked about. "And? What am I missing here?"

"We decided that between the distance and both of us starting new jobs—with all the added work demands and getting settled on opposite coasts—it might be best to step back from planning something more permanent. Stay friends, take a break until we got ourselves situated. Then, who knows? It's really the best for both of us."

Tori planted her fists on her hips like a schoolmarm. "Olivia Penn, you're egregiously lame. What does that even mean? Take a break? Are you in high school?"

"Always appreciate the support."

Sophia leaned against the table. "Is it really over? You

were together for what—two years? That's a long time. Don't you still have feelings for him?"

Olivia glanced at Tori, judging whether going with a "no comment" would clear or convict her. "As far as I'm concerned, it's over."

Tori shook her head, smirking. "Liv, would you like a shovel to help pile up your—"

"Okay, fine. I'll admit, sure, it's been upsetting. We're just heading in different directions. We're both in good places. This was mutual. We had a great run, and I wish him the best. I really do. But I'm moving on with my life. He's moving on with his life. End of story."

"Well, my dear, you've written yourself into a tragedy then. Regardless, these unfortunate circumstances have blocked your heart chakra. We must clear and rebalance."

"Although generous of you, I'm certain that would involve one of your infamous cleansing smoothies. We all remember what happened last time with your no-fail, go-to recipe."

Tori put her hands on Olivia's shoulders. "Liv, first, you've gotta let that go. Statute of limitations. Second, I won't hold your ignorance about your own energy flow against you. My calling, my mission, is to educate." She abruptly spun Olivia a half-turn and lightly shoved her forward, causing her to stumble.

"Hey! Tori, what the—"

Preston stood on the welcome mat just inside the entrance. "Ms. Penn."

"Sorry. I wasn't saying hey to you." *That sounded really dumb.*

"Okay."

"I mean, it's not that I'm not saying hi to you now."

"Oh, Liv, ever the wordsmith," Tori said as she gauged Preston from hat to toe.

He removed his Stetson. "Ms. Penn, I need a word with you."

Tori grabbed his arm and lead him in. "She'll be delighted to give you a word." Olivia rubbed her forehead, shooting her friend a silent sideways warning.

"I understand you saw Ms. Warner yesterday?" Preston said.

"That's right. I was in the Grossman's office when she came in."

"What did she talk to you about?"

"We planned to catch up later. I had just arrived in town and stopped by to pick up a soil tiller. She said she was going out to Grove Manor."

"Did she say why?"

"Something involving pictures."

"When did you last speak with her prior to yesterday?"

The pendulum on the wall clock clicked a steady beat as she hesitated. "We've mostly texted and e-mailed over the past couple of months. We met for lunch in mid-February."

"So, you two were not particularly close?"

Olivia stood her full height. "She was my friend, Detective Hills. We've both been busy. That's all."

"You're visiting town. Is that right?"

"Yes."

"What do you do for a living?"

She hesitated, but Tori did not as she stepped behind Olivia, grabbed her elbows, and presented her like a spelling bee champion. "She's 'Dear Ms. Penn.'"

"Excuse me? What does that mean?"

"She's a celebrity. She writes the preeminent advice column in the entire country. New York publishers are in a bidding war for her debut novel."

Olivia fixed her sight on the ceiling, longing for aliens to abduct her on the spot.

"So, you write about relationships. Is that correct?"

"It's more than just relationships. People send questions to me about their problems." The more she spoke, the sillier she thought she sounded.

"Okay. I see. Ms. Penn, where did you go after you left Grossman's yesterday?"

The question caught her off guard. She shifted her weight, gathering her hair off her shoulders. "Why?"

"Where did you go?"

"I came here, and then I drove to my dad's house."

"You didn't stop anywhere between the clinic and your father's place?"

"That's correct."

"Did anyone see you after you left here and before you arrived at his house?"

She curled her fingers, brushing the blemished skin from her knock-down yesterday. "Not really."

"Okay. How long will you be in town?"

Tori grasped Olivia's wrist, yanking her forward. "As long as you need her." Olivia unleashed the death stare. Tori rose to the challenge. "You should take her cell number in case you desire more information—or anything else. She has many talents."

Sophia pursed her lips, biting back a smile, but Olivia had had enough. She glared at them both, plotting who to kill off first in her next thriller. "As pleasant as your company is, I have to go to the inn to pick up something for my dad."

Preston's attention was diverted to Tyler's giggles as he celebrated another three-block tower takedown in the treatment room. Seizing the opportunity, Sophia stepped behind Olivia, lowered a shoulder, and love-tapped her forward. Preston flinched, extending his arms, and caught her before she face-planted into his chest.

"Oh, Liv. I'm so sorry," Sophia said. "I've had a case of klutzy all day. Are you okay?"

Olivia quickly backed away from him, allowing Sophia's engendered fuse to fizzle. She opened her mouth to reprimand Sophia for playing with her like a marionette, but her words would not coherently align. Tori awarded Sophia a fist bump for her performance.

Olivia huffed and turned toward the front door. "I'm leaving now."

Preston matched her movement. "You said you were heading over to the inn?"

"That's right, Detective Hills. Since it seems I need to account for my whereabouts, I'm picking up zucchini bread that Beverly Styles has for my dad. Is that okay by you or should I have witnesses?"

"No. I mean, yes. That's fine. No, to the witness part."

Tyler crawled into the foyer, stopping every few feet to yell "pow." Tori lifted him from the ground. "Say bye to Auntie Liv, baby. Someday, hopefully soon, she'll have her own little bundle of joy, and then you'll have a playmate."

Olivia waved to Tyler. "Ba-bye." She said nothing more to either of her friends.

"I'll walk with you, Ms. Penn. I'm heading over to the inn myself."

"Really? You have zucchini bread waiting for you as well?"

A dimple appeared on his left cheek, visible through the short stubble beard framing his face. "No, ma'am. Although, I understand it's first rate. I need to see the owner."

"She a suspect too?" Olivia could not believe she let that fly from her mouth. The entire scene had not been one of her finer moments.

"No. At least I hope not. Beverly Styles is my mama."

CHAPTER 10

Olivia always found something oddly charming about a grown man who called his mother "mama." A half-smile softened her eyes as she eased her stance. She allowed her friends to exalt in their good-natured ribbing for now, scheming for the day she would exact payback in kind. Tyler grabbed her sleeve and mischievously tugged, pulling the shirt's neckline halfway across her shoulder. She tapped his fingers until he loosened his hold, and rumpled his hair when he tried to reclaim his aim. "Fine, Detective Hills. Go with me if you need to. I'm leaving."

They turned to exit, with only Preston exchanging parting pleasantries with Sophia and Tori. He opened the door, insisting she take the lead. "We can drive if you'd prefer. My truck is right out front."

"I prefer not to be in a police vehicle under any circumstances."

"Understood."

They walked three feet apart, Olivia outpacing him as if their destination was not the same. As they passed the Grossman's Construction office, she saw Cassandra sitting on the inside window ledge, instantly sparking "What's Love Got to Do with It" to loop in her head. A pair of business-attired Gen Xers approached from the opposite direction, compelling Preston to draw closer to her as they neared Flora's Florist Gallery. She turned toward him without minding the gap.

"You're wrong about A.J. You're wasting time. I've known him since we were kids, he would never hurt—" She startled as a postal carrier zipped out of the flower shop, spurring her to quickstep into Preston's side. "Sorry. Anyone."

He gave a faint smile, holding up his hands. "No harm, no foul."

She let her defense of A.J. rest as they continued in silence, shifting from the shadows to the sunlight as they crossed the corner on their way to the inn.

Olivia remembered last September when Paige had won a contest sponsored by a mid-Atlantic tourist magazine for an article she had written about the inn. The publisher had sought submissions on small-town hidden gems. Her entry on the history of the inn had earned the top prize and had been featured in the November issue. She had sent Olivia a signed copy of the magazine with the inscription "Next up, the Pulitzer."

Jeremiah Jackson's grandfather had built the hotel when the town was a junction stop for the railway. The former Jackson Depot Lodge provided overnight accommodations for those traveling lengthier routes from the East Coast to the Midwest. A restaurant, gift shop, and general store soon followed. Apple Station's expansion from a mere railroad crossway to a thriving borough served as the legacy of the Jackson family. The building swapped hands several times over the years until Beverly Styles renovated and rebranded the premises as a modern boutique inn, appealing to tourists on weekend getaways. The trains stopped decades ago, but whenever a full moon hung high in the night sky, locals said they could still hear the rails rattle. That was the story that Beverly spun on the inn's website. Ghost stories made for superb sales copy.

Olivia and Preston entered through the historic building's double French doors. The fragrance of freshly brewed coffee and the subtle scent of baking bread paired to permeate the lobby with a welcoming air. Beverly stepped out from behind the reception desk and greeted her son.

"Preston, it's about time you visited your mother." He bent forward, kissing her cheek. Then she turned to Olivia.

"Hi, Mrs. Styles. I'm Olivia Penn—Bill's daughter."

"Call me Bev, please. Your father didn't tell me his daughter was as fetching as you." Her laugh compelled her entire torso to bounce. "Isn't that right, Preston?"

She slapped his bicep. "You failed to inform me you were bringing a guest."

Olivia sheepishly smiled and shook her head. "You're so kind. It's a coincidence—us coming at the same time. My dad has told me so much about you. I appreciate you thinking of him."

"Dear, my pleasure. Bill told me all about you too." She grabbed her son's forearm, addressing him as if dramatizing an aside. "She's a writer. She lives in D.C.— alone." Then she smiled, reopening the stage to all the players. "The zucchini is straight from my greenhouse garden. Preston here helps. He's strong as a lumberjack. When you plant zucchini, it's a modern-day miracle of loaves and fishes. The darn things won't stop growing. That's right, we're a farm to table establishment here." She beamed, glancing back and forth between her son and Olivia. "Yes, indeed. Your father told me so, so much about you too."

"Farm is an overstatement, Mama."

Olivia stifled an amused smile. "My dad and I planted a garden this morning."

"We have something in common then. Yes. So, so much in common." She winked at Preston.

How is she his mother? "I didn't realize the connection between you two when I first met your son."

"Naturally, you picked up on me being a Styles and my boy being a Hills. You, sweetie, are so perceptive and brilliant. Isn't she brilliant, Preston?"

"We should get Ms. Penn her father's bread and let her be on her way."

She persisted, as though his suggestion was neither heard nor under consideration. "My dear departed husband, may he rest in peace, I loved him with all my might, but to take that name when we married, to become Mrs. Beverly Hills—can you imagine?" She cackled, clapped once, and added a foot stomp for emphasis.

Olivia grinned, peeking at Preston. "Excellent point."

"Oh, yes. My son takes after his father—an exemplary family man."

"Okay, Mama. How about we get that bread now?"

"Nonsense, my dear. We won't be rude to our guest. Let's all have lunch." She grabbed Olivia's forearm and Preston's elbow, leading them to the inn's dining room with an impressive show of strength and determination.

Preston pulled out chairs from a rustic, round oak table for both Olivia and his mother. A youthful server wrapped in an indigo apron arrived soon after they settled in their seats.

"Olivia, you must try our special of the day," Beverly said. "We have country ham glazed with an apple-garlic reduction, whipped sweet potatoes, and julienned green beans. How does that sound?"

"Delicious. You had me at ham," Olivia replied.

Preston chuckled as he removed his hat and hung it on the wall beside him.

Beverly turned to Preston. "That okay for you?"

"You had me at ham, too." He unfolded a corn-flower-blue linen napkin and spread it across his lap as Olivia admired the three framed black and white photos of the inn aligned next to his Stetson.

Preston kept angled away from Olivia, looking at the table, at the ceiling, at the entrance to the dining room. "Do you have full occupancy for the festival?" he asked his mother.

"Oh yes, son." She flashed an enchanting smile, grabbing Olivia's hand and squeezing it as though they were lifelong friends. "We've become famously popular. It's all the five-star reviews."

"It's been years since I've eaten here with my dad. The renovations are lovely."

"Thank you. With a name like Styles, the decor demands a bit of panache. Perhaps you would like a tour after we eat? Preston, you can show her the greenhouse garden—that you planted."

"I think Ms. Penn probably has better things to do."

"It's Olivia. Please call me Olivia, Detective."

He turned, meeting her eyes. "In that case, please call me Preston."

Beverly gleamed with delight, as if they had just guaranteed her grandbabies. As they waited for lunch to arrive, she recounted morsels of the inn's history for Olivia's sake, and narrated tales of unexplained nightly noises dating back to the mysterious death of a banker in a room on the second floor in 1910. Beverly used that story in a pop-up on the inn's website every October, converting like catnip for Halloween bookings. Two servers arrived as Beverly urged Preston to escort Olivia on a tour of the haunted hallways after lunch.

"You have an old building with old wooden floors, Mama. No ghosts. Food looks good."

"Where's your imagination? Forgive my son, Olivia. He needs to be more open to possibilities. These beans are the first harvest from the outer garden. Preston planted them in early April. Perfect timing for today. I'm partial to yellow wax, but these green bush Blue Lake will do in a pinch. Now, before we dig in, let's join hands in prayer."

Preston's spine straightened as he micromanaged his silverware's placement. "Since when do you pray before——"

"It wasn't a question, son. We need to always be grateful for what we have, especially for our loved ones."

He raised his eyebrows, but kept his mouth shut. He gently grasped his grinning mother's waiting palm, and then, with apologetic eyes, reached for Olivia's fingers. She smiled to soothe his discomfort as his hand enveloped hers.

With the circle complete, Beverly led the invocation. "Let us have a moment of silence." A blissful aura lit her face.

One minute turned into another. Then another. Olivia bowed her head, rehearsing the rote prayer she learned as a child, in case called upon to lead grace. She could tell from Preston's touch that he was no stranger to manual labor. She detected a callus on the inside of his palm, and she caught herself tracing its outline with her thumb. Her cheeks warmed, and she desperately needed a sip of water.

Preston eyed his mother with waning patience. "Mama, are you actually going to say a prayer?"

"Oh yes, of course. Thank you for the meal, dear Lord. Amen."

Olivia and Preston answered in unison. "Amen."

He sighed. "Wow. That was beautiful."

The sarcasm did not faze her as she winked at Olivia. "It's important to give thanks for our blessings, son—for food and family."

While they ate, Beverly shared as many embarrassing stories from Preston's youth as she could until he halted the history lessons. Olivia found herself captivated by the tales, and for at least an hour, she did not dwell on what troubled her. At the close of the meal, she declined the offer for the grand tour but accepted a rain check and an open invitation to dinner whenever she visited town.

"Thank you, Bev. Lunch was wonderful. My dad will enjoy the bread. I have it on good authority that it's the best."

"Preston, why don't you drive Olivia to where she needs to go?"

He pointed vaguely toward the lobby. "We walked over here from the clinic."

"Then walk back with her."

"No, I'm good," Olivia said. "There's no need. Your son is busy. Thanks, though."

"You're very welcome, dear. See you soon. Don't be a stranger—to me or my boy."

CHAPTER 11

Olivia secured Beverly's zucchini loaf on the center console armrest of her Expedition. She rested two fingers on the push-button start, but kept the engine idle as she leaned back, easing into the leather seat. The homemade bread's sweet aroma swathed the cabin in a cloud of warm, tempting cinnamon spice. She had never baked for Daniel. He was a gluten-free, sugar-free, fat-free wonder. *It's amazing he ever ate anything at all.* Her last foray with baking coincided with her visit home over the holidays, five months ago. Christmas cookies. Tray after tray. She smiled, replaying how A.J. had devoured at least a dozen straight from the oven. He burned his mouth on each one he pilfered when he thought she was not looking.

Why won't he talk to the lawyer? She stared at the police station, dismissing Billingsley's insinuations of guilt from this morning. *What was that between A.J. and Paige yesterday?*

She fastened her seatbelt, pulled away from the curb, and drove the fifteen-minute trip to her father's house in unsettled silence.

She inspected the morning's enterprise when she arrived home. All the delicate seedlings had survived their transitions. Puddles lingered in hollows near the house's foundation, and the hose remained stretched along the garden's border, ready for when next needed. Buddy slumbered on the porch, but when the bread's scent saturated his subconscious, he woke and bounded to greet her. She cupped his lower jaw in her hand. "Hey, little fella. You've been catnapping? Let's go see Dad."

She entered through the front, finding her father asleep on the recliner with the television tuned to a World War II movie. The morning had taxed him. She slipped out of her shoes, sidled into the kitchen, and set the bread next to the stove. Buddy followed, gently weighting his paws, ensuring his claw taps did not wake his owner. He fetched his ball by the back door and bounced it off the top of her foot, watching as it rolled under the table. Air-raid sirens wailed from the living room, followed by the haunting whistling of dropping bombs. Explosions signaled impact, heralding destruction and casualties along the ground. She grabbed a pad of paper and a pen from the junk drawer as Buddy nudged her shin with his nose and whimpered.

"Yes, I see you," she told him. Then she wrote a note for her father.

*Bread is on the counter. Didn't want to wake you. I have
Buddy. Be back soon.*

She squatted, rubbing his chest and chin. "Let's go,
little guy."

Buddy understood that "let's go" meant a car ride.
He shifted onto his hind legs and lifted his front paws,
imparting his version of a high-five. Then he crawled
under the chair, snatched his ball, and followed her
outside.

Olivia drove the same route to Grove Manor she and
Sophia had traveled last night. Today, though, no other
vehicles or barricades barred access to the property. She
crept along the gently sloping, lengthy drive to where it
curved back in the roundabout in front of the home. The
police had lifted the cordon off the grounds, removing all
evidence of their investigation.

She let Buddy loose from the rear compartment, and
he immediately bounded across the weed-infested lawn,
sniffing about a sea of dandelions and buttercups.
Daylight revealed a decrepit manor. Unmanaged over-
growth of boxwood topiary obscured both sides of the
entrance. Ivy inundated the right front corner, climbing
from foundation to rafters. A similar long-dead patch on
the left side stained the masonry with a rust hue. Each of
the four columns that supported the roof over the portico
bore vertical, snaking cracks. Chunks of concrete lay at
the bottom of the steps leading to the entry's double
doors.

Olivia weaved a steady path on the crumbling stairs to the porch and tested the lock, turning the handle and shoving the door with her shoulder. She glanced back, ensuring that Buddy was busy policing the grounds, and then, stepping forward, she crossed the threshold.

The entrance opened into an expansive foyer. A stately fireplace faced her fifty feet from the front door. She imagined, when in full glory on a winter's evening, the heat generated from the hearth may have warmed the entire first floor. To her left, a staircase of nearly two dozen steps led to the second level. The landing split left and right. To the right, an extended aisle followed the length of the foyer below. A three-foot high railing with worn white wooden posts bordered the corridor. Most of the decayed pillars were detached from either the top or bottom, no longer protecting the passage. To her right, on the ground floor, was an empty room with walnut wood paneling. Inside, a dilapidated fireplace half the size of the one in the foyer aligned opposite the doorway. She conjectured the side-suite may have once been a study or parlor.

Though she stepped lightly, the eerie silence amplified creaking from the frail floorboards. Sparrows and wrens cautiously glided inside, dipping from the second-level railing, swooping above her as she angled toward the empty room. Last night, she had noticed the extensive damage to the front windows. The interior view revealed entire portions missing. Someone had placed plywood over the lower halves of the absent panes, but as the barriers lacked full coverage, debris from outside littered the floor. She counted multiple holes in the ceiling that allowed thin streams of light to filter through from the room above. The breaches aligned with rotting oak flooring below, suggesting long-term leakage. She understood now why no renovations were underway and appreciated what Frank had said yesterday about the property's condition. Though once a noble home, the manor's neglected past left little hope for a fate other than demolition.

She went back into the foyer, examining the dirt that soiled the floor. All lay indistinct except for her own footprints and a conspicuous blemish by the staircase. The oddity that caught her attention was a patch of mud imprinted with a quarter-inch of shoe tread. A smaller remnant of mud sullied the third step. More marred the fifth. *Probably the police from last night.*

She followed the trail, stopping every few strides as she ascended the staircase, listening for anything besides the sparrows that now serenaded her with their chirps and trills. Upon reaching the second floor, she first looked left into a narrow hallway leading to seven rooms. The suite at the far end was open, but five of the other six remained sealed by termite-damaged doors. The standout allowed for a partial view of the room's empty interior through a skewed plywood sheet supported solely by a smattering of nails along both sides of the doorframe. To her right, across the landing above the foyer, a twin hallway aligned. The muddy footprints lay in an unmistakable path.

When she approached the threshold of where the aisle over the foyer yielded to the hallway, she discovered that the passageway mirrored the layout of the other side. All doors on this end, though, were open. The footprints led into the second room on the right. She peered inside, observing a hole in the floorboards large enough to swallow the unlucky limb of a misplaced step. Multiple rifts in the ceiling exposed the interior to the elements. She glanced back along the hall, judging the distance to the staircase, and listened for any movement. Still just her.

Only a dresser to the left of the entrance furnished the threadbare room. A fractured window on the opposite wall provided a panorama of the front lawn and driveway. A soiled circular carpet served as the room's sole adornment. Olivia walked toward the window, and as she crossed over the heirloom covering, the floor sagged without warning. She hopped off the worn, woven rug and rolled it to expose a cannonball-size breach guarded by a lone sheet of warped and moldy particle board. She knelt on both knees a foot from the gap, keeping her weight balanced on her heels. She peered through the rotted holes in the fragile support, viewing the parlor six inches below, and then scooted back and returned the carpet to its prior placement.

Standing, she surveyed the dresser. The barren drawers hung open in a haphazard array. A framed photo of a young woman standing beside a well-dressed, white-haired man occupied one corner. A pint-size toy fire truck and a powder blue rattle rested on the opposite end. In between lay a disassembled and broken picture frame. Careful to avoid the jagged glass, she flipped the frame, finding it empty.

A fragment of glass matching the missing piece lay on the ground. She reached for the shard and the sparrows' songs silenced. She peered around the doorframe's casing for a protected view of the hallway, seeing no one. She stepped into the corridor and edged back toward the landing, listening for the slightest hints of any creaks or cracks. Though faint at first, she attuned to the sound of Buddy barking outside with a steady, agitated rhythm. She quickened her pace, rushed down the staircase, and exited the manor.

By the time she reached the porch, Buddy's barking had escalated in pitch and frequency. As a mother can interpret the tone of her child's cry, Olivia knew he was announcing a threat. She hastily descended the front steps, turned the corner bordered by the boxwood, and stopped dead in her tracks. Buddy stood on guard in rigid fury twenty feet from the tree line, staring at the path where the police had extracted A.J. yesterday.

"Buddy, come," she called. He postured in full alert with his tail outstretched, reaching straight skyward. She yelled louder. "Buddy, let's go."

She inched forward, as if wading through a minefield

with leaden legs. Buddy growled, and his entire body shook with each yelp.

"Buddy, here. Now." He bolted for the tree line. "No, stop!"

He halted his charge at the forest's edge. She no longer hesitated, hustling straight away to retrieve him. She hoisted him from the ground, peering into the tangled backwoods brush. Buddy ceased his warnings and licked her cheek, panting from his labored efforts.

"You chasing after a squirrel, little pup? You about gave me a heart attack."

She rubbed his neck and was about to turn back toward the manor when two twigs snapped in the dense, dark foliage opposing her. Her pulse spiked, alerting Buddy, and he snarled as he fought to vault from her arms. She held him tight, stepping back without diverting her eyes from the tree line. She retreated in this manner the entire distance to her Expedition. After securing Buddy in the cargo hold, she fixated on the forest for several minutes, wanting to show that she knew she was being watched.

She hit the lock switch as soon as she was behind the wheel, allowing the seat's cushion to absorb her full weight. She closed her eyes, breathing in while counting to five. Her phone rang, and she jolted, focusing immediately on the tree line through the passenger window. She scanned all sightlines, double-clicked the locks, and put the call on speaker.

"Hello?"

"Olivia, it's Beverly."

"What can I do for you?" She started the engine and released the emergency brake.

"I hope you don't mind me calling. Ms. Maria gave me your number."

She pulled away, imprinting the decrepit manor in her memory. "No, Mrs. Styles, I mean Bev, that's fine."

"Good. I meant to ask earlier if you'll be around for Saturday's festival."

She glimpsed the backwoods in the rearview mirror, seeing Buddy on alert with his nose pressed against the window. She thought of the photo of Paige with her mother, celebrating last month at the inn. "I'll be staying."

"Splendid. Please come and sit with us at our table for the luncheon. Preston will be there. Bring your dad, too. Okay, sweetie—it's a date. We're so glad you're here."

CHAPTER 12

Olivia woke before sunrise Wednesday morning, weary after a sleepless night alternating between sitting on the edge of her bed and lying, staring at the ceiling. The *Downton Abbey* theme played at its preset daily alarm time, but she was already awake, curled up in her childhood reading nook since four o'clock. She had spent endless hours through the years in this same spot, propped against these same pillows, captivated by her books and writing her stories. The overgrown branches from an oak tree tapped on her window, but they no longer scared her the same as when she was a child.

She had not spoken to her father about her visit to Grove Manor yesterday and had no plans to do so over breakfast. She rubbed her tired eyes and scrolled through her e-mails, leaving them all unopened as the words in the subject lines blurred, transforming the text into hieroglyphics. By the time she joined her father in the kitchen, he had finished his first cup of coffee and progressed to the editorials in section A of the newspaper.

"Good morning, honey. How'd you sleep?"

She grabbed a mug from the cabinet and a spoon from the drawer. "Great. Glad to be home."

"I'm inspecting the garden before I go for seconds. See if everything survived. You wanna come?"

She stifled a yawn and dumped her scoop of espresso blend into an amber glass jar sitting next to a similar, smaller one for tea bags. "Sure. I hope the squirrels didn't dig at the roots. They always think something's hidden when the soil gets turned over."

"I sprinkled cayenne pepper at the base of all the plants after you left yesterday. That'll keep them away." He stood, setting his glasses on top of the opened paper, ready to resume reading the Metro section upon return-ing. "I have a feeling this will be our best year yet."

They exited through the front and surveyed the plot. "It looks wonderful, honey. You did a spectacular job."

"You always say that, Dad."

"It's the truth." He wrapped his arm around her shoulders, pulling her in close. "I added something special to the cucumbers."

"Not the nitro patches."

"They worked with the habaneros. Nitrogen is good for a garden. It's called fertilizer. Everybody knows that."

She bit at the bait of his playful cast, luring her to shake her head and sigh. "That's not how it works."

"You watch. We'll get so many I'll be selling them at

the farmer's market on Saturday mornings." They traversed the garden's length to the sweet potato patch at the back boundary. "You should spend some time in your mother's office while you're here. Why don't you take something of hers with you? A memento from home for your new place."

"You mind if I do that now?"

He reached into his pocket, pulled out his key ring, and handed it to her. "Just lock up when you're done. Spend as much time as you want."

He walked back to the house, leaving Olivia alone to make her visit. After her mother died, she spent countless quiet hours in the cottage, surrounded by her mother's books and writings, to ease her grief. She had not been inside, though, for nearly a year. The interior remained unchanged—her father never wanted to move a thing. Her mother's glasses lay on the desk in the same spot she last placed them. One of the four bookcases housed collections of her mother's writing, while the other three sheltered an ample, diverse library. A glider chair bided its time by the front window, waiting for a willing partner to sit a spell and share in the sun's radiant warmth.

She read the spines of her mother's binders, each one labeled by form, genre, theme, location, or season. *Fall: Poetry, Short Suspense, Tasmania—1995*. The case was full of them. She selected a volume titled *Memories, Olivia*, and flipped to a random handwritten page.

Olivia,

Today, you were a most enchanted child. As Daddy and I
sat on the porch enjoying a fine evening, you saw your first
firefly. With you sitting on my lap, one of our little summer
friends came to rest on your arm. You gazed at it, and
when it glowed, your eyes widened. You looked at us in
amazement! When the glow disappeared, your smile left,
and you turned sad. When the glow returned, your face
beamed as if you had discovered something magical.
Daddy and I laughed, and then we carried you to the back-
yard where hundreds of fireflies danced in the night sky.
You pointed to as many of the lights as you could until you
fell asleep. May you always be looking for your lights. Even
the darkest of night skies can never extinguish the glow of
the smallest light.
Love,
Mom

Olivia held the binder close, knowing the last person to
touch it was her mother, her hands now where her mother's
hands once were. She traced the signature with her finger,
recreating the moment her mother left behind this memory.
A blue-lacquered fountain pen lay idle on the desk. She
removed a box of gold-bordered cream stationery from the
side drawer and drew the pen several times across the page
to test it, leaving behind two solid lines. She recapped the
pen, shoved it into her pocket, and replaced the letterhead
underneath her mother's address book in the drawer. As
she did, a slip fell from the petite book, with the name M.

Matthews and a phone number. She retrieved the wayward scrap from the ground and opened the book to put it back in place. An entry for Martha already existed, but the phone number differed. The ten-number sequence in the address book she remembered from her childhood, but the one on the slip belonged to an adjacent area code and was not in her mother's handwriting.

She checked her phone for the time. An hour had passed. She promised herself she would return before she left on Sunday to select a sampling of her mother's poetry to take with her to New York. She ran her fingers across the spines of the binders and then knelt, lifting the lid of a cardboard storage box on the bottom shelf. She could inventory the contents from memory. It held mementos from her youth: a cloth Red Riding Hood picture book, a pink teddy bear, a painted rock she gave to her mother as a gift. Scratching on the screen signaled Buddy had found her and wanted to play. She locked the cottage, picked up Buddy's ball, and threw it past the garden, toward the front of the house.

Then she entered the kitchen through the door off the back porch and placed her father's key ring on the counter. "Dad, question for you."

He held up his hands. "This pepperoni plate isn't mine. I wouldn't dare to eat something so unhealthy— when you're not here to supervise."

"So it's for?"

"Buddy."

"We'll circle back to that later. I want to ask you about A.J."

"Okay." He motioned for her to sit, sliding the appetizer arrangement closer to her. "Feel free."

"I thought that was Buddy's."

"You never know about that beagle. Better eat it before it goes bad. What's on your mind?"

"I guess I was curious more about his mother, Mrs. Matthews."

William aligned a slice of pepperoni and a piece of pepper jack on a cracker. "Martha. Friendly woman. She was our neighbor for over twenty years."

"Where did she live before she moved next door?"

"Not sure." He bit off half of his hors d'oeuvre, continuing as he chewed. "She was already living here when we bought the house. Why do you ask?"

"I found two phone numbers for her in Mom's address book. The home number I recognized, but the other one I didn't."

He leaned back, placing his empty glass by the sink. "Could be for a cell."

"Yeah, you're probably right."

"Find anything special to take with you?"

She pulled the pen from her pocket. "This one was her favorite."

"She would love that. Penn's pen." He laughed as he fashioned a triple-decker cheese tower. "Your mother would be very proud of you. Working in publishing in

New York. A signed author. Everything she wanted for you."

"Not signed yet." She selected a cracker and a slice of sharp cheddar. Her doubts festered. Wasting her mother's sacrifices weighed on her.

"It'll happen, sweetie. You know, I've been thinking. I don't believe any of this about A.J. for one minute. I can't see him hurting anyone."

"Let's say, Dad, hypothetically, that he did it. Why? What might his motive be?"

"She had something on him."

"What do you mean?"

He stacked two slices of pepperoni and dipped them in a finger bowl of spicy mustard. "I mean she had dirt on him. She knew something. Saw something. Uncovered something. You can find out a lot of things that shouldn't be found by searching the internet these days."

Olivia rolled her cracker across the table, pinning the square-cut cheese to its base with her thumb. "That gives me an idea." She pushed her chair back and palmed ingredients from the plate to bolster her meager breakfast. "I don't think Buddy will mind if I take a little extra. I'll be home for dinner." She kissed her father goodbye and grabbed her keys from the counter, plotting a course to find and confront Cassandra.

CHAPTER 13

Olivia parked her SUV two stores down from Paige's office, in front of Carol's Comforts. The boutique gift shop, a fixture in Apple Station for over twenty years, stocked stationery, specialty home decor, and seasonal wares. She visited whenever in town to replenish her supply of local hand-poured candles and load up on greeting cards for holidays and birthdays. Daisy's Feed and Saddlery occupied a suite between the store and Paige's office. Olivia popped in from time to time to chat with Sawyer Weston when he held hours to repair tack. They had dated for six months after high school, but then had gone their separate ways as their college choices landed them on opposite coasts. They had tried to make it work, but the distance proved to be an insurmountable barrier to the budding relationship. Still, they remained friends, and met every year for a trail ride through the Shenandoah Valley during autumn, using horses from his father's stables. This past October they celebrated their tenth anniversary of the tradition with a picnic at the summit of Hawksbill Mountain. Today, though, she paused in passing only for a moment, admiring the artistry of the custom-crafted saddle in the storefront window.

The preparations for Saturday's festival were underway. In the town square, red, white, and blue bunting draped from the gazebo's roof and railings. A half-dozen workers labored, constructing the hosting stage for the weekend's headlining entertainment: the hometown bluegrass trio, The Pickle Barrels. Five pallets of stacked folding tables lay behind two bleacher sectionals, and a white box truck stocked full of matching metal chairs waited by an impromptu dock near the tiered seating for unloading.

Olivia eased open the door to the low-lit, quiet office of the *Apple Station Times* as if testing for a trip wire. The clang from a cluster of bells froze her mid-entrance as the suite's lone occupant startled, knocking a capped water bottle onto his keyboard.

"Hey, Cooper."

The bright-eyed twenty-two-year-old shoved the sleeves of his blue button-down oxford above his elbows and smoothed his wavy chocolate-brown hair. He sprung from his seat, circled his desk two-arm's length from her, and extended his right hand, offering a professional, collegial greeting. "Ms. Penn, an honor to have you in our humble office."

"Come on, Cooper, it's always Liv to you."

He grinned, wrapped his arms around her like a Burmese python, and laid his head on her shoulder. "I've missed you. I heard you were in town. I always read your columns. Every word of every single one."

She coughed as he dialed up the pressure on her rib cage. "Thanks, Cooper. I can always count on you. Missed you too. It's been a while. How've you been? How's your mom? How about letting go?"

He cut her loose, but kept well within her personal space, spurring her to inch back. "I'm good. I finished my exams at the community college last week. I'm working here for the summer. Mom was tidying the RV, getting ready to roll into retirement, but after what happened, she'll be staying." His shoulders slumped, and his smile faded as he eyed the empty desk opposite his, across the open-plan office. "We're all gutted about Paige. She was the nicest. We'd go to lunch together once a week. She read my drafts, gave me pointers. She always had time for me."

"That sounds like her. I'm still in shock myself." She gently squeezed his hand. "We'll get through this together. We'll all need time. That's great news about you finishing school. Congratulations. You writing now for the paper?"

He scrunched his nose, rolling his quill-print tie halfway to his collar before unfurling it back to his belt buckle. "Mom doesn't assign me actual articles yet. I write the copy for the free item classifieds. Gary out on

Orchard Trail—you know where you keep going past Hamilton's and then take the right where the road dips over the bridge? He has twenty-eight bunnies that need a home. If you're interested."

She propped herself on the edge of his desk, casually crossing her arms. "New York winters and my lack of square footage, or grass, wouldn't suit them. I'm sure you'll find a taker. You and Paige were close, then?"

"She'd always call me Coop."

Olivia smiled, recalling last year when Paige served as a reluctant fill-in judge for the youth poultry show at the State Fair and announced the Blue Ribbon Hen Award while waving fried chicken at the runners-ups. "You work on any stories with her? What about the piece she was writing on Grove Manor? Know anything about that?"

He pursed his lips, puffing his cheeks like a chipmunk. "Not too much. Sometimes she let me help with research, but not on that one. After Mom named her an assistant editor last week, she asked me to gather the details of the library's summer reading program. I'm writing the copy for it in next month's calendar column. She treated me to pie at Jillian's that day. They had pecan on special."

"I didn't know that."

"Usually it's apple on Fridays, but lately, it's been pecan or shoo-fly."

"No. I meant the promotion. What about Cassandra?"

He trained his sight on the grid lines of the ceiling's acoustic panels. "She didn't want to come."

"No, I meant—never mind. I imagine Cassandra wasn't happy with your mom's decision."

"When she heard about it, she stormed out of the office." He pointed toward the wall by the entrance. "Slammed the door so hard, that mirror fell. The frame cracked, and it won't sit square, but I put it back up anyhow. C'est la vie."

She aligned her head with the slanted decor. "Oui, monsieur."

"Huh? What?"

"Nothing. You were saying?"

"Can I ask you a question? A personal one. Since you're a professional columnist, I could use your opinion —strictly off the record."

"Sure. What's on your mind?"

"Do you think I have a chance with Cassandra?"

"And by chance, you mean?"

"If I asked her to dinner. Don't get me wrong. If you were younger ..." He gestured back and forth between them. "The age gap makes it weird."

"Cooper, Cassandra and I are the same age."

"Really?" He briefly raised one eyebrow. "Can I ask you something else?"

She interlaced her fingers and cracked her knuckles. "Go for it."

"Paige was helping me with my writing, and I was

wondering if you had any advice. I'm trying to convince Mom to let me work on feature articles."

"I'm sure she will, Cooper. Your future's bright, brighter if you leave Cassandra out of it. I think first——"

"Wait. Hold on. I should write this down." He pulled a plastic-wrapped reporter's notebook from his back pocket and flipped it over and over and around every which way, struggling to locate a cooperative corner to tear. "Where's the pull thingy on this?" He snatched a pair of scissors from his desk caddy, held the notebook against his chest, and attempted to pry open an end by thrusting the twin points like a dagger toward his throat.

"Whoa! Please, stop. Here, let me try."

He passed her the pad, and she peeled the plastic with exaggerated effort, sparing him any embarrassment.

"I guess you've had practice with that. Can you repeat what you were saying?"

"I think you first——"

"Wait. Lighten the throttle." Cooper scribbled as he spoke. "Think—you—first. Okay. Go."

She eyed him, standing there with pen and paper at the ready. She was filled with dread, envisioning him yanking the emergency brake every time she picked up speed. "Have to practice writing——"

"Hold on. Practice—writing. Now go."

She felt herself age. She adored Cooper like a puppy —not like Buddy, more like a lost doe-eyed stray wandering the streets, searching for his family. She wanted to help, but she did not have time to fill his inkwell drip by drip today. "Can we pick up on this later? I have deadlines for my weekend columns—"

"Say no more." He crossed his arms, opened his eyes wide, and heavily sighed. "Deadlines. I get it. It's the life we chose, right?"

She nodded, matching his expression, echoing his exhalation.

"Let the pros write the prose," he said. "I just made that up now. You're free to use it."

She could not help but smile. "Thanks. It was great to see you, Cooper." She headed for the door, but stopped short of the exit. "One more thing. Paige said she was taking pictures of Grove Manor on Monday."

"Pictures—no. Anyone who shoots photos for a feature uses a DSLR from here. I log them. She didn't check any out. I was here all day. Lots of folks getting rid of things on account of the rain keeping everyone inside over the weekend. I'm sorry I don't have more to tell you about the story she was writing. Ms. Jess at the bank is in charge of the sale. She'd have details. The low-down, the nitty-gritty, the whole—"

"Thanks, Cooper. That's actually very helpful. We'll catch up later, okay?"

He beamed with the compliment, gesturing a surfer's double "hang loose" as she turned to leave. "Hook 'em horns."

She waved as she walked out the door. "Aloha, Cooper."

"Dear Ms. Penn, we're not hiring." Olivia spun to see

Cassandra nearing the office, passing the round-post hitching rail in front of Daisy's next door. She sported a messy top bun perilously close to unraveling with each step.

"That's a shame. We might work well together."

"You need experience to work here. Actual reporting experience, that is."

Olivia tried to maintain eye contact, but the physics-defying cohesion of Cassandra's giant ginger topper astonished her. "I suppose you're right. What are you working on now?"

"That's privileged information."

"Privileged for whom?"

"Members of the press."

"I see. Then let me ask you this. Do you think Cooper's mother will now make you an assistant editor?"

Cassandra shifted her weight onto her back foot, thrusting a finger toward Olivia's chin. "You're awful. That's not a concern of mine. I've got a crime to cover."

"You investigating?"

"Why are you here? Shouldn't you be addressing someone's heartache? Perhaps something you can write with authority on?"

"Are you and Junior dating?"

Cassandra ripped a lanyard with her ID and a key from around her neck and wedged it into her front pocket. "Shove off to New York. You'll flame out like a hack."

"I'll take that as a yes. I'm guessing you know full well A.J. had nothing to do with what happened to Paige."

Cassandra stepped around Olivia, knocking her shoulder back in passing. She flung the office door open, triggering a cacophony of bells and shattered glass. Cooper hastened to retrieve the fallen mirror as Cassandra trampled over the broken bits, brushing right by him.

CHAPTER 14

Olivia balanced on the edge of the curb, cooled by the shade of a cherry tree rooted in a square patch of soil on the sidewalk fronting the newspaper's office. A near-pristine aspen green Crown Victoria cruised by, observing a school-zone pace. She assumed the sedan had a driver, though she discerned only the headrest and the hint of a hand at the top of the wheel through the rear window. A circular saw's whirling buzz blended with the ruckus of two laborers working in tandem in the town square, securing the bottom boards to the stage's steps. She strolled across the trimmed lawn, watching as one carpenter knelt, holding the planks in place as the other drilled the freshly hewn lumber into stair stringers with decking screws. The kneeling worker jumped to his feet and yanked the final board off the stage, revealing a familiar profile outfitted in a black T-shirt and work-worn jeans. He glanced her way, and she quickly looked up at the low, lumpy clouds. Within two strides, her ankle rolled in a shallow hollow of ground, paining the outside of her Achilles.

"Olivia, over here!" Dorothy Peabody waved. She tapped her husband, Floyd, sitting beside her on a bench bordering the town lawn. Floyd looked at his wife and then in the direction she was pointing as Olivia walked toward them. He smiled and joined in with his wife's welcoming wave.

Olivia swore under her breath at the sunken patch that had tripped her as she limped over to the sidewalk. "Mr. and Mrs. Peabody, how are you?" She lifted her right foot, rotating her ankle a half-dozen times in each direction.

Dorothy reached out and grabbed Olivia's hand, squeezing it like a ripe lemon. "The knees are cranky today. You can't reach our age without aches and pains. I'd stay young if I were you."

The long-married couple laughed and playfully elbowed each other. Floyd fanned his book on the bench and scooted to the edge of the seat. He rocked forward once, twice, stood halfway, then fell back. He tried again. One, two, and as he extended his legs, Dorothy pushed on his backside, boosting him straight to his feet. He shuffled to Olivia, hugging her as if she were a paper doll.

Dorothy removed a receipt from her purse, inserting it as a bookmark in the propped paperback next to her. "How long are you in town, dear?"

"Through Sunday."

Floyd lowered himself back onto the bench in slow motion. "Splendid day, isn't it? I've got a question for you."

"Now don't bother her, honey."

"I'm sure she'd know what to do. You said she writes a column."

The rising tang of beef brisket from the smokers of Sweet Moe's Pit Stop suggested that the assembled crowd by the stage would soon stake claim to the choice cuts of savory, smoked meat. Olivia's stomach rumbled, reminding her that she had only eaten four crackers and three slices of cheese for breakfast. "Know about what? It's okay. What's your question?"

Floyd leaned forward, removing his glasses. "We've got this coffee pot."

Dorothy grabbed his arm, placing her other hand along her own cheek. "Olivia, the darn thing is ancient. I call it T-Rex." The couple giggled. "I've been on him to get one of those fancy machines that use those pods. They're just like science fiction."

"I don't trust them the same as the wife does. I bet they overflow. Cause a mess. Give me a good old Mr. Coffee pot any day. You can't go wrong there."

"My dad shares your sentiments," Olivia said. "But I'm with you, Mrs. Peabody. I have a single cup brewer at home. It suits my needs."

Dorothy poked Floyd in the ribs. "See. I told you. I'm finding one on the web this afternoon."

"The wife here shops for everything now on the computer. Yesterday, the mail carrier delivered water to us in a box. Water, in bottles, delivered in a box. What do you think of that?"

"Forgive him, Olivia, you've heard what they say about old dogs."

"You trying to teach me new tricks, dear?"

"No, sweetie. Old hound dogs get fleas the same as young puppies." Floyd chuckled and clutched his wife's hand, tenderly kissing her as if she were a fairy-tale maiden. Olivia grinned, charmed by the knightly gesture, admiring the compatibility and companionship the couple shared.

Floyd turned back to Olivia. "This coffee pot we've got, won't come clean. Have any pointers?"

"You shouldn't put her on the spot," Dorothy said.

He jabbed his thumb toward Olivia. "You told me she writes those advice articles."

"Oh. No, Mr. Peabody, it's not a column quite like that."

Dorothy scooted sideways, inviting Olivia to sit in between them. "You do a recipe column, don't you? I've been hunting for a new sheet cake recipe. Last one I baked raised flat as roadkill."

Floyd reached across Olivia, playfully poking his love in the arm. "That's the truth. I bet I could've slipped it through the mail slot."

Olivia propped herself on the edge of the bench, sweeping her hair behind her shoulders. "I don't do many—any—recipes either. I'm guessing vinegar may work for both. It handles just about everything."

He nodded, tapping Olivia's knee. "I knew she would have the answer. Whoever wants only one cup of coffee anyhow?"

Dorothy dismissed him with a wave of her hand. "I saw you across the street talking to Cassie Collins. It's terrible about June's daughter. I can't recall anything like that happening here before. Do you, sweetie?"

"Remember what? Who are you?"

She grinned, patting him on the cheek. "This guy here—he's a keeper. They're saying that fellow who works at Frank's did it."

"They got it all wrong, darling."

Olivia glanced at Floyd. "What do you mean?"

"A.J. couldn't hurt a fly. Nice fella. He patched our roof last year after the insurance appraiser said we had damaged shingles. Guy came out and told me the whole roof needed replaced, but A.J. took a look and shored up a few leaky spots. Got it to pass inspection. Saved me a lot of money, that's for sure. No, he didn't do it."

"The police don't share your opinion, Mr. Peabody."

"Steve Sharp—the ex-mayor. No doubt about it. He did it."

"I hate to say it, but my husband may be right."

Olivia balked, lost by Floyd's left turn, debating whether to entertain his hypothesis or dismiss it like her father's nitroglycerin theory. "The ex-mayor? Why would you think he did it?"

Floyd frowned, folding his arms. "It was that article June's daughter wrote. He wasn't paying his taxes. She found out he hadn't done so for years and wrote two and a half pages about it. He had to resign afterward. I can't imagine he was too happy with her."

Olivia stood facing them. "When did this happen?"

"Oh, what, Dorothy, three, four months ago?"

"Yes, that seems about right."

"What happened to him?"

"He got a lawyer. Billingsley. That slick fella. His office is by the police station. They worked something out. That's what having money will do for you. He has to pay back what he owes under what they're calling court supervision. I would've gotten the slammer. Now, he's been doing construction around town."

Dorothy nodded. "Out at that Grove Manor place, too. Rose from the beautician shop has a sister whose daughter works at the bank. Her niece told her they've been fixing up things to prepare for the sale on Friday. You might not remember it. You're so young. The house used to be magnificent. Like you'd see in the movies. Such a shame. It would be a perfect wedding venue, but the cost of the renovations would be more than most anyone around here could afford."

Floyd picked up his paperback. "I've seen him working in town, too. Last Wednesday, he was with Frank's boy, repainting walls at the bookstore."

"My husband here loves his books."

"I'd rather have a book in my hand any day than be staring at one of those tablet things like you."

As the Peabodys contested the merits of paperbacks versus e-readers, Olivia wondered if the police were aware of the connection between Paige and the ex-mayor. She glanced toward the station and then across the street. A preschooler with a four-wheel walker bull-dozed her way out of Sophia's clinic, racing ahead of her mother toward the sweet treats in the cafe's window. Floyd waved his murder mystery as if preaching from the bible while Dorothy mocked him with her cell, completing payment on her next e-book. *How did I not know? I should've called Paige sooner.* She looked back at the Peabodys, who mirrored her stare.

"I'm sorry," Olivia said. "What was your question?"

Floyd shook his cell at his wife. "Blue light. They say it strains the eyes. What do you make of that? I tell you; no blue light is coming out of my books."

"Mr. Peabody, you said Steve Sharp is still in town?"

"Yes, that's right."

"Do you have any idea where he's working this week?"

He pointed toward the end of the square. "Our illustrious former mayor is the one standing by the johns."

Olivia followed his direction, identifying the man in question. Steve Sharp, dressed in a black T-shirt and work-worn jeans, stood by the completed stage, super-vising the unloading and placement of a dozen porta-potties, thanks to Paige's exposé.

CHAPTER 15

Olivia's rapid-onset nausea had little to do with her meager morning meal. Her stomach soured, twisting in knots as she reconstructed Monday's timelines. Steve may have been on his way to Grove Manor not long after their much-too-close encounter outside the clinic.

Floyd and Dorothy rose in sync and excused themselves, relinquishing their prime seating to a pair of chickadees, citing places to go and people to see. They interlocked arms, stepping deliberately across the short span of grass until finding firmer footing on the sidewalk.

Olivia scanned the length of the lawn from end to end. A doting mother in a yellow floral sundress cooed close to a swaddled baby in a stroller she rocked back and forth while waiting to cross the street. The Peabodys moseyed in the opposite direction, holding hands and sharing sweet nothings, in no hurry to get home. In between, she saw herself as a twelve-year-old playing soccer on weekend afternoons with A.J. and his buddies. As a team captain, he always picked her first, though she was the slightest and youngest among them all. On the night of their high school graduation, she and Paige promised each other they would be friends forever as they sat side by side, soaring higher and higher on the square's playground swings. Now, a short skip from the slides, Sharp perched on the edge of the stage with a plate of Sweet Moe's barbecue in hand, bantering with Chief Payne like a barstool pal.

Olivia crossed the street and headed for the clinic to see if Sophia had finished her morning sessions. Maria embraced Olivia as soon as she stepped through the door. "Mija, I'm so sorry about Paige. Ernesto described the awful scene to me when he arrived home. I know Alexander is like a brother to you. We have to keep our faith and stay strong for his sake."

Olivia nodded, not knowing what to say. The clinic always served as a cozy sanctuary for her whenever she visited town, never failing to ease the stress and strain from the hustling pace she kept herself to in the city. She could find her way around the space even if blindfolded. Her eyes drifted to the framed photo of her and A.J. amid the collage of family keepsakes arranged on the wall next to the children's play corner. The snapshot memorialized the day the clinic opened for business.

Sophia leaned out of the treatment room. "I'm finishing up a note. Give me a second."

Josefina set her recipe binder aside, stood, and

strolled past Olivia, pushing the sleeves of her forest-green cardigan to three-quarter length. "You need to eat. I'll start lunch." She sauntered halfway down the hallway before Olivia could summon a single word to decline.

Maria smiled softly, taking her hand and leading her to the sofa. "It's useless to protest when you come here. I should make sure she leaves us room for dinner. Please sit while you're waiting."

Olivia melted into the couch's cushions, lifting her legs and drawing her toes toward her. Her hamstrings ached from the hours spent on her knees in the garden yesterday. She leaned back, closing her eyes. *I have the online chat tomorrow, the call with New York on Friday, and then . . .*

She jerked her head forward, waking from a two-minute doze. Josefina's recipe collection lay opened beside her, bookmarked on a page for tres leches cake. She stifled a yawn as her stomach rumbled, craving a plate full of carbs.

"Hey, Liv. Sorry to keep you waiting. I'm running behind today." Sophia settled on the sofa, gently twisting her lower back a quarter turn to each side. "I'm so tired. I barely slept the last two nights. I can't stop seeing every-thing from Monday—the ambulance, police, Paige's mom."

"Me too. I nodded off for a sec, sitting here. Ques-tion for you—do you know anything about the article Paige wrote that led to Steve Sharp's resignation?"

Sophia stretched her arms overhead. "That

happened about three months ago. He got off pretty easy. He lost his job, of course, but they never filed charges against him. Still can't understand how that works. You think that's somehow related?"

"I don't have a clue. The Peabodys told me about it before I came here. I went out there yesterday."

"Where's there?"

"Grove Manor."

"By yourself?" Olivia nodded, earning a back-handed whack to her arm. "What possessed you to do that? Why didn't you call me? I would've gone with you. You shouldn't have done that." Sophia readied for a follow-up smack, but Olivia's recoil confirmed she had duly noted the disapproval.

"The inside is a mess. And—I wasn't exactly alone."

She related all that occurred, and when she finished, Sophia's silence and stern stare prompted her to scoot out of striking range. "Congratulations, Liv, on earning a doctorate in dumb. Stick it on the wall next to your other degrees. What were you thinking?"

"First, I'll take that—only because I know you care." She flashed a campy smile worthy of a teeth whitening ad, cracking Sophia's stoic pose. "I know. You're right. I should've let someone—"

"Someone?"

"Okay, I should've called you. I'm sorry," Olivia said. "Something's really off about Junior and Cassandra, and I don't mean the nightmare of them playing the dating game. Can't put my finger on it. Murder is a tough tale to pin on her though. Even on him. He's been working with Sharp, but I don't know if that's something or nothing."

Sophia peeked toward the hall and leaned closer to Olivia. "As long as we're sharing—my dad told me when Payne called for the ambulance, Paige may have already been dead."

"What? How could he possibly know that? That doesn't make any sense. If it's true, why would he ask your dad to come?"

"He wouldn't—couldn't—go into any details. But he told me to stay away from the investigation unless the police needed to question me. He said you should do the same."

Olivia nodded. She wanted to tell Sophia about her plan for finagling a meeting with the bank manager in charge of the auction. After Sophia's reaction to her visit to Grove Manor, though, she kept it to herself.

Maria stepped into the foyer, waving at them to follow her to the kitchen. "What's all this whispering, you two? Esto no es bueno. Come on, let's go. We're ready."

Olivia allowed the warning to steep as they settled around the table for a leisurely lunch. Josefina arranged a hearty spread of leftover slow cooked pork and garlicky white rice with an avocado and tomato salad, and conchas baked in the early hours of the morning. Sophia streamed a playlist from her phone through speakers installed on the underside of the cabinets above the counter. The soothing flamenco rhythm of "Aqua Azul" was like an antenna tuned to allay the static from Olivia's tangled thoughts.

Maria passed her the platter of pulled pork. "You must be excited about moving to New York."

"Sort of."

Josefina piled more meat onto Olivia's plate and handed her the bowl of Mexican sweet bread. "You should stay home, take care of your father. Get married."

"Ay, ay, Mamá. These two are a different generation. You should be proud they're such independent women. They'll do what they want. They make their own choices."

Olivia turned toward Sophia, genteelly dabbing her mouth with her napkin. "This pork is fantastic."

Sophia hummed and nodded. "Isn't this salad the best?" Neither of them would dare contradict her grandmother in matters of marriage, family, or children.

Maria pointed her fork at them both. "You two— peas in a pod. It's true, though, Olivia. Your mother would be proud of you, no matter what decision you make for yourself. I thought you wanted to move. Are you reconsidering?"

"Yeah, Liv, what's up with the doubts? Is it because of Daniel?"

Olivia swiftly kicked Sophia's shin under the draped tablecloth.

"What's this about Daniel, mija?" Maria asked.

Olivia stared Sophia down. "We aren't together anymore. He's moving to California."

Josefina dropped her knife on her plate, grasping Olivia's wrist as if catching her pilfering from the church's poor box. "That man you were to marry? You two are no longer together?"

"No, Abuela. We've separated, but we were never engaged."

"Eres increíble." Josefina scooted back from the table and made the sign of the cross, invoking both the seraphim and cherubim. She stood, tossing her napkin onto the table, and walked over to the counter. She uncovered a cake on a silver serving tray and removed a serrated knife from a cabinet drawer.

Maria leaned forward, resting her forearms on the table, and pushed her plate away from herself. "Mija, I'm sorry to hear about Daniel. Whatever happened, though, he's a fool to let you go. You're better off without him. Doors open and close for reasons. When you're ready, you'll find the one who is ready for you." She rested her hand on Olivia's wrist. "Keep your heart open. Don't mind Mamá. She just wants you settled and to have support wherever you are. We all do."

"Thanks, I know. I'm okay, though. Really. He and I decided—"

Josefina lifted the tray and then turned toward the table. "La familia lo es todo."

"This is what I keep telling her, Abuela. Family is everything, Liv. You're not getting any younger."

Maria popped up from her chair. "Mamá, let me help you with that."

Sophia slid a clean fork from the center of the table toward Olivia. "That's Abuela's tres leches cake. It's the best. She's the best. You should eat a piece, Liv—before you go."

Olivia picked up the fork and sparked a diplomatic smile. "I'll take one now and one for the road." Bloating her way downstream would be far easier than back-stroking against the current to redeem herself and regain Josefina's good graces. "Everything is scrumptious, Abuela. One of the best meals I've had in a long time. What's your secret?"

Josefina made the sign of the cross, pointed at Olivia, and squeezed Maria's hand. "Strong faith, a loving marriage, and respectful children." She pulled at the waist of her linen blend skirt, letting it snap back against her skin. "And, elastic."

They all laughed, and the temporary truce enlivened the air. They spent the next thirty minutes schooled by Josefina on how to bake the perfect creamy caramel flan. At the end of the meal, Olivia expressed her gratitude and beelined for the foyer, dodging any further flare-ups over her former intended.

Sophia walked with her to the front of the suite and opened the door, handing over the tote bag of take-home treats. "You won't be going back out to Grove Manor, right?"

"No. I promise."

"Don't you think you should tell that detective about your little field trip?"

"No. Not after what your dad said. I'm staying clear of Preston for the time being."

"Interesting. He's now Preston to you. That didn't take long."

Olivia brushed a scuff off the side of her shoe, recalling the awkwardness of Beverly's impromptu prayer circle. "Thanks for your inspiring performance yesterday. I owe you and Tori for your dog and pony show."

"First, I can't fathom what you're referring to. Second, you shouldn't be investigating—doing anything—alone."

"I need to find out why."

"You mean why someone wanted to hurt Paige?"

"Even before that. What was she doing at Grove Manor? She didn't take a camera from the office. She was up to something else. I have to find out more about the sale on Friday."

"How do you plan on doing that?"

"It's time to raise the stakes and lay odds on some town gossip."

CHAPTER 16

Olivia departed Sophia's clinic, strolling three blocks along the shop-side sidewalk, past Jillian's Cafe to the far end corner across from the post office. The sight of Steve Sharp installing safety-orange event fencing next to the gazebo nixed shortcutting through the town square to save time, so she elected for the roundabout route, hanging a right turn to pass both the police station and Billingsley's office on her way to the bank.

She walked up a half-dozen steps and entered the bank's enclosed vestibule. A wall-mounted ATM flashed scenes of possibility: a family celebrating at a backyard barbecue, newlyweds embracing on a Venetian gondola, three friends sunbathing on a white sand beach. The ceiling vents over the display streamed a cool current, coaxing an abandoned, curled receipt to drift from a slot to the ground to join a pile of likewise orphaned slips. She peered into the lobby from inside the mantrap, assessing anyone flaunting a managerial air. A customer crowned with a pillbox hat exiting the lobby hit the automatic access switch, springing the door, startling and pushing Olivia back until she shuffled by with her cane.

The bank's decor evoked the feel of a frontier Colorado mining town. Three teller windows aligned four feet apart behind a faux wood grain counter. Ornate wrought iron frames with a manufactured patina fronted each window. Sepia toned, mass-produced photos of cattle, trains, and cowboys almost outnumbered the signage for mortgage rates, retirement accounts, and checking services. Though contrived, the design conjured the conceit that a stagecoach chased by a gang of masked robbers could appear at any moment.

Olivia entered the lobby and was greeted immediately by a customer liaison sporting a blue plaid skinny suit. He rushed toward her as if magnetized, with his hands folded and head tilted, showcasing a Broadway-ready smile. "Hello, ma'am. How can Piedmont Valley Bank be of service to you today?"

"I'm here to speak with Jess."

"I'll be delighted to help you with that. Thank you for being a loyal customer. Is your appointment with our manager, Jessica Nichols?"

"She's handling the sale of Grove Manor, correct?"

"Yes, ma'am, she is. What time is your appointment?"

"Now."

"Absolutely. I'll inform her you're here, right away.

Thank you for your business today. Pardon me for one moment." He bowed, pivoted a one-eighty on the ball of his left foot, and glided to the nearest teller window, peeking over the counter. A whiff of woodsy vanilla cologne trailed in his wake, reminding her of the candle Daniel had given her the week before everything between them fell apart. The associate returned to her with a palm-up extended arm, directing her to a corral of empty chairs. "She's currently on the phone. It'll be a few minutes. Please have a seat. Coffee or tea while you wait?"

"Nothing for me. Thank you."

"Olivia, how are you?" Frank lumbered toward her from a narrow corridor between a set of cubicles. "What are you doing here today?"

His glasses slipped to the tip of his nose as he bent forward and grazed her cheek with a kiss. "Are you doing okay? Please don't take this the wrong way, but you look tired."

"I'm fine. It's been a long couple of days. Any word on A.J. from your lawyer?"

"I wish I had better news. Ben tells me Payne wants to transfer him to a more secure facility."

"Where? How soon?"

"I don't know—about either. I've been out of the office all morning. I came here to deposit checks so I can pay my vendors." He waved a file full of papers. She settled into a rustic leather wingback chair as Frank propped himself on a saloon stool next to her, his legs straight and feet crossed on the laminate wood flooring. "I still can't believe A.J. was there. Ben says the police confirmed his truck was involved."

She scooted forward, feeling like a Lilliputian engulfed by the double-wide chair. "None of this makes sense."

"I asked Junior this morning before I left the office if he knew anything more that could help. He says A.J. and the girl—there was something between them. I had no idea. I'm as lost as you. I've never seen him violent in any way."

"You said the other day that you've worked at Grove Manor in the past."

"Yes. Why do you ask?"

"Does Steve Sharp ever work for you?"

Frank retrieved a receipt that fell from his file to the floor. "No. Not for me."

"But Junior has worked with him, right?"

"Yes, that's true. What Steve did, that tax situation—now that was terrible. Not to mention illegal. He asked me for a job a couple months back. Maybe it's wrong for me to think like this, but I couldn't trust having him around the office. I knew he owed a lot of money. So, I offered him smaller projects that came our way. I loaned Junior out if the work required a two-man crew."

"Did any of those involve Grove Manor?"

"The bank here contacted me. They wanted a few windows boarded up—other little odds and ends, too.

Wasn't worth my time for the pay, so I gave him the opportunity. Why the interest in Steve?"

An authoritative brunette attired in a navy pantsuit accessorized by a key-laden wrist coil approached, extending her hand toward Olivia. "I'm the manager, Jessica Nichols. I hear you're asking for me."

"Olivia Penn." She rose, shaking Jessica's hand. "Thank you for seeing me today. I have a few questions about the sale of Grove Manor."

"Sure. Did you get your business taken care of, Mr. Grossman?"

Frank stood, fanning through his folder. "Yes, thanks, Jess. You bidding for that place, Olivia? New York must pay well."

"Not quite that well."

"Mrs. Penn, please follow me. We can speak privately in my office."

"Go ahead," Frank said. "I'll get in touch if Ben has any new information. Give my best to your dad, will you? Tell him we're on for Saturday morning coffee at the cafe. I'll come pick him up at nine." With that, Frank left the bank, and Olivia followed the manager to a glass-enclosed room next to the vault.

Jess perched on the edge of her executive chair with her hands folded and elbows pinpointed to well-worn landing marks on the desk's varnished surface. "Okay, Mrs. Penn. I'm sorry to keep you waiting. Somehow, your appointment missed my schedule. I apologize for that. What can I help you with?"

"No worries. It's Ms., not Mrs. I've gone back to using a paper planner myself." Jess stared at her, remaining still as a statue. "Pen and paper—can't go wrong there, right?"

Her counterpart raised her eyebrows, twisting her watch to reorient the face. Olivia slid forward and swiveled Jess' brass business card stand, highlighting her name with her finger.

"You're Rose's niece, aren't you? I was talking earlier to someone about her beauty shop. She's a local legend. I always had my hair cut there when I was a child."

Jess dropped her direct demeanor and relaxed in her chair, resting her head against the seat's high back. "She'll never retire. She's such a hoot. If you ever want to hear what's happening in town, sit awhile around there any morning, and you'll be up on everyone's business in no time. We may have met before. I hung out there after school when I was younger."

Olivia eagerly laughed. "Perhaps we did. What are the odds? I bet when she and Mrs. Peabody get gossiping—"

"Dorothy is the ringleader of the crew. She goes in there twice a week whether or not she gets her hair done." Jess opened the tray drawer under the desktop. "I've been in back-to-back meetings all morning. I'm starving." She pulled out a fistful of lollipops. "Would you like one?"

Olivia's eyes rounded to match the offered confection. "Yes, please."

Jess leaned forward, sparking a glint from a ruby ring as she extended the bunch toward Olivia. "Would you like red or green?"

"Red always."

"Me too." She plucked a pop from the assortment, handing it to Olivia, and then unwrapped one for herself. She spoke with the stick dangling from the corner of her mouth. "What can I tell you about Grove Manor? Are you thinking of submitting a bid?"

"No. I'm helping to finish a story for the paper. Cooper gave me your name, said you're the go-to, in-charge, boss lady. I just need to verify the basics."

"Oh, that Cooper. He's a cutie. Boss lady may be an exaggeration, but if the shoe fits …"

"By the way, those heels—killers. Gucci, right?"

Jess twirled her ankle, admiring the shine of her pump's black leather. "Thank you, but no, they're not. Similar in style, though. Maybe not so much in price."

"Well, us girls can dream, can't we? So, you were saying about the sale …"

"Yes. The property includes the house and thirteen acres of ground. We expect a developer will buy it and petition for rezoning. Most likely for single-family resi-dences. The local real estate market has seen an uptick in demand for larger estates with included acreage. We have quite a few clients from Washington who want a weekend home in the country. If that describes you, we could help with financing. There are several properties out near Hamilton's that are steals right now."

"That sounds lovely. I'll keep it in mind. How did Grove Manor come to auction?"

"The former owner passed without heirs. The estate collected debt from unpaid taxes. Dead or not, the county wants its tax money. The attorney who probated the will located no other assets. We foreclosed on the property, and it's being auctioned to satisfy the back payments."

"How many bids do you have?"

Jess removed the lollipop from her mouth and inspected the remnant, waving it like a magic wand. "The bid details are confidential, but I can tell you interest hasn't been high. Please don't print that though."

"I won't mention it at all. And what happened there on Monday—will that affect the sale?"

"No. The police gave us the green light to proceed. Though, it might scare potential buyers. A homicide occurring on a property could cause some to reconsider. I would have serious heebie-jeebies about it myself."

Olivia nodded. "You and me both."

The customer liaison tapped on the glass and timidly cracked the door, daring to place only one of his tri-tone wingtips onto the office's low pile, gray gridded carpeting. "Your next appointment is here. Should I tell him to come back?"

Olivia rose. "I don't want to take up any more of your time, Mrs. Nichols. I appreciate your help today."

"It's been a pleasure chatting. We apologize again for the schedule mix-up. Don't we?" She shot a stink eye toward her dapper colleague, silencing him before he could proclaim another mea culpa. "And I'm a 'Ms.' too. I haven't had the inclination to be a 'Mrs.' yet."

Olivia extended her hand. "You and me both."

Jess escorted her to the lobby where three customers queued for the lone open service window. A retiree sporting a straw fedora seemed to be considering joining the line by ducking under a stanchion's retractable belt. Jess rushed forward and lifted the barrier for the senior patron, avoiding the need to add calls to both paramedics and insurance adjusters to her to-do list. The liaison flitted toward Olivia with flushed cheeks, brimming with a bobblehead grin. "Thank you for banking with us. Have a pleasant day."

She reflexively returned his show-stopper smile, catching blended, fuzzy fragments of customer conversations and the promotions Jess was pitching: refinance, cupcakes, closing costs, apple pie, fixed rate, dog walking. She glanced at the teller counter, at the wingback chair, at the cubicle offices. Jess removed a leather case from her jacket pocket, pulled out a business card, and extended it toward Olivia, who stared right through it.

Jess lifted the card higher and closer to Olivia. "My contact information, for when you want to discuss financing."

"Of course. Thank you." She snatched the card from Jess, eyeing the embossed logo with no effort to decipher the details. *Paige, what did you get yourself into?*

CHAPTER 17

The town had resumed its cozy, quiet charm by the time
Olivia left the bank. The workers setting up for the
festival had completed their assigned tasks and were
dispersing for the day to rest their weary muscles and
aching backs. Car doors, departing pleasantries, and
caroling robins were all that remained to enliven the late
afternoon soundtrack. A border collie sprinted across a
stretch of the lush, deep-green lawn and leapt with adept
timing, snatching a disk thrown by its proud owner from
twenty yards away. A pair of rowdy twins chased each
other around the gazebo until the pacesetter reversed
course, knocking them both to the ground. The hour was
later than she expected. *What am I even doing?* She lent
half a thought to visiting A.J., but with the police motor
pool at full occupancy, she opted out. *Tomorrow. I'll try
tomorrow.* She crossed the square to her Expedition and
headed home.

She coasted to a quiet stop at her father's house, parking halfway up the gravel driveway. Buddy frolicked behind the azalea shrubs that lined the porch, zipping over to greet her when she stepped off the SUV's running board. Her father stood near the front bricked border of the garden, pondering the cucumber patch's day-old growth. "Hey, Dad. How's the crop holding up?"

He waved, walking with caution along the uneven ground, using his downed dogwood limb as a trekking pole. "Everything's doing great. I watered this morning. I was getting worried about you. I didn't think you'd be out so long."

She bent forward, straightening a tomato plant that had tilted from perpendicular, and compacted the soil around the base until the stalk realigned. "Sorry, I lost track of time."

He pointed to a seedling in the next row. "That one too." She repeated the procedure. "What've you been up to in town?"

"I saw Soph and had lunch with her mother and grandmother. Visited with the Peabodys, too. I haven't talked with them for a while. They're doing well."

"Floyd and Dorothy. Those two are older than me."

"Mr. Grossman wanted me to remind you about coffee on Saturday."

"You went to his office?"

"No. He was at the bank."

He turned, facing her. "What were you doing there?"

She scratched the back of her neck and looked over

her shoulder, feigning interest in an HVAC service van passing the house. "I was checking into a few details about the sale. That's all."

"This is about Paige, isn't it? Let the police handle it. I know you wanna help. I'm with you, I hope A.J.'s not involved in any of it."

She wiped the dirt from her hands and gathered the hose, moving it out of his way. "He's not involved. He's innocent."

"Honey, you're leaving in a few days. It's enough for you to manage your own life, between your job and getting yourself settled in New York. What's happening here … you don't need this now."

She hooked her arm with his, inviting him to escort her along the cleared path toward the back end of the garden. "No need to worry, Dad. I was asking a few questions. Nothing more." Buddy scampered in front of her and pawed at her shins. "Not now, little guy. We'll play later." He barked, working his way between her feet. "Hey, stop that. Go. Shoo." She bent forward and nudged Buddy aside. He got the message and scampered off toward the backyard. "How about we focus on getting dinner ready? I'm not leaving until we get you bulked up a bit."

"Sounds okay by me. But let the police do the questioning from here on out. And remember, I don't need vegetables with every meal." She smiled, holding the kitchen door open for him. "Meat and potatoes. That's good enough."

William relaxed on his recliner, watching the BBC news as she prepared his favorite weeknight dinner: meat loaf with mashed potatoes and gravy. When she called him to the table, he dramatically spooned a token portion of Parmesan broccoli onto his plate, ensuring he received credit for partaking in the full menu. She pretended not to notice when he went back for seconds, scooping up every last bit of the cheese between his fork and fingers. During the meal, she avoided further conversation concerning either her investigation of Paige's murder or her ambivalence toward New York. She wanted to relish a simple evening with her father, free from all else weighing on her.

After dinner, they settled on the sofa, enjoying back-to-back episodes of *Doc Martin*. Buddy slumbered by the recliner, lost in dreams of endless fields, crimson balls, and bacon treats. They both dozed on and off during a documentary about the lemurs of Madagascar. At eleven, she stirred and woke her father. They said their good nights, and he left her alone to lock up and turn off the lights. Twenty minutes later, she tiptoed upstairs, partially closed the door to her room, and pulled out her laptop, initiating a search of public records for Jeremiah Jackson.

At first, the noise that roused Olivia was vague. She opened her groggy eyes, confused by the still lit bedside lamp. She stared at her sleepy sideways reflection in her laptop's hibernating screen and blindly reached for her phone on the nightstand. *It's after midnight. I must have fallen asleep.* She darkened the room and fluffed her pillow, drifting off for a minute before she startled awake again. "Oh no!"

She scooted out of bed, scurried through the hallway, and dashed down the stairs. "Buddy, quiet. Stop barking." She skated past the couch, misjudging her trajectory in the unlit living room, and rammed her foot into an end table. The impact knocked over a framed photo of her atop the Continental Divide in Colorado and threatened the stability of one of her mother's crystal vases. She limped into the kitchen, flipping the switch for the dome light above the sink.

"Buddy, shush. You'll wake Dad." He barked twice more, pawing at the door. "It's okay, guy. What's going on? You need to go outside?"

She stroked his back as she twisted the deadbolt, hesitating before rotating the worn brass knob. Buddy, now on hind legs, scratched his claws on the door's lower panel, whining with escalating urgency.

"Okay, okay." She opened the door, and he bolted straight across the deck and disappeared around the side, hauling double-time for the front of the house.

She tracked him past the garden, rounding the corner as he darted onto the porch. He scoured, nose to the ground, from one end to the other and then bounded down the steps, crisscrossing the close-cropped lawn in a grid-like pattern. When he detected a deviation, he altered his course to follow the trail. Her throat tightened, and she stepped back several feet, scanning from the road to the neighbor's house. His sweeps extended to the mailbox where he reversed direction, shadowing a scent along the driveway toward her SUV. She fixated on her father's darkened bedroom window, watching for any movement of the miniblinds. A bat swooped at her from above and she ducked, anticipating a second pass within seconds. Buddy's pants grew louder as he neared her Expedition, and when he reached the rear bumper, he suspended his surveillance, shook his head, and sneezed twice.

"Buddy, come." He sat with his hind legs tucked under him. "Buddy, house, go." He yawned and lay on the driveway, belly-crawling a few inches forward. "Buddy, here, now." He rolled to his side and rubbed his forepaw over his nose.

She swiped at her shin. A squadron of mosquitoes had homed in on her position and were dive-bombing her exposed legs. She shooed a pest away from her left ankle, only to sense it land on her wrist. She scratched her calf and swatted at a buzzing near her ear.

She checked behind her again and cautiously walked to where Buddy lay, keeping her eyes alert and fists curled. She hoisted him up, propping his head and forelegs over her shoulder.

"Good job, little guy. You chased whatever—or whoever—off."

He fidgeted and fought her grasp, gaining leverage to launch from her hold. She clutched his right leg before he could leap and readjusted her grip.

"Fine, you want down? You've got it." She lowered him to the ground where he faced her and barked three times. "Please, work with me here." He lay sprawled as his breathing eased. She prompted him to stand, lifting his shoulders, but he resisted all her efforts. "Sorry, Buddy. We've got to go in now."

He whimpered, staring past her, and she squatted and turned, following his gaze to the front passenger tire. Flat. She swiveled her feet toward the rear tire. Flat. She circled the back bumper to the driver's side. Flat. Flat. All four tires lifeless. She swiftly surveyed a three-sixty view, swooped up Buddy, and hustled back inside to call the police.

CHAPTER 18

Olivia deployed in the living room, on the couch with Buddy in her lap. She had lit the entire first floor, every lamp and ceiling fixture beaming as if aiding in a search for a lost, precious treasure. She had also grabbed the aluminum bat her father stashed by the end table next to the staircase and leaned it against the sofa, ready to rouse the muscle memory of her home run swing. William remained asleep. She envied his ability to slumber through all manner of maelstrom. If she had inherited the trait, she had not yet discovered the epigenetics for its expression. She scratched at multiple bites on her lower legs and arms, leaving her skin reddened and streaked, and craned her neck to peer through the sliver of opened curtain and sheer panel she had aligned for an optimal sightline of the driveway. Twenty minutes after her call, high beams blazed a laser line through the bay window. She guided Buddy to the ground alongside her father's recliner and widened the view between the drapes, watching Preston as he exited his truck and bounded up the front four steps with two strides.

She opened the door, joining him on the porch. "Thanks for coming. I was upstairs when I—"

He held up his hand. "I'll talk to you when I'm done. Stay inside and lock the door. I'm going to search the grounds. When I'm finished, I'll come back and knock. Don't open this door otherwise." He stood firm, waiting until she fastened all three locks.

She sheltered Buddy on the woven rug below the coffee table, offering him a bone chew toy as a distraction. Then she parted the curtains and sheers, providing her with a panorama of the porch. Preston illuminated a long-barrel LED flashlight and unlocked the retention that secured his Smith & Wesson pistol in the duty holster on his belt. She shadowed his path, moving from the living room to the kitchen as he traced the house's perimeter. He inspected the home's windows and locks and then conducted the same examination of her mother's office. He returned to the front of the property and circled her Expedition in a wide radius, meticulously scanning the ground. After a complete go-round, he scooted his brawny frame beneath the undercarriage as far as his shoulders allowed. When he finished his inspection, he rolled and stood, snapping photos of each tire from multiple angles with his phone. After half an hour, he headed back toward the house where Olivia waited, peering through the peephole until he signaled.

She opened the door. "Please come in."

"Thank you. Is anyone else here?"

"My dad. He's upstairs. He's slept through everything so far. I didn't want to wake him." Buddy mobilized from his temporary bunk, mustering between them. "This is his dog—well, puppy. He's just about nine months. He wants to be a German shepherd when he grows up."

"I'm not sure he's got the genes for it." Preston shuffled sideways, stepping toward the living room, but Buddy mirrored the movement and entangled his feet. "Maybe we should keep that to ourselves, though."

She lifted the dog and held him between them. "Come on, little fella, it's okay."

Preston held out his palm, allowing Buddy to rest his head in his hand as he softly scratched his neck. Then she lowered him to the ground, and he trotted off toward the kitchen.

"Did your search turn up any evidence?" she asked as Buddy paced back to them, dropping his ball between Preston's boots. "I'm sorry. It's a game we play. Another time, Buddy."

She reached to retrieve the toy as Preston bent forward with the same aim. Her hand landed on his, and they froze for a beat as if locked in a panel of a graphic novel. She released her hold, and they stood in sync. He rolled the ball toward the kitchen, spurring Buddy to chase after his quarry.

"Careful, or you'll find yourself with a new best friend."

Preston rested his hands on his hips, slightly dipping his chin. "By the way he protects you, no doubt I'm the safer for it."

She stifled a smile, keeping her cheeks from rising as her eyes narrowed. Buddy gauged the pair from inside the kitchen with his tail playfully swaying. Although ready for another round of fetch, he deemed his charge otherwise occupied and no longer threatened. He dropped the ball and lay back at his guard post.

"A fixed blade was used to slash your tires. My guess —a bowie or hunting knife." He scrolled through the captured images. "You can see here the slice along the sidewall." He enlarged the photo, pointing to the damaged tire. "Here too. That large of a gash requires muscle. The Escape—is that your father's?"

"Yes."

"What's that building in the back?"

"That is—was—my mom's writing office. She's deceased."

He removed his hat, wiping the sweat from his brow. "The doors and windows of both your house and the office show no signs of tampering. I'll have Cole come out when it's light and dust for prints, but I doubt we'll find anything useful. Sometimes we see tires slashed around the time of the high school's graduation—mostly pranks—but this doesn't seem like some random, youthful indiscretion."

Olivia listened without so much as blinking. When he

finished, she scrambled for something to say. "I'm sorry, please have a seat."

He waited for her to select a spot on the sofa, and then he situated himself a cushion width away. "This seems personal."

"I thought you'd be more comfortable on the couch rather than standing."

Preston's dimple appeared as his lips parted. "I meant the slashing."

"Right. Of course." She felt like when she mistakenly chose the kilt over the ewe sign and walked into the men's restroom at a pub in Edinburgh.

"You have issues with anyone in town? Someone who might want to scare you?"

Names were not an endangered species. Cassandra and Junior. Maybe Payne. Perhaps even Steve, though she was uncertain if he knew of her connection to Paige.

"No. But something may have happened yesterday."

He balanced on the couch's edge, propped forward with his forearms on his thighs and fingers interlaced. She brushed her hair behind her ears and recounted her visit to Grove Manor with no sparing of detail. When she finished, he said nothing. One minute of silence turned into another. The veins on the back of his hands distended as he unbuttoned and rolled the cuffs of his dark-blue denim shirt.

"Did the police go inside the house on Monday night?" she asked.

He stared at her as if she had spoken in Mandarin.

"Let me see if I understand this. You trespassed on a property where a murder occurred the day before. Placed yourself in danger. Now, you're asking me about the investigation? Is that correct?"

She leaned away, widening the neutral zone between them. "When you put it like that, I realize it doesn't sound so good."

He shoved his sleeves above his elbows. "I don't know which offense to address first. Did you even consider that whoever was in the woods might have hurt you?"

She calculated the permutations of answering yes or no, debating whether he meant that rhetorically.

"Stay away from Grove Manor as long as you're in town. You understand?"

She nodded.

"No. Say it for my sanity."

"I will stay away—from Grove Manor."

"I want you to be careful wherever you go. Make sure you lock up at night, and don't venture anywhere that could get you arrested—or worse. If anything happens, contact me." He grabbed her father's pencil from the table and wrote his cell number on the crossword puzzle left beside it. "I'll give Jed a call in the morning. He'll tow your vehicle to his shop and have your tires replaced. Nobody will bother you further tonight. Try to get some sleep." He stood and aligned his hat so that the brim was in perfect parallel with his cognac brown eyes.

"Thanks again for coming."

"You remember what I told you."

He opened the door and stepped onto the porch, pausing a moment before turning back toward her. "I want to apologize about Tuesday—my mother and lunch. She can be presumptuous."

She flashed the same smile that had disarmed his discomfort that day. "No need. Your mother lives up to her name. It helped take my mind off everything that's happened. You should know that she invited me, and my dad, to sit with your family at the festival on Saturday."

He glanced at the ground and sighed. "That sounds like her. Please don't feel obligated to come." He wiped some lingering dirt off his jeans and checked the retention lock on his gun's holster. "Get back inside and lock that door. Goodnight, Olivia."

"Goodnight, Preston."

CHAPTER 19

Olivia double-checked the front door locks and tracked Preston through the bay window as he climbed into his F-150. He lit the interior with the driver's side dome light and placed a pair of phone calls. Within five minutes the cab faded to black, and he rolled out of the driveway, executing a tactful retreat, disturbing only a handful of stones.

She breathed easier. She set her father's bat back by the stairs, no longer feeling as though she was at home plate with bases loaded, two outs in the bottom of the ninth. Buddy lay by the sofa with heavy eyes. She squatted, stroking between his ears.

"Did we wake you?" She yawned, and he followed her lead. She had not stayed up past two since her visit to Vermont with Daniel in December.

Buddy propped himself up on straightened forelegs and then stood with an unsteady weariness that suggested he too needed sleep. He whimpered, and she knew what that meant. Together they shuffled to the kitchen, where Olivia snatched his leash from the hook rack next to the refrigerator. She clipped the navy nylon cord to his collar, unbolted the door, and stepped to the end of the porch, allowing him onto the grass no farther than the tether extended. He did his business, and she led him back inside where he toddled to his near empty water bowl by the sink and lowered to his belly.

"Let's get you some fresh water." She pushed the door shut, reached for the bowl, and filled it from the faucet. "Good night, Buddy. Sleep well, little guy."

She returned to bed and her laptop, resuming her search on the Jackson family. The hour, though, soon got the best of her. She abandoned her efforts after she read the same paragraph three times and still could not recall the name of Jeremiah's wife. *E-mail. Forgot.* Her inbox displayed nearly fifty messages. Most were from readers who submitted questions for her column. Angela had sent two reminders of the online Q&A scheduled for later today. She skimmed the preview lines, but the letters and words blended. Her eyes shut for extended lapses, and she had to back-skip the text each time she woke. After another futile five minutes, she closed the screen without logging off.

She lay her head on the queen-size goose down pillow, allowing the Euro top mattress to swallow her limbs in a cotton cloud. Gravity's pull felt infinite. The house echoed sporadic creaks accompanied by a cycle of hums from the air conditioner and refrigerator when each unit's motor rallied for duty. All else was quiet. *This bed is better than what I have. I should replace mine. How did Dad sleep through everything?* Three thoughts and she was out.

Olivia quarter turned onto her right side, pulling the bedsheet higher to blanket her arms, and peaked at the clock. The hour approached three. She settled into a cozy cocoon, snuggling her neck into the cooling pillow. Within seconds, the sheet slipped from her shoulder to her elbow. She fumbled for the linen, grasping twice for the layer before gathering it back to cover herself. She drifted off immediately, but the sheet slowly inched down her arm, all the way to her wrist. A heavy grunt shattered the silence, startling her awake. She kicked with both feet and her heels caught the mattress, launching her straight back into the headboard. She swung her arm sideways, grasping for the lamp on the nightstand, but her errant aim smacked the shade, causing the light to teeter. She floundered for the switch and lit the room, finding Buddy on alert by the bed, staring at her with his glacier blue eyes. She leaned back against the bedpost, burying her head in her hands, hearing her heart thump in her throat. Buddy braced his front paws on the box spring as far as he could reach and barked.

"Come on. Quiet." She reached over the edge, lifted him onto the mattress, and stroked his neck. "I guess things got to both of us tonight." He grabbed her shirt with his incisors and tugged. "Hey, stop that." She nudged him, and he released the cotton tee. He tried again, but she parried his advance. Undeterred, he dodged her counter, nipping at her sleeve near her shoulder. He secured a snippet, yanking it toward him. "I'm not playing now. Go to sleep."

He alighted from her side, scampering toward the hall. When she made no effort to follow, he scurried back to the bed and leapt, but fell short of hurtling the height. He looked up, whimpering, and then turned, pranced to the room's entrance, and defiantly barked. Olivia sighed, biting her tongue, and swung her legs off the bed to fetch him before his antics woke her father. She peeked at the pitch-black bottom of William's closed door and then at the opposite end of the hall where Buddy jingled his collar tags, nuzzling next to the banister.

"You need to go outside again?" He rounded the corner post and started down the steps. "Okay, Buddy. I'm coming." She trailed him through the living room, careful to avoid a second assault to the end table. In the kitchen, she snagged his leash and lowered to a knee, grasping for his collar, but he backed out of reach. "Hey, stop." As she scooted forward, he spun and faced the door, growling at heavy footsteps on the deck. "Shh. Quiet. Come here."

She seized his hind legs, dragging him closer to her as the knob slowly turned. She stood, hoisted Buddy, and gently shoveled him into the living room. The door cracked open. She scanned for a weapon. The leash, a spoon, a mug. She saw a hand. She lurched toward the counter, grabbed a Dutch oven, and flung it toward the gap as the door swung open and the intruder entered. A heavy thud from the pot landing on the floor alerted that her toss was well short of her target.

She flipped the switch for the light over the sink, illuminating Preston with his Smith & Wesson drawn, targeting her center of mass. They scowled at each other as if sworn enemies at the O. K. Corral. The Dutch oven had landed midway between them. He holstered his firearm as she planted her hands on her head.

"What are you doing here? Why are you breaking into my house?"

His eyes narrowed as he thrust a finger toward the door. "Why is that unlocked?"

"You scared me to death! What are you doing on my back porch?"

"Why are you throwing a pot at me?"

"I thought you were breaking in."

"No need to break in when you don't bother to use the locks." The lines between his brows deepened as his lower lip tensed. "That's your home defense? A pot?"

"Yeah, that's right. It's eight-quart cast iron. It would have left a mark."

"On the floor, no doubt."

They stood in stalemate six paces apart, glaring without blinking, daring the other to crack. Buddy swiveled back and forth between them. He sniffed the enameled cookware and ambled over to Preston, lying by his feet. She relaxed her arms, venting a full boiler of steam.

"That's wonderful. Take his side."

Preston ran his hand through his hair twice before firmly resetting his Stetson with the brim dipped low. He pushed the door shut as if to rip the hinges, stopping short, though, of allowing it to slam.

"We went out for a minute. I kept him on a leash. I must not have locked up."

"You think?" He retrieved her improvised weapon from the ground, transferring it to the counter. "You need better means of defending yourself."

She brandished her best Mr. Olympia biceps pose. "You don't rate my guns SWAT team ready?"

His amusement betrayed his countenance. "We may need to get you some more training, Gunny." She relinquished her siege with a modest smile, and a tenuous truce established between them. "I'm sorry for alarming you. I've been down the street watching the house." He jabbed a thumb toward the door. "I came to check that you locked up, like I asked you to."

"Oh. I didn't realize. I thought you left." Other than her father and A.J., no man ever treated her as though she needed protection. She was unsure whether to fume or feel flattered. "So, anything amiss, or can we all sleep safe?"

His jaw's brief softening faded as he removed his hat and gestured for her to take a seat at the table. "I asked you before if you could think of anyone who would want to send you a message. Did any names come to mind?" She ran through her mental list, shook her head, and shrugged. "What about Junior—you two got any history?"

She leaned back in her seat, searching the ceiling for the least complicated nutshell explanation. "We've known each other since we were kids. I haven't seen him much over the years after I moved away."

He allowed the silence to hang. When she failed to fill in the blanks, he prompted further. "Anything else?"

She tucked her hair behind her ears, speaking as if pained by a spear in her spleen. "We dated for a moment when we were in high school. That was long ago, though. It didn't go or end well. He took it hard, and we never got back on decent terms."

He leaned forward, laying his arm on the table. "How was he acting on Monday when Paige came into Grossman's?"

"His usual self. Standoffish. Churlish. I borrowed his father's tiller for our garden. He carried it from the office and put it in the Expedition. He said he wanted to catch up while I was in town. Why are you asking me about him?"

"Because within the past hour, he's driven by your house three times."

CHAPTER 20

Olivia invited Preston to stand guard in the living room for the remainder of his watch, but he declined, insisting on keeping to his post outside. He showcased his truck in front of her Expedition as a warning to anyone harboring plans of further predawn visits. She camped on the couch, venturing a second pass at her e-mail, but soon fell victim to the hour, dozing off with her cell cradled in her palm. She woke at five and checked the driveway. The silhouette of Preston's F-150 pitched against the sunrise eased her mind, and she snuggled back into the sofa with a hoodie draped across her eyes, blocking the morning's encroaching light.

She slept without stirring for the next three hours. She woke to gentle tapping on her toes, poking out from under the cotton throw blanketing her. She yawned and rolled to her side, reaching for a bottle of water on the coffee table. "Dad, what time is it?"

"It's after eight. Why are you sleeping on the couch?" He picked her phone up from the floor, tilting the screen so she could see. "You've been buzzing for over an hour. I didn't wanna wake you, but I thought I'd better in case someone was calling you from work."

Olivia stood and stretched, drawing her shoulder blades together. She stepped a few feet toward the window, peering at the empty spot in front of her damaged Expedition.

"Whatcha looking at?" he asked.

"Dad, you're one sound sleeper." She sat back down and related all that had transpired during the night in the least dramatic fashion she could. She excluded the details of Junior's drive-bys as she had no evidence he had any role in the slashing.

He listened to her entire recounting before saying a word. "Why didn't you wake me? You shouldn't have been outside by yourself."

"I came in when I saw the tires. I called the police as soon as I could. I thought you'd hear us and come downstairs. Preston stayed in the driveway until, I guess, he decided it was safe to go. I'm not sure when he left."

William remained silent, refusing to look at her. He picked up his pencil from the table, turning it end over end several times before tossing it next to the remote. "Is he going to watch you the rest of the time you're here too?"

Olivia kept her head bowed, speaking as if stranded

on a lake coated by thin ice. "It probably was local kids, pulling a prank. Random vandalism."

He sprung to his feet, snatching his crossword puzzle from the coffee table. He rolled the folded paper into a tube and pitched it toward his recliner. "Olivia, four tires on your vehicle is not a prank. That's not random. This was directed at you. I know that. You know that." A lump rose in her throat, seeing him as angry as when she told him about Daniel's move to California. "I want you to pack up and leave today."

The blow stole her breath. She swallowed hard, rising in slow motion. "What do you mean, leave?"

"Take my car back to D.C., and I'll get yours fixed. We'll worry about swapping later. Take it to New York if you need to. I can always drive up—"

"Dad, no. Just wait a second. Hold on. You're over-reacting."

"Olivia, this business that you got yourself involved in … well, it's not your business. I understand Paige was your friend. What happened last night is related to your poking around. No, Olivia. This has gone too far. You need to leave. Today."

She held up a hand. "Dad, stop. First, I'm not poking around anywhere. I just—"

"Why were you at the bank then? Asking questions about Grove Manor. Don't tell me you're not poking around." He bent forward, swiping his fallen paper from the floor, and slapped it on the table, leaving no doubt that was where it belonged. "Olivia, you're not the police."

"I'm aware of that, Dad." She wrapped an arm around his shoulder. "Please, calm down. You know, if it had been me, instead of Paige, who was—"

"Stop. Stop right there. Don't even say it." He turned away, waving his hands in front of him. "Don't you ever, ever say that to me."

She tipped her head back, drying her cheeks. Then she interlocked her arm with his, leading him to the couch. "Please, Dad, sit. Let's just both take a breath here. You know I won't do anything stupid, right?" He rubbed the back of his neck and wiped his eyes, nodding and exhaling from the full depth of his lungs. "Preston is sending someone to tow the Expedition this morning. I have work-related things today and tomorrow. We have the luncheon on Saturday."

"It seems you'd be safer if you left. I can't believe I would even say that. Safer alone in New York. If I can't protect you here, who will protect you there?"

She scooted closer to him, reaching for his hand. "Is that what this is about? Are you still worried about me moving there?"

"Of course I am. I always worry about you. What sort of father wouldn't?"

"I don't have to go. I don't have to leave Washington."

"No. You need to move. You need to go there and write. It's everything that you've always wanted and worked so hard for. Don't stay in D.C. for my sake. I'm okay here. I've got all that I need."

Her cell rang, and she glanced at the screen, hoping to see Preston's number display as an unknown contact. She pushed the phone away, but it rang again.

"Go ahead," her father said. "You probably should answer that."

She picked up the phone. "Hi, Angela."

"Olivia, I want to give you a heads-up. I just talked to my contact with the publishers in New York. They're having an in-house conference next Friday, so they're rescheduling that day's meetings, including yours, for Monday. So, plan accordingly."

"I can't be there on Monday. I'm not planning to leave here until Sunday."

"You don't have a choice. Look, just cut your vacation short. Come back to D.C. on Saturday, get a cheap flight for Sunday, and meet with them on Monday."

"It's not that simple, Angela."

"Well then, you do what you have to do to make it that simple. I have to get moving to the staff meeting."

Olivia shook her head. "Okay. I don't want to hold you back. Thanks for the warning. Bye." She flipped her phone over and slid it across the table.

"Problems?"

"No. It's fine. Minor conflict with a meeting. I'll get it sorted tomorrow."

"It doesn't sound like nothing. If you need to go—"

"No. I need to be here. I need to make sure the

garden lasts through the weekend and that you don't turn my room into a gym."

The reference to his letter softened his disposition. "I thought you'd be happy if I started exercising. Maybe I'll buy myself a treadmill and some of those kettles you use."

"Kettlebells, and I'm fairly certain you'd end up putting a hole in the wall or window if you tried."

They shared a conciliatory smile, and she leaned in close, kissing his cheek. "Look, I only have a few more days here with you. I don't want to—I'm not going to leave."

"I'm sorry, sweetie. I don't want you to leave either, until you planned to. I'm just worried. I want you to be ..."

"I know, Dad. It's all right. I understand. How about we get the morning going, get the coffee on, and check the garden—see if we need to get any replacements before all the stock sells out at the nursery."

"Okay, honey. Yeah, it's getting to be slim pickings, especially with the tomatoes. They had plenty of habaneros, but we're not doing that again. All right. Let's do that." He patted her knee and stood. "Olivia, you know you mean everything to me."

She grasped and gently squeezed his hand. "And you to me. Go on and get things going. I'll be right in." She leaned back against the sofa, wedging a throw pillow between her hip and elbow. Angela had sent multiple texts after their call ended. She watched her father refilling the coffee brewer's water reservoir and then read: "You come on their terms, not yours," "One chance only," "If they pass, so will the others," "1:50, please," "Thanks."

She had waited eight months, through fall, winter, and spring before receiving word that her novel had generated interest among the publishing houses in New York. Angela championed her cause with her connections, both for her potential book contract and the position at corporate. Though the two were not interdependent, her employers were planning a marketing strategy around her as a national columnist and best-selling author.

She opened her phone's browser, checking for flights on Sunday night. *I shouldn't be worrying about New York.* She glanced again into the kitchen. Her father had set her favorite cobalt blue mug on the table next to a plate of Beverly's bread, ready for them to share. He wanted to make everything perfect for her. She scrolled through the departures, staring blankly at arrival times, convincing herself she had at least tried. *I need to see A.J. before he gets transferred. What was he doing in the woods?*

She pocketed her phone and joined her father for breakfast, detailing her morning plans, promising to be safe, until he no longer protested.

CHAPTER 21

Olivia and her father waited on the porch until Jed arrived and inspected her Expedition, confirming the fatal diagnosis. The sidewall damage proved beyond repair, and the only remedy was replacement. He scrolled through his supplier's inventory on his cell and called several regional retailers, trying to find a set of tires deliverable by Saturday. Coming up empty, he vowed to continue searching back at his shop, but warned that with the station closed for service on Sunday, he may not receive and mount the tires until Tuesday.

They watched in silence as he winched her SUV onto his flatbed tow truck and then departed as if leading a funeral procession. They stood side by side at the end of the drive until the wrecker's flashing lights vanished.

William retrieved his key ring from his pants pocket and handed it to her. "Here." Then he walked past the garden and around the back of the house.

She drove in to town and parked her father's Escape two stores down from the cafe. Her hands lingered on the wheel as she kept the engine idling. She tipped her head back against the seat, eyeing her mother's memorial prayer card, which her father kept tucked in the sun visor's pocket. A wayward breeze meandered through her half-open window, lightly tapping a gas receipt a few inches across the dash. *What am I going to say to him?*

A gunmetal-gray pickup stopped alongside her, and the driver reversed course, parallel parking in the vacant spot between the Escape and the end of the block. She remembered three summers ago when she and A.J. packed up his silver crew cab, venturing out on a day trip to Lake Anna. He swore she would learn to love fishing before the sun set. He baited her hooks and removed the modest largemouth bass she reeled in on the last cast before sundown. After they had packed their tackle in the bed of his truck, they shared a picnic dinner on the shoreline under a full moon, speculating on where life may take them in five years.

She eased her grip on the wheel and relaxed her hands on the seat. The preparations for the weekend's festival had resumed. A five-man crew worked along one length of the lawn, assembling the canopies for the artisanal crafters set to sell their locally made breads, jams, and wines. Four men stabilized the poles of each shelter as Steve pounded the stakes to anchor the tie-down ropes in place. The well-rehearsed assembly followed a familiar layout used for every large-scale town event during the year. The white tents, pitched side by side, aligned across the square from the row of food vendors that would be there early Saturday morning.

When Olivia was ten, she had begged her father for a tent. That Christmas, when she found an extra-large red-ribbon package tucked deep under the tree, there was no happier child anywhere in the world. She recalled the countless nights she and A.J. camped in the backyard, protected by that shelter. They spent easeful summer evenings under the stars with all the requisite supplies: sleeping bags, pillows, flashlights, canteens, books, and brownies. As they waited for her mother's curfew check, they sat side by side in the tent with the flaps parted wide, watching the fireflies dance in the night sky.

She unfastened her seatbelt, but remained behind the wheel. *Why didn't Paige tell me about A.J.?* Then, thinking she heard someone call her name, she glanced in her rearview mirror and then out her window toward the town square.

"Over here." Dorothy waved from where she sat on one of the wooden benches lining the lawn.

Olivia got out of the car, locked up, and crossed the street. "Good to see you, Mrs. Peabody. Are you alone today?"

"Right behind you." Floyd patted her shoulder. "Got them, sweetie." He lifted a handled paper sack from Jillian's as proof and then settled next to his wife, situating the bounty between them.

Dorothy retrieved a doughnut from the bag and

offered it to Olivia. "Can I interest you in one? They're apple cinnamon."

She held up her hand. "No, thank you. Maybe I'll get a dozen before I leave on Sunday."

Floyd snatched the glazed doughnut from his wife. "I'll take it. We always start our mornings with something sweet. These are my favorites. Her Boston creams are good too. Make sure if you buy a dozen, you get your free one. Yesterday, I put vinegar in the coffee pot like you told me, and what do ya know, it worked. Clean as a whistle."

Dorothy unfolded a napkin and rummaged through the bag. "I'm still getting a pod brewer. It's coming this afternoon."

Floyd grumbled, shaking his head as he chewed. "And a box of bottled water too, I'm sure." He looked up at Olivia. "You should write a book with tips like that. People would pay good money for that kind of thing. Vinegar—who'd a thought?"

"I can't take credit for the idea. Others have more experience with those sorts of issues. That's not in my wheelhouse."

He wiped his chin with the back of his hand. "You've got to believe in yourself. I see books in your future. I've been working on a novel myself."

"Please don't bother her, dear." Dorothy chuckled and then turned toward Olivia. "He's been lost in chapter one for thirty years."

He tapped a finger above his ear, and pointed the

remaining half of his doughnut at Olivia. "It's all up here. You make them do a large print. I had to get a new prescription to read the paperbacks they're making these days."

Dorothy snickered, dabbing the corner of her mouth with a fresh napkin. "I can change the size of the text on my tablet whenever I want."

Olivia smiled, scanning across the sun-bathed lawn from the inn to the gazebo. "Who knows, perhaps one day I'll—"

Her words sunk like a jettisoned anchor. Steve was heading straight for her on a laser-line course, the distance between them less than fifty feet. Dorothy and Floyd's conversation faded into the background and she nodded at random phrases while tracking his every step. Thirty feet, twenty feet. She steadied herself, aligning square to him. Ten feet, five feet. She took a deep breath, and he stomped right by. He kept his sight fixed on her, though, until he reached a rusty truck parked behind the Peabodys' bench. He stretched into the pickup's bed, retrieving a ragged polyester black duffel. Then he retraced his steps, strutting back in her direction. Neither broke eye contact. The tools in his bag clanged, jostling against each other in their cramped confines.

He stopped a few paces from her. "You seem more attentive today. It's Olivia, right?"

She shuffled her feet, widening her stance. "It's Steve, right?"

"Was that your Expedition Jed was hauling through

town earlier? Something happen to it? I'm a pro at fixing things." He raised his duffle, shaking it as the contents clattered. "You should've called me. I would've given you a discount. Oh well. I guess Jed can take care of whatever ails it. Maybe next time."

"How do you know it's mine?"

"Black SUV, Washington plates. Seems a bit out of place. You know—out of its element."

The Peabodys peeked at one another as Floyd reached into the paper bag for a second helping. They scooted forward on the bench, ensuring they heard every word of the theater before them.

"You seem a bit out of your element."

He stepped toward her. "Is that right? How so?"

"A mayor now in construction?"

"Former mayor."

"Because of Paige?"

He dropped his duffel drawing closer. He glanced at the police station, sneering with a laugh laced with a razor's edge. "They caught the creep who did it. I'm sorry that she's dead. It's a shame. Something like that— terrible for the town, for business. The publicity could impact attendance this weekend. Probably drive down the sale price for that property too. What's most important, though, is that our streets are safe again. The police got their man." He dismissed her with a mock salute, walking backward two steps, and reached for his tools.

Olivia stepped forward, clenching her jaw. "Did they?"

Steve stood straight, dropping the duffel again. Metal clanked with agitation as the weight of the bag crushed the tall fescue by his side. "You got something to say?"

"You've been doing work at Grove Manor?"

He placed his hands on his hips. "That's right. What's it to you?"

"You're familiar with the grounds then."

He yanked his gear from the ground. "As I said, glad you're paying more attention to your surroundings today. Keep up the good work. Best of luck with the car. Give me a call next time." He turned and strode toward the tents.

She tracked his departure until he was over halfway across the square and then spun around to apologize for the disruption. "Mrs. Peabody—"

"Olivia, that man is awful. I wouldn't be talking to him if I were you."

"Listen to my wife," Floyd said. "Stay away from Steve. If he did it once, he'll do it again."

CHAPTER 22

Olivia traversed the block to the police station without once glancing in Steve's direction. She wanted to. She wanted more, though, to deny him the satisfaction of paying him even an ounce of attention after they separated to their neutral corners. She exchanged pleasantries with a postal worker passing by and vacantly watched a trio of millennials exit the cafe. A toddler dressed to the nines in red and white gingham scampered toward the sidewalk, chasing after a runaway pink balloon. Olivia quick-stepped onto the grass, snagging its curled, white ribbon, and returned the treasure to the rosy-cheeked, strawberry-blonde cutie.

She entered the police headquarters and rapidly reconned the workroom, verifying that only Cole, Bert, and A.J. were present. A.J., clad in an orange jumpsuit, was hunched forward in a folding chair in his cell, leafing randomly through a magazine. Cole had his back turned toward the foyer as he balanced on his tiptoes, stretching for the rear contents of a file cabinet's top drawer. Bert sat at Preston's desk, wearing wired earbuds while working on a laptop, bobbing his head to a rhythm all his own.

"Hey, Cole."

He turned abruptly, bumping his forehead into the corner of the cabinet. "Ms. Olivia, wow—that smarts. I didn't see you come in." He winced, gritting his teeth. "Detective Hills—oh, that hurts—isn't here, if you came to see him."

"You okay?"

He nodded with a pained Cheshire cat grin, poking at a reddened patch of skin below his hairline. "I've hit myself harder."

She bit back a slight smile, imagining the memes that may conjure such a caption. "Maybe you should put ice on that. Actually, I didn't come to see Preston."

"Okay, well, if you didn't come for Detective— Preston ... Am I bleeding? Do you see blood?"

"Definite bump. No blood. Maybe you should sit for a minute."

"Gonna take a lot more than a little lump to knock this deputy down." He donned his campaign hat, cringing with the band's compression. "What can I help you with?"

She peeked over her shoulder toward the cell. "I want to speak with A.J."

Cole and Bert glanced at one another. A.J. tossed his

magazine next to a pancaked pillow on his cot. He stood, and his eyes met Olivia's, but neither spoke as if the distance between them was as wide as an ocean and as unbridgeable as the deepest of canyons.

Cole removed his hat, tossing it onto the desk. "Sure, fine by me."

Olivia had envisioned finding A.J. looking like a bedraggled convict with craggy stubble and tousled hair, rocking on the floor of his cell with his knees to his chest, proclaiming innocence. Instead, his rounded cheeks lacked any hints of growth, and he presented properly groomed. Her heart dropped like a pail that had lost its tether in a well. *He's not guilty. He's not. He didn't do it.* "I see they gave you a change in clothes."

Bert snapped his laptop shut and swiveled his seat to gauge A.J.'s profile, yanking his earbuds out with the quick spin. "I got those over in Luray last year. Me and the Mrs. drove down Skyline Drive when the leaves turned, and we chanced upon a mom-and-pop offloading Halloween get-ups at half-price. They had that orange one and an extra-large with stripes. I bought them both, and me and my cuz here used them a week later for Fall Fest costumes."

Cole drummed his stomach. "I wore the zebra suit to accommodate my abs. We won the adult category—beat Jillian's grande double espresso latte. The *Times* printed our picture with the trophy above the fold."

Bert closed a manila folder and saluted Cole. "That pumpkin swirl she designed on top of her foam—downright impressive, though. You should have seen it, Olivia. She could squat, pull her arms in, and voilà: a four-foot-tall coffee cup sitting on the grass. Everybody wanted a picture with her. She probably should have won." He gathered the papers spread across the desk into a loose pile. "Can't help it now—I need a quad shot. You want anything, partner?"

Cole gazed into a far distant realm, as if pondering the meaning of life. "I'll take an iced brew and one of those cake pops. Make it two. The ones with rainbow sprinkles."

"Olivia, can I bring you a coffee?"

"No. Thanks, though, Bert."

Cole renewed his quest in the file cabinet, leaving her alone with A.J. She reached her arm through the cell. "How are you doing?"

He grasped her hand, holding on as if never wanting to let go. "They're moving me sometime. They didn't say when."

"What did the lawyer say?"

"I should plead."

She recoiled. "Plead to what? Why would you plead to anything? You didn't do this." She peeked over her shoulder. Cole stood on a stepstool and plunged neck deep into the drawer. She lowered her voice. "What happened that night? Why were you at that place?" His shoulders rounded as he reluctantly released her hand. He backed away and slumped in his rickety, off-kilter chair. "A.J.? Tell me what's happening."

"I can't."

"What do you mean, you can't? They're charging you with murder. It's me. Talk to me, please."

He rose, returning to where she stood. "They have my truck, and I don't have a stellar alibi." He glanced at Cole, who was now fixating on his reflection in the wall mirror next to the water cooler, inspecting his injury. "I don't know what to do." Tears moistened the corners of his eyes.

"Were you and Paige—more than just friends?"

He rested his forehead against the bars, softly nodding.

"I'm so sorry. I didn't know." *I should have known.* She sheltered his cheek as he fought to keep from sobbing, but his chest heaved with each stifled breath. She reached into the cell to embrace him, but the five-inch spacing between the grilles blocked her from encircling him with full support. "Listen. We'll figure this out. You need to talk to me. Were you there to meet her?" He shook his head. "Then why?"

"I can't tell you."

Olivia withdrew her arms, feeling as though trapped within the inner circle of a roundabout. She wanted to scream, "Help me, help you."

"Paige left me too."

"What do you mean?" She double-checked Cole's proximity. He swiped at a pair of flies with a procedural manual, meting out justice for their buzzing about his desk. "You weren't together? I don't understand."

"Liv, don't get involved. You'll end up getting hurt or worse. Everybody does."

"How can I not be involved? What's Junior's role in this? What aren't you telling me?"

He white-knuckled the steel and sharply sighed, diverting his gaze to her right. She traced his path, flinching as Cole thrust a bottle of water toward her chin.

"Would you like a chilled beverage? It's getting steamy out there today. I can get you a straw."

She tilted her head back, readying to bob and weave, fearing he may swat at the flies that had followed him over. "Thanks. That's sweet of you." She accepted the bottle and then raised it slightly in a toast. "Cheers, Cole. No straw necessary."

"Okey-dokey. I'll just be back over there if you change your mind."

They watched as Cole sauntered back to his desk.

"Junior liked Paige," A.J. said once he was out of earshot. "He asked her out a few times—dinners, movies, even a Nats game once when New York was in town at the end of last season. But she wasn't interested."

"Did he know about you and her?"

"We tried to keep it quiet. Sorry, we were going to tell you this week. We started spending time with each other around the beginning of the year. I know we weren't together as long as you and Daniel, but we kind of hit it off. One day, Junior saw us having lunch at the inn, and the next morning, he came into work hung over, started throwing punches. Frank dragged him into his office and yelled at him for twenty minutes. We've never talked about it since. It's like it didn't even happen. His dad always treated me well, so I wasn't about to leave the company. Besides, I needed the job. I was saving money to buy Paige something special."

Why didn't she tell me? "Did Junior know you would be at Grove Manor on Monday?"

"Yeah, he knew. I was there to meet—" His eyes darted behind her. "Liv, you gotta leave. Now. Go. Be careful. Don't trust—"

"Ms. Penn, what are you doing in my station?"

She peeked over her shoulder. Payne stalked toward the cell like a drill sergeant ready to break a fresh recruit. She turned in her own sweet time. "I'm visiting my friend."

"Visitation over. You're not to come here again. Is that understood?"

"He's allowed visitors. You can't stop me from—"

"Liv, don't. Please, just go."

She glanced back at A.J., acquiescing only for his sake. Payne stepped between them and escorted her to the gated divide as Bert returned, carrying his provisions from Jillian's, followed by Preston hauling an evidence box bearing Monday's date.

Bert raised his double-cupped venti quad. "You leaving, Olivia?"

"Yes. Good to see you, Bert. Enjoy your coffee."

She scooted sideways past Preston through the entrance, with the concealed contents retrieved from the crime scene separating them. They swapped subtle head nods, mutually gauging the tenuous trust forged last night. Payne retreated inside the station once Olivia was clear of the door, but Preston trailed her out onto the sidewalk.

"Olivia. What's going on?"

She turned, facing him. "I'm not sure." Two warnings about trust. She bet all-in that she did not need to worry about Cole or Bert. Payne, yes. But Preston …

He stepped toward her, and she matched his progress equal and opposite, as if repulsed by a magnetic field. He stopped, and she halted. His eyes narrowed at the riddle before him.

"Olivia. What's going on?" he asked again.

She could not script a lie. She could only question and doubt her judgment. "Preston, I can't—I need to go."

"Olivia, wait. Please."

"I've gotta go." She turned and walked away, wasting no time in putting daylight between herself and the station.

CHAPTER 23

The hour approached eleven, and with time to spare before her scheduled two o'clock online Q&A, Olivia drove back to her father's house to prepare for the afternoon session and research public land records related to the Jackson property. She rolled up to a crossroads not far from where she nearly collided with Cassandra on Monday and idled at a four-way stop, feeling adrift at sea with no shore in sight. She rested her head against the seat and ran her fingers through her hair. "Don't trust them? Who are you talking about?" The driver of an Ecosport watched and waited from the intersecting lane, assuming the right of way when she showed no signs of budging. A pickup's horn blasted from behind, and she glanced in her rearview at a baby boomer holding his hands high as if in Sunday worship. She flipped on her turn signal, and waved, mouthing "sorry," certain his pointed response was not one of praise.

Olivia rounded into the driveway, catching sight of the porch, and slammed on the brakes, leaving her rear bumper hanging in the roadway. A white cargo van from the Grossman's fleet was stationed at the upper end of the drive with its rear panel doors opened. Ratchet tie-downs secured two ladders on the roof, and a box of tools with its tray drawer extended rested at the bottom of the front steps. She unfastened her seatbelt, scanning the porch, and shifted into park once the Escape was out of harm's way. After snatching her cell from the center console cubby, she walked cautiously toward the van, twice considering skirting the side of the house to enter through the kitchen. Her father strolled around the front corner of the garden, carrying a spray nozzle, and waved. He bent forward, lifting the end of the garden hose, and fastened the two together. "I expected you'd be out at least another hour."

The screen door swung wide as the visitor reversed out of a crouched position. She returned her father's wave, keeping her eyes glued to the porch. "Hey, Dad. Yeah, turned out to be a quick trip." *Please don't be Junior.*

"Hi there, Olivia." Frank stood, bracing himself against the doorframe as he wiped his brow with his shirtsleeve.

"Hi." Her cheeks softened with a half-smile. "What are you doing here?"

"He's installing a second deadbolt on the front and back doors. On your mother's office too."

"Do you think that's really necessary?"

Frank leaned with his hands on the wood rail that ran the porch's length. "Your dad told me what happened last night. You can't ever be too safe. Nobody will get in after I'm done. I guarantee that."

Her father shuffled up the steps, tightly gripping the banister. "Honey, I'm making lunch. Do you want something?"

"Sure. Anything's fine. Call me when you're ready."

"Two for chicken soup, coming right up."

She followed his route to the porch and reclined in the rocker to the left of the door. Frank knelt, resuming the installation. "Can I get your help here? See that screwdriver—the one with the blue handle? Could you please hand me that?" She rose and picked up the screwdriver that he was pointing to among an assortment just out of his reach. He took the tool from her and affixed a strike plate to the doorjamb. "Your dad teared up when he told me about your tires. He said you've been asking around about that reporter's death. We both believe A.J.'s innocent, but that means whoever hurt that girl is still out there. I didn't wanna scare your dad any more than he is already, but I'll say it to you. This happening with your truck—that's not a coincidence. You can't convince me of that. Your dad's not buying it, and neither am I." He placed the Phillips head on the ground next to him, resting his palms on his thighs. "There, that should do it. That's solid now."

Olivia stood and strolled to the patio table, centering

a bouquet of miniature yellow roses she had cut from bushes fronting her mother's office. "I appreciate the concern. I do. This was probably random vandalism. There's no need to overreact."

Frank rose and rubbed his hands together, wiping away the dirt from his endeavors. "All I'm saying is watch yourself. Spend the rest of your week with your dad here and then enjoy New York. Live it up. You deserve it. Come back and visit whenever you can. Next time you're in town, I'll take the two of you to dinner for a real celebration."

She buoyed him with a warm smile. "I'll definitely hold you to that. Like I was telling my dad, I'll be back before anyone misses me."

He walked over to where she stood by the petite round-top table, and she backed into the corner to make room for him to sit in the bistro chair beside her. "I also want a first edition of your book, inscribed and signed."

She grinned and nodded as she crossed her arms and leaned against the side railing, and it immediately gave way. She tumbled off the porch, falling three feet to the ground.

"Olivia!"

She lay dazed, slammed against the sod. Gravity pinned her motionless as searing, sharp pain pierced from the base of her right thumb straight through her wrist. A wave of nausea crested and broke over her within seconds.

"Olivia! Are you okay?"

Light flashed when she closed her eyes, and a throb beat a surging tempo in the dead center of her head. Frank leapt from the porch and dropped to the ground by her side.

"Olivia, don't move. Bill! Bill!"

She rolled to her back, struggling to lift her shoulders as the thumping between her eyes deepened. She heard the screen door squeak open and Buddy barking from inside the house.

"Did you need me? Where are ya, Frank?"

"Over here, Bill."

She tried to roll to her side as her father came down the steps. He quickened his pace as soon as he saw her looking up at him from the ground.

"Olivia? Why are you—? What happened? Why's the railing—did you fall? Sweetie, are you hurt?"

She tried keeping pace with his questions but could only grimace, unsure of what or how to answer.

"I'll call an ambulance," he said.

"No, Dad. Don't. I'm okay. No, don't call. Please." She took two deep breaths, fearing she may pass out.

"No, we're going to the emergency room. What's hurting? Did you hit her head?"

She tried sitting again, pushing up through her hands, but the pressure jolted her wrist, and she fell back to the ground. "Ah, I might—I think I, ah, need some help here."

Frank supported her shoulders while William eased

her up. She squinted at the sun's overwhelming bright-ness, bracing her injured wrist against her rib cage.

"Let me see, honey." She gingerly extended her fore-arm, inhaling short, shallow breaths. "It's swelling, sweetie. Let's go to the hospital."

"No, Dad. Please, give me a minute to rest here."

Frank propped her forward, supporting her lower back. "You could've broken something. Your dad's right. We can all go in my van."

"No. Please. Everyone, stop. I just need a minute. Dad, could you bring me a bag of ice?"

"Don't move. I'll be back in a second. Can you stay with her?" William stood as fast as he could, almost losing his balance in his haste.

Frank kept his arm around her. "Keep still. How much pain are you in? Hey, Bill! Bring her some water, too."

She tried touching her thumb to each of her fingers, but could not come close to connecting. "Prob-ably just sprained it. I'll be fine. I'm feeling steadier now."

"You sure? You're not gonna nosedive on me if I let go, are you?"

"No. Promise."

He pushed up from the ground and stepped a few feet over to where the railing dislodged from its anchor mount to the house. Her father returned with a bag of frozen carrots wrapped in a paper towel and held them out to her."

"Hold on, let me try to get up first." She rotated onto her knees and slowly stood, fending off a wave of vertigo.

"Take it easy, honey. Are you dizzy?"

"Little bit." She made her way to the porch with her father by her side and slumped in the rocker, testing her jaw and tasting metal. Her father pulled out a water bottle from his short's front pocket, twisted off the cap, and handed it to her. She drank a few cautious sips, and after ensuring they settled okay in her stomach, she downed half of the rest in several large gulps.

Frank dropped the failed railing to the ground and walked halfway to the steps. "Bill, a word." He pulled his cell from his shirt's front pocket.

"Please, Mr. Grossman. Don't call an ambulance. I'm not going to the hospital."

"Frank?" her father replied.

"Bill, can you come over here for a second?"

"What is it, Frank? Go ahead. Tell us both."

He lowered his phone, looking back and forth between her and the busted bracket. "I'm not calling for an ambulance. I'm calling the police. That railing coming away from the house like that—" He cleared his throat, choking back anger. "The screws from the anchor mount—they've been yanked from the wood sheathing under the siding. That doesn't happen by itself. You need a drill to reverse those screws to loosen them enough to get 'em to pop like that. This wasn't an accident. If I find out who did this—" He lifted the cell to his ear. "This is Frank Grossman. Get Ray on the phone now."

William's face drained to pale. Olivia reached for his hand, smiling as much as the pain allowed. His skin was cold and clammy. "I'm okay, Dad. It feels better already. I'll be fine. The police are on their way. I'm sure Preston will be here any minute."

She bowed her head, closing her eyes, and remembered A.J.'s warning. *Is Preston one of them?*

CHAPTER 24

Preston arrived within twenty minutes of Frank's call. He rounded his F-150 into the driveway without a hint of subtlety, skimming past the Escape and stopping three feet shy of impacting Grossman's van. He hurried from the pickup to the porch where Olivia and her father waited, watching him as he scanned the yard, rapidly surveilling the crime scene. Frank irately approached, preparing to present his evidence, but Preston pushed right by him, pinning his focus on her. "What happened?"

Frank stood midway between the steps and the corner of the house, pointing to where Olivia had tumbled from the porch. "The railing. It ripped away from its mounting. Someone loosened the anchor bracket. That's what happened." He started toward the steps, but reversed course and stomped back to the felled support, indignantly shaking his head as his cheeks flushed scarlet red. "Where's Payne? Why isn't he here?"

Preston glared at him and then focused on the open end of the porch for a moment before turning back toward Olivia. "You should go to the hospital. I can call for an ambulance or take you to the ER."

"No, please. It's calming down." She hiked her shoulder and leaned to her left, raising her wrist off her lap as fabricated proof. "I fell awkwardly. That's all."

"Did you hit your head?"

She kneaded the back of her neck, feeling her muscles inflamed and taut. "I'm not sure."

"Let me see." He dropped to a knee, and she entrusted her hand to him, lifting the compress as if protecting a baby bird. She handed the carrots to her father as Preston supported her wrist, sending a rush of soothing warmth across her frozen skin. "No bones sticking through. That's a good sign."

She rubbed her temple and rolled her eyes, sighing at the rudimentary diagnosis. "Thank you, doctor. Your true talents are being wasted in law enforcement."

His lips thinly parted, coaxing his dimple out of hiding.

William leaned forward, holding the carrots between them. "She should keep this on her wrist."

"You're right, Mr. Penn." Preston cradled her elbow, tenderly guiding her arm into her lap. His hand lingered on her fingertips as he looked across the porch toward

Frank, who was hoisting one end of the sabotaged railing. "Can you put that down? That's evidence."

William tapped Preston's bicep with the softening crinkle cuts, and he promptly withdrew his hand and rose, retrieving his cell from his jeans front pocket. He held the phone to his ear while descending the steps. "Cole, listen up ..." He peeked over his shoulder at Olivia, lowering his voice.

Frank waited by the fractured railing as Preston carried on with his call, out of earshot and with his back turned to all. When Preston had finished, he walked over to Frank, who was examining where the busted bracket had ripped away from the house. Preston squatted next to the debris, snapping pictures with his cell.

As Preston stood, Frank retrieved the fractured end of the railing from the ground, highlighting where the securing bracket splintered. "See—those screws had to be reversed out of there. No way that happens by itself." Frank turned away from Olivia and recounted the malfeasance, orchestrating the players with full role play of positioning and sequencing of events.

She leaned forward, eavesdropping, but the ringing in her ears drowned out the fragments she caught, rendering the dialogue murky. She glanced at her father. *Thank heavens it was me.*

"Honey?" He patted her shoulder. "Are you doing okay? I asked if you wanted more water."

"Sorry, Dad. Yes, thanks. I could use a refill."

He opened the screen door, and Buddy bolted out

with his ball loosely hanging in his jaw. He scurried past Olivia to where Frank and Preston were still talking, dropping the well-worn, wet toy between them. Preston bent forward and threw the ball clear to the mailbox as Frank's volume escalated, peaking in a diatribe punctuated by coarse allusions to Payne and departmental incompetence.

Buddy retrieved his target in no time, racing back to Preston, but withdrew from the game as the vibe between the two men infected his play. He climbed the front steps and settled on his belly next to Olivia's chair. She leaned down over the armrest, massaging above his collar as her father returned with a bottle of water and a throw pillow from the living room couch.

"Are the carrots still frozen?"

She scooted forward, making room for him to jam the embroidered cushion behind her. "They're fine. Soggy, but they'll do. Guess we'll be having these for dinner."

"I won't complain. I like them with salt and butter." He opened the bottle and handed it to her.

"Thanks, Dad. Grab a seat." He slid the other rocker over, sitting beside her as Preston and Frank walked measuredly back toward them.

Preston joined Olivia and her father on the porch while Frank waited by the bottom step. "Mr. Penn, I have to agree with Frank's assessment. Appears there's been tampering with that mounting. Deputies Lee and Branch are on their way to assist with evidence collection. If you don't mind, right now, I would like a word with your daughter."

Her father angled his seat so that his armrest abutted hers. "Go ahead."

Preston raised his Stetson, running his hand once through his hair. He shifted his weight, looking first at Frank and then directly at her. "I would like to question her alone."

William clenched her armrest, shifting to the edge of his seat. "Question? What about my questions for you? Let's start with what you were doing at my house last night without talking to me. Is that how you do things by the book now or are you some renegade cowboy cop—"

"Dad, please. It's okay."

He catapulted to his feet, scowling and drawing his shoulders back. "This isn't right. What exactly were you watching last night? Because it sure doesn't look like it was her."

"Please, Dad. Give us a few minutes."

The creases bordering his eyes deepened as he looked back and forth between them, seething while waving Frank over. "Come on. Let's wait in the living room. Sweetie, you call me if you need me out here."

After they walked inside, Preston pulled the door shut and ensured the screen was closed. "Seems your father doesn't have a high opinion of me at the moment."

She stared past him, softening her gaze on the purple and fuchsia petals of her mother's azaleas, envisioning A.J. in his cell. "He's worried. He's very protective."

"Grossman tells me you've been asking questions concerning Ms. Warner's death."

"Paige. Her name was Paige. And she was murdered."

"Olivia—"

"Do you think whoever slashed my tires did this to the railing last night?"

"Possibly."

"You think there's more than one person involved?"

He removed his hat and held it against his thigh. "You need to stop this."

She snapped her sight from the azaleas. "Is that an order?"

"Why do I sense you're not one who reacts well to orders?"

She poked at the puffiness around her thumb, counting how many seconds the skin stayed indented.

"Don't leave home at night by yourself," he said.

"Excuse me? I'll go where I want, when I want, and with whom I want."

"What were you doing at the station this morning?"

She hesitated as she repositioned the pillow behind her. "I was visiting A.J."

"Seems you ruffled Payne, and that's difficult to do. He lit into Cole and Bert about you being there."

"I'm sorry for that. I didn't mean to cause them any trouble."

"I'm stationing them outside your house tonight."

She shook her head, leaning forward. "No. That's unnecessary."

"It's not your call." He aligned his hat and pointed to the compress on her hand. "You're not going to the hospital, are you?"

She peeled the saturated paper towel from the carrots and hung it over her rocker's armrest.

"You'll have that wrist examined tomorrow if it gets worse overnight, right? Will you at least promise me that? Olivia?"

"Yes, doctor."

"Cole and Bert will be here soon to collect evidence and take your statements. I need to check into some things at the station. You stay put until they arrive."

"What's happening with A.J.? When is he being transferred?"

"You have my number. Use it." He tipped his Stetson and retreated to his truck.

After Preston pulled out of the driveway, William and Frank returned to sit with her on the porch. "Everything okay, honey?"

"Yes, it's fine. There'll be police outside the house tonight. The good doctor–detective insists."

Frank lay his hand on her shoulder. "That's the first smart thing he's done this whole time."

She rose from the rocker, tossing the thawed carrots on the slatted seat. "I'll be back."

Once inside, she headed straight upstairs to the hallway bathroom where she grabbed an elastic bandage from the medicine cabinet. Sitting on the edge of the tub, she anchored the fabric between her hand and leg and encircled her palm and wrist with the wrap until the roll reached its end. Then she secured the support with two metal clips and flexed her fingers, ensuring the compression did not compromise her circulation.

She returned to the living room and retrieved her briefcase from her father's study, flinging it onto the couch. She grabbed the keys for her mother's office from the hook rack by the refrigerator and exited the house through the kitchen, hoping Frank had not yet installed the additional lock on the door.

She hurried across the lawn and breathed a sigh of relief when she was close enough to see a single deadbolt. She unlocked the door, heading straight over to the desk, and pulled out the address book she found yesterday. She removed the scrap of paper that had fallen to her feet, stuffed the note into her pocket, and locked up. Then she retraced her route to reenter through the back door.

William stood as she stepped onto the porch with her bag slung over her shoulder and his key ring dangling from her thumb. "Where are you going?"

"Sorry, Dad. I'll have to miss lunch. Keep a bowl for me in the fridge. I have an online chat for work soon."

"You can't do it here? Honey, you're not in a condition to go anywhere. The only place you should go is to the emergency room."

Frank nodded. "Your dad's right. You shouldn't be driving."

"I'm fine. I put a wrap on to help with the swelling."

"Honey, can't this wait? Can't you reschedule?"

Olivia waved him off. "I have to do this. I'll be all right."

"Your dad and I were just talking about the time I took you to the hospital after you fell off your bike when you and Junior were racing by the ball fields. I remember it like it was yesterday. You were ten. It was a month before your birthday. I thought you had broken your leg."

Olivia turned slightly, looking at him, replaying the scene. *He ran into me.*

"You had me scared. I was shaking like a leaf when I picked you up. I won't ever forget how panicked your mother was when she got to the ER. Now, I understand what she must've been feeling." Frank eyed the damaged railing. "Let us drive you, at least. I don't have anything pressing this afternoon."

"Yeah, honey. We'll all go."

"No, Dad. Thanks, but I'll be fine. Sometimes Dr. Reyes stops by the clinic for lunch. If I go now, maybe I'll catch him, and he can look at my wrist." Olivia kissed her father on his cheek and hurried down the steps before either of the men could protest further. Buddy barreled after her, trying to leap into the Escape when she slid into the seat, but she held him back as she carefully closed the door. "Sorry, little guy. You stay here. I have to do this alone."

CHAPTER 25

Olivia headed straight for Paige's office—her true intended destination. The late morning malevolence had prevented her online probe of the Jackson property, so now she amended her fact-finding strategy to pursue a hunch informed by her twenty-year friendship with Paige. First, though, she made a pit stop at Sophia's to hijack the Wi-Fi for her Q&A, which was set to start in less than an hour. Angela had texted twice amid the melee of the past forty-five minutes: the first a warning, the second a reminder of the warning.

She entered the clinic, finding herself alone in the foyer. Josefina was absent from her customary afternoon reading encampment on the couch, and there was no commotion or clamor from the offices or kitchen to hint at who else was there.

"Hello? Anyone home?" She leaned sideways, peering into the empty hallway. Sophia peeked around the doorframe from inside the treatment room as Olivia slung her briefcase onto the sofa, wincing as the weight fell from her.

Sophia stepped into the foyer holding an opened folder. "Hey, Liv. Sorry, I was finishing paperwork. What happened to your—"

"I hope I'm not interrupting a session." She rotated slightly, keeping her wrapped wrist behind her back, pretending to scratch an itch she had difficulty pinning down.

Sophia closed her file and tossed it onto the table. "No. I'm free." She stared at Olivia, who kept up her charade, scanning around the foyer and out through the suite's window.

"So, where's everyone?"

Sophia stepped closer, pointing to Olivia's side. "What are you doing?"

She turned further and reached for her bag, developing a sudden need to remove something, anything, from the exterior pocket. She tugged twice at the zipper with her left hand, but the slider stuck, refusing to budge around the reinforced top corner. "I have this work thing, and I—wow, this is a little sticky here." She lifted the briefcase by the pull tab, trying to shake it loose.

Sophia grabbed and held Olivia's hand, lifting her fingers from the slider, and unzipped the pocket. "Go ahead, Liv. Get what you need."

Olivia forced a grin, gritting her teeth, unable to break free of Sophia's grasp.

"No, how about using your other hand? You know, the one you're hiding behind your back rather pathetically."

She reached around Olivia and coaxed her right arm forward, then supported the wrapped wrist as she squeezed the swollen thumb and palm. Olivia flinched with each press.

"What in the world happened to you?"

"I had an accident, but I'm fine—probably a minor sprain. Don't make a big deal of it. I have an online chat for work, and I need access to—"

"Stop talking. You walk in here playing hide and seek with a wounded wing and expect me to believe you're fine? Tell me, did you leave your unicorn under the rainbow outside?"

"That's a bit aggressive."

"Tell me right now what happened."

Olivia relaxed her shoulders, breathing out two days' worth of tension. She related all that had occurred, and when she finished, Sophia led her to the foyer's table and pulled out a chair.

"Sit. Put your arm up. Let me see. Did you wrap this yourself?"

Olivia nodded, expecting at least a modest commendation for her ingenuity.

"Fascinating technique. Wherever you trained, ask for your money back."

"I learned by watching you." She winced as Sophia pinched the tip of her thumb. "Ow!"

"Did that hurt?" She mirrored Olivia's grimace. "My bad. Go ahead, keep it up. Zero to ten—rate your pain."

"Quite the compassionate bedside manner you have. Before your assault, six and five-eighths."

"How wonderfully precise. Do this." She modeled various motions, instructing Olivia to imitate each one twice. "You should have x-rays taken. You need to go to the ER."

"That's not happening."

"You're incredibly stubborn sometimes. You could have structural damage."

"It's fine. I'm feeling better. It must be the ambiance in here."

"Okay. In that case, you won't mind if I move it around a bit." Sophia reached for her wrist.

Olivia retracted her arm as if about to be shocked by a live wire. "No-no-no. I mean—I appreciate your concern. I have an online chat for work in ten minutes. That's why I came here. I was hoping to jump on your Wi-Fi."

Sophia leaned toward her. "So, that's how this works. You stroll into my clinic, with what just happened, like no big deal, wanting to bum off my bandwidth."

Olivia angled away, massaging the back of her neck. "I didn't mean it like that."

Sophia pressed her palms together, allowing Olivia to sweat out the contrived offense for several awkward seconds. "You know I'm kidding. Seriously Liv, you have me beyond worried. Your dad's right. You should leave.

Let the police do their job. I don't know what I'd do if something—like Paige something—happened to you. What did Preston say?"

"He wants me to stop asking questions. Travel with company until I leave town."

"By company, does he mean himself?" Olivia flicked her fingers, clipping Sophia's arm. "What's so wrong with having a special ... bodyguard?"

"He's got that taken care of for the night." When Sophia raised her eyebrows, she added, "Not like that. He has Cole and Bert stationed outside my dad's until I go."

"You still planning to leave on Sunday?"

"Unsure. It's complicated. Look, I have this chat real soon. Is it okay if I set up out here?"

Sophia pushed back from the table and walked to the closet opposite the treatment room. "Sure. This is the plan. We'll let that swelling settle overnight. Come here in the morning. If I'm not happy with your motion and pain tomorrow, I'm driving you to the hospital myself." She lugged a thirty-quart latched plastic container out from under a shelf.

"Soph, I love you, but I'm one hundred percent positive any therapy tomorrow would be unpleasant. Please don't take offense."

Sophia rummaged through the bin, checking the sizing on the side panels of several cartons. "Here we are. Found it. Your lucky day, Liv." She severed the seal and removed a splint, pointing it at Olivia. "Full offense taken. Up." Olivia placed her forearm on the table. "This will keep your wrist in a neutral position. It has metal stays, so it's rigid. Slip your thumb through the hole and secure it with the straps. Don't make it too tight. I want you to wear this for the rest of the day and while you sleep tonight. If it causes more pain, take it off. Otherwise, leave it on. And I will see you tomorrow. If you refuse, I'll tell my grandmother you've sworn never to get married or have children."

Olivia scooted back in the chair, letting her splinted wrist rest in her lap. "You're being ridiculous. How's that even related? Why would you do that to me?"

On cue, Josefina emerged from the hallway, carrying her recipe collection and afternoon cup of herbal tea.

"What's it going to be, my friend?" Sophia asked.

"This is blackmail, and so beneath you."

"You have no idea how far I'm willing to go."

"I'll get you back."

Sophia greeted her grandmother with a hug. "Abuela, Liv says she's starving. Do we have any leftovers for her to eat?"

Olivia rubbed her eyes, wondering precisely when today she lost control of the narrative.

"Sí." Josefina set her binder on the couch and retraced her steps, carrying her steaming cup back to the kitchen.

"I swear, Soph, if you weren't my best friend—"

"You're lucky I am your best friend. I don't get paid enough for your drama. Now, go put on a smiley face and be 'Dear Ms. Penn.' Help others with their problems even though you, yourself, are a mess."

Olivia grinned at the playful jab, conceding there may be more fact than fiction in that assessment. "Thanks ever so much for your professional medical diagnosis and courtesy."

"Licensed and specialist certified, always at your service." Sophia executed an exaggerated stage bow, leaving her alone in the foyer.

Olivia plugged in her laptop and dialed Angela's number on her cell while inserting a pair of earbuds. Typing with the splint proved painful and awkward. She reverted to a hunt and peck strategy to log on, but even with the deliberate approach, she backspaced four times to enter her password correctly.

"Thanks for showing up, Olivia, a minute before we go live. I guess I can call off the Saint Bernards."

"Sorry, Angela. I had problems with the connection. Everything's on target now. I'm ready."

"Okay, the feed is up and questions are pouring in. You should be able to see your name up on screen."

"Got it."

"We have a few seconds here. Olivia, the publishers want to meet on Monday. You need to get up there."

"About that—"

"Hold the thought. We're on. Batter up."

She studied the first question. Her wrist throbbed, and her head hummed with a dull pain as she strained to focus on the blurred edges of the text on the screen.

Out of Bounds: I received a job offer with a higher salary, but I'll have to work longer hours and on the weekends. I like the people on my team now, and I'm not interested in riding the management track. Should I give it a go? Take the paycheck and see what happens?
Ms. Penn: No.

Angela grunted. "Olivia, although a brilliant response, your readers want more than one-word answers."

Ms. Penn: No, I don't think so.

"Real cute, Olivia."

Galactic Trooper: I caught my girlfriend in a serious lie, but she doesn't know that I know she's lying. I'm thinking of breaking up with her, but maybe I'm overreacting? Thoughts?

Olivia stared out the window at the newspaper's office across the town square. Cassandra's car blocked a full view of the entrance. *I need to look through Paige's—*

"Olivia, hello? Is your connection okay? What's up? The question is there. Do you see it?"

"Sorry, Angela. Things froze for a moment."

"I knew you'd have problems connecting from out there."

Ms. Penn: People who want control will manipulate others to fulfill their own wants and needs. She'll continue to lie until she's forced to admit the truth. Your girlfriend has shown you who she is, believe her.

Feisty Fox: When hubby and I got married, we agreed we wanted kids. Now he's unsure. He suggested getting a dog as a trial-baby. What do you think?
Ms. Penn: That's lunacy.

"Olivia! You can't write that. What's going on with you today? Get your head in the game."
"Yes, of course. You're right. Head's in the game."

Sara-Ann-Dipity: My boyfriend of eight months and his ex-girlfriend remain best friends. They dated for two years. He wants to go away with her to celebrate her birthday for the weekend. Should I be worried? Thanks.
Ms. Penn: Literally slapping my head right now.

"Olivia! That's it. You're done." Her name vanished from the screen. Angela's alias appeared in its place.

Auntie Angel: "Apologies, folks. We've lost Ms. Penn for the moment. She's having technical difficulties. Keep sending in your questions while we work on getting her reconnected."

"Angela, the connection is fine here. Put me back on."

"No. This is over for today. I don't know what's been going on with you since you got there, but you're acting as if you couldn't care less about New York or the publishing contract. Olivia, people are watching you. You're hurting yourself. You're digging your own grave. I'll talk to you tomorrow."

The line went dead. Olivia tried to flex her wrist, but the splint restricted the motion. Sweat trickled down the small of her back, and her pain measured a nine on Sophia's scale. She texted Angela: "Sorry, not feeling well today. Thanks for covering for me."

A reply arrived before the screen dimmed: "Okay. Get better soon. Talk later about Monday."

She pulled the laptop's plug from the wall and wrapped the cord around the adapter. Sophia's grandmother returned, placing a petite ceramic bowl of sweet bread in front of her. "Gracias, Abuela."

Josefina nodded, patting Olivia's braced wrist. "Eat. Don't worry. You'll be okay."

She shuffled to the sofa, settling in the corner with two pillows propped behind her back so her feet could rest flat on the floor. She paged through her recipes as Olivia stared out the window, sweeping the length of the town green while savoring the vanilla sweetness of the midday snack. As she polished off the last of the mini-morsels, Cassandra emerged from the newspaper's office, threw a messenger bag in the backseat of her Fiesta, and drove away.

Olivia wasted no time. She packed her laptop, gave Josefina a quick hug, and set out straight across the square.

CHAPTER 26

Olivia burst through the entrance of the *Apple Station Times* like a Navy SEAL breaching the bunker of a most wanted combatant. Cooper darted out from behind the flung door, barely dodging a blow to his heavily bandaged hand. "Holy moly, Liv. How about a little warning next—hey, that's weird. What happened to yours? Wait, let me guess—the carpal tunnel."

"Sorry, Cooper. No. I didn't mean to scare you." Her attention about-faced to June standing behind her daughter's desk as she shoved aside the lid of a corrugated file box. The purple-grey circles and puffiness under her absent eyes reflected a string of sorrowful, sleepless nights. "Mrs. Warner, how are you holding up?"

She slowly lowered herself into Paige's seat and tenderly rested two fingers on the lip of an oversize bubblegum pink coffee mug. "Hour by hour. I came to collect her belongings. The police have everything from that night. They were here Tuesday morning and took what they needed. Her laptop, files. Even a sweater I gave her to wear here. She told me one time, it gets cold in the summers with the air conditioning. Now, why did they need to take her sweater? Why couldn't they leave that for me? This is all that's left." Her voice faded as she placed a thermal travel tumbler from Sweet Briar College into the storage box. "I don't know when or if I'll get any of it back."

Olivia stepped around the desk and embraced June with strength enough to hold them both. "They'll return everything when they're done investigating. It'll just take time."

June unsnapped her purse, retrieving a pocket-size pack of tissues. "I'm having her mass and burial on Monday. Will you be able to come? You were one of her dearest friends."

Olivia swallowed hard. "I—I'm going to—"

"I understand if you can't. She would understand. I wasn't sure when you'd be leaving for New York."

"I'm going to try. I want to be there." She nodded slightly toward Cooper, who was hunched over his desk repacking a first aid kit. "Do you mind, can we talk more in a second? I need a word with Cooper."

"Go ahead. I'll be here."

Olivia turned and walked cautiously across the room, high-stepping over droplets of blood and a pair of scissors ripe for a crime scene evidence flag. Crumpled wads of scarlet-stained gauze lay on Cooper's desk alongside a tube of superglue, pre-cut squares of duct tape, and a bottle of activated charcoal. Self-adhesive wrap covered his thumb from tip to palm, lending the impression the finger was twice its actual size.

"Hey, Cooper." She raised her wrist as exhibit 1A. "I had a minor accident. What happened to you?"

"This is super freaky. Me too. My stapler wasn't working. I thought it had jammed but turns out, it hadn't."

She cringed, spying the scissors, and suppressed a wave of nausea as she loosened her splint's top strap.

"Some good news, though," he continued. "Mom is letting me write captions for the festival's photo spread."

"Don't you think you should see a doctor? Please tell me you didn't use glue."

He squeezed his thumb along the entire length, flinching with each pulse. "Just to seal the edges around the tape."

"Tape? Not as in duct tape, I hope."

"I'm a bleeder."

She picked up the activated charcoal and read the back of the bottle, electing not to ask. "I saw Cassandra leave a few minutes ago. Do you know where she went?"

"She drove out to Grove Manor."

"Did she say why?"

"No. I didn't ask. I should have asked. What sort of reporter doesn't ask questions? That's why I'm not a reporter. I will never be—"

"Don't worry, Cooper. I'm just curious, that's all. Are you sure you'll be all right?"

"This isn't my first rodeo with that stapler."

She curled her lips and nodded, at a loss for how to follow up on that. "I'm going to talk to Mrs. Warner, okay?"

"Absolutely." He waved his hand over the splayed contents of the first aid kit, channeling his inner David Copperfield. "I'd better make this disappear before Mom gets back."

She backpedaled and turned, rejoining June at Paige's desk. "These all her belongings from here?"

"Yes. There are some office supplies in the drawers, but I'm not taking them."

"Would it be okay if I looked through her things?"

June stood, offering her Paige's chair. An array of items lay scattered on the desk: two reporter's pads, a lotus flower necklace, a framed photo of Paige and her mother, several quart-size baggies, a menu from Jillian's, business cards from Materials Core Innovations and Jed's Auto Body, a box of salted brownie protein bars, three empty sample vials, a pair of latex gloves, reading glasses, and a writing style manual.

Olivia examined the notebooks, perusing each one for relevant clues. Paige's precise penmanship reflected a love of calligraphy she had cultivated while spending a semester abroad in Japan. The first notebook cataloged research for stories in progress, but none mentioned any connection to the auction. Olivia inspected the second notebook. It was empty except for the "if lost" contact information on the thick cardboard front cover. She aligned the blank book on top of the first. A narrow band of ripped paper lingered in the top pad's spiral binding. She spun the notebook around and flipped through the pages again. Though they were still devoid of content, the entrapped, coiled remnant told her that the last sheet was AWOL.

She scrutinized the business cards for notations of any sort, but there were none. The Materials Core Innovations card showed a mailing address in Saskatchewan, Canada, with headquarters based in Saskatoon. *Why would Paige have this?* She snapped a picture of the card with her phone and entered the company's website URL in a browser. The page stalled, and she reloaded and set the cell to the side, allowing the network more time to connect.

"Mrs. Warner, had Paige been to Canada recently?"

"No. Canada? Why? Do you think she visited—" Her phone rang. "This is my sister. I'm going to take it outside."

Olivia nodded and carried on with her survey. She set the business cards on top of the notebooks and angled the framed photo to temper the ceiling light's glare on the glass. The picture was recent, taken in March judging by the Spring Fest signage in the background. June stood behind Paige on the gazebo steps with her arms wrapped around her. Paige beamed a captivating smile, wearing her favorite "I do it protected by the First Amendment"

T-shirt. Olivia studied the photo, tapping the desk with her finger, and then flipped the frame and dislodged the backing. She removed the cardboard cover and a thin paper protective sheet, but the five by seven print was the only item in the housing. She reconstructed the components and slid the frame aside.

Then she picked up the style manual, recognizing that the same edition occupied a corner of her desk at work. Her own copy was dog-eared, but the near pristine condition of Paige's guide suggested she seldom used it. *That's strange.* She fanned through the pages until the simulated flip book hesitated three-quarters of the way through the animation. She repeated the test, and when the speed bump recurred, she marked the irregularity with her index finger. Stuffed deep into the binding between pages 276 and 277, she discovered a miniature key perfectly scaled to unlock a dollhouse. She glanced at Cooper, who was looking into a wall mirror as he converted the knot of his quill print tie from a half to full Windsor. June continued in conversation outside.

Olivia checked the desk's two side drawers for a mechanism to partner with her find. The bottom of the pair featured a protruding lock head with a diminutive slit. She slid the key into the slot, gaining access. The drawer contained dozens of manila folders spread from front to back. She selected several, opening each one, but all were empty. She riffled through the remaining files without extracting them, but they appeared bare as well. She submerged her left hand under the entire array, rummaging about, hoping the haphazard arrangement concealed something worth hiding. Still, nothing. She removed all the files, gathered them in a straightened pile, and pressed down on the spines, examining the stack for any subtle inconsistencies. One was not like the others. She skewed the folders atop the anomaly and slipped the deviant from the mound. Inside, she discovered four sheets of paper folded three times.

The compilation revealed a photocopy of a distillery license and related transactional receipts from the Virginia Alcohol Beverage Control Authority, issued to Benjamin Billingsley. She leaned back in the chair, trying to piece together why Paige would have this as the clock's second hand circled twice around the dial. She read the details of the permit three times and stared out the window at June. The search on her phone's browser had stalled again without offering the slightest hint of a homepage.

She sprung forward and pulled out the top side-file drawer, running her palm along the interior surfaces, but found nothing. She tried the pencil tray under the desktop, reaching as far as she could through the narrow opening, but again came up empty. When she rotated her shoulder to withdraw her arm, her elbow pinned into full extension, triggering a twinge of pain under her collarbone. A twist and a dip of her upper trunk loosened her limb, and as she shimmied free, her hand brushed against heavy paper on the underside of the desk. She traced the edges of the paper and then ran her hand across its width, finding it slightly thicker than the sides. She pressed up on the middle, feeling a protrusion through the paper, and realized it was a large envelope. She searched for an opening, finding a clasp, and unfastened the metal prongs to liberate the safeguarded contents.

A photocopy of a newspaper column from the *San Diego Sun* lay on top of the collection, which was held together by a small binder clip. The story detailed the death of a Virginia woman in a car accident while visiting California. The victim was Anna Jackson. Next was a five by seven photo of a young mother sitting in a rocking chair, cradling a newborn. The last item, a lined sheet of paper ripped from a spiral-bound pad, recorded a familiar telephone number. Olivia pulled out the slip she had removed from her mother's address book. *How— and why—did Paige have Martha's number?* She gathered the materials, placed them between the small of her back and her waistband, and covered them with her shirt. Cooper ducked into the storage room with his first aid kit, and she seized the moment to bolt.

Her abrupt departure startled June, who was pacing by the window. She angled her cell away from her ear. "Are you leaving? Did you find anything useful? Is every-thing okay?"

"I'm sorry, Mrs. Warner. I have to go. I'll catch up with you."

Without waiting for a reply, she turned and hurried back to the Escape, entering the area code for M. Matthews on her phone as she unlocked the SUV's door.

CHAPTER 27

Olivia dialed the last seven digits of the phone number before she settled behind the wheel, but after the fourth ring, an answering machine picked up. She locked the Escape's door, staring at the screen's prompt to redial. *I must have called his house hundreds of times over the years.* When she and A.J. were children, and after they had completed their homework on schooldays, they romped around the unpartitioned yards between their houses for an hour before, and sometimes after, dinner. Every afternoon she called and asked his mother, "Can A.J. come out to play?" Together, they created galaxies and imagined distant lands where they took turns portraying the hero of the stories they fashioned. In the summer evenings, they frolicked in the twilight, catching fireflies in mason jars. They were unconcerned running about in the dark, as they knew all the dips and bumps along the ground and had no fear of falling.

Now, a fence separated the properties. The house had sold twice since Martha's death, and a widow whose husband perished in combat moved in two years ago. Olivia had never met the new neighbor. William exchanged polite greetings with her near the holidays and offered casual waves when their outdoor activities coincided. Otherwise, he said she kept to herself, though she made quick work of clearing his porch steps whenever snow fell.

She hit redial on the screen, and after three rings, the line opened. "Hello?"

She straightened in her seat. "Hi. My name is Olivia Penn. I found this phone number for Martha Matthews and—"

"I'm sorry. Martha passed years ago."

"Yes, I know. She and my family were neighbors in Apple Station."

"Aha."

"I pulled this contact information for her from my mom's address book."

The sound of an oven door snapping shut punctuated a pause from the other side. "Well, Martha never lived here. We're out near Oatlands. I don't understand why anyone listed this as her number."

"But you remember her?"

"She was my aunt."

Olivia ran her fingers through her hair, staring at the scrap of paper propped in the cup holder. "I was unaware she had a sibling."

"Excuse me, but who did you say you are?"

"Olivia Penn. I'm friends with Martha's son, A.J. We grew up together."

"Okay, right. That sounds vaguely familiar now. This is my mom's house. She's not in the best of health, so my family moved in to help her about two years ago."

Olivia felt as deflated as her Expedition's tires. "I guess I misunderstood. The number is for M. Matthews, so I assumed it was hers."

"That's how it's listed?"

"Yes."

"My mom's name is Mary. So M. Matthews may refer to her. Does your mom know mine?"

Olivia pinned her phone between her head and shoulder as she started the engine. "My mom is deceased. I'm not sure if she knew your mother." She checked the time. It was almost four o'clock. She made a U-turn in the intersection and drove east. "May I come and speak with her? I can be there in forty-five minutes."

An extended silence lingered, and she glanced at the screen, checking her connection.

"I guess that's okay," Mary's daughter replied. "My mom tires in the afternoons sometimes, though. What's this concerning?"

"Her nephew, Alexander."

Olivia ended the call after Mary's daughter gave her directions and texted the home address.

The two-lane road that connected the towns wound through Virginia's horse country. When Olivia was younger, she ventured along this route whenever she needed to clear her head: the day before moving away for college, the night of her breakup with Sawyer, for weeks following her mother's death. Expanses of rolling meadows dotted with scenic estates lined both sides of the roadway. Wooden railed fences stretched for miles. The road undulated and followed the curvature of the land, requiring a cautious pace. Unexpected bends and sudden turns often led those unfamiliar with the path astray, while blind hills obscured views and were dangerous to those who were not prepared to react to what waited ahead.

Olivia arrived at the address she had received and parked in front of a spacious farmhouse-style home with a wraparound covered porch. A thirty-something-year-old man, who she assumed to be Mary's son-in-law, was hunched over the engine compartment of a candy-apple red Mustang in the driveway.

"Hi. I'm Olivia. I spoke to your wife on the phone. She's expecting me."

"I'm Able. I would shake, but ..." He held up his hands, caked with layered dirt and grease from his poking about the belts, hoses, and fluid reservoirs under the vintage car's raised hood. "Go on in. Hope is inside."

The dwelling's mahogany wood door was propped wide open, allowing for the occasional late afternoon breeze to filter through to the interior. The sweet smell of lavender planted in a galvanized metal bucket at the top of the porch steps welcomed Olivia with a cleansing aroma that reminded her of a flower farm she used to visit with her mother near Catlett. For the last ten years they had together, on Olivia's birthday, they would drive an hour southeast to the gardens to cut lavender stems to make sachets. Her mother kept a petite bouquet from each outing in a vase by her desk until the blooms faded. She always told Olivia that the sweetest words graced her verse when she had that fresh lavender by her side.

Now, Olivia peeked through the screen door, knocking on the aluminum frame. An elderly woman wearing a royal-blue cardigan overtop a yellow and white print dress sat on the sofa with an opened novel in her lap. Hope walked out of the kitchen, removing a pair of oven mitts as she headed for the door. "Hey, Mom, your visitor is here." She opened the screen. "Hi, I'm Hope."

"Nice to meet you," Olivia said. "Thanks for letting me come over."

Hope shook her left hand in an awkward exchange, solidifying Olivia's resolve to ditch the wrist brace ASAP. "No problem. Mom perked up when I told her you were coming. If you don't mind, I have cookies browning. I'll let you two chat. Pop into the kitchen if you need me." She donned her mitts and glided across the oak floor as a timer signaled for her attention.

Olivia turned to Mary, smiling as she walked tentatively to the sofa. She bent forward, drawing close, and spoke louder and slower than usual. "Hi. I'm William Penn's daughter. I lived next door to your sister when I was a child."

"When Hope told me you called, I had to think at first. But then I remembered—when you were a baby."

Olivia felt like her train had derailed fifty feet from the station. *She doesn't know who I am. This was a bad idea.* "I'm sorry, but I don't believe we've met before. Perhaps you're thinking of someone else."

"No. I recall you very well. You were so small. Your mother brought you here once with Alexander. You two sat right over there on that old braided rug and played together. That's the exact one. Different TV, of course."

Olivia had no recollection of ever visiting the home, though she dined with her father in a nearby historic district once or twice every year. "I'm sorry. I don't have memories from here as a child."

Mary waved a hand in front of her. "I wouldn't expect you to. You were only a few years old. I used to have a brown beanbag chair by the window there, and the day you came, Alexander kept putting you right in the middle of it and then cheering you on as you tried to get out. After five or six times, you got pretty upset. I gave you each a piece of chocolate cake, and all was forgiven between you two."

Olivia relaxed her stance and laughed. "That's kind of how we still handle things."

"I haven't seen or heard from him for quite some time. My James and I moved to Vermont when he was about five. My husband worked with the forestry service up there for almost twenty years. We rented this house to a young family—nice couple, they had twin boys. When those two left for college, the parents bought a smaller home in Purcellville. A widower moved in next. When my James passed, we were still in Vermont, up around Rutland. I stayed there for a while, but then moved in with my sister-in-law in Pennsylvania. Now, when she passed, I came back here—oh, it's been over ten years now. My daughter and her family moved in about two years ago. Please sit, my dear. You don't need to be standing."

Olivia sheepishly smiled, embarrassed that she had been hovering over Mary, tenuously tracking the timelines. She sat on the sofa, angling toward her. "I'm sorry to ask, but does A.J. know you live here? When your sister passed, I don't remember—"

"We couldn't make it back for the funeral. That was an awful winter season. A terrible nor'easter came up the coast, and we got three feet of snow over thirty-four hours. Closed the roads for a week."

Olivia's thoughts drifted to the blizzard that kept her and Daniel in his family's Vermont cabin for two days this past December.

"I don't think Alexander has too many memories of me," Mary continued. "I'd send him a card on his birthday when he was younger, but we lost contact over the years. After Martha's house sold, I no longer had an address for him. I wasn't even sure if he still lived in Apple Station. What about you? Do you still live in Washington?"

The question jolted Olivia from a flashback of being

curled up with Daniel, sipping cocoa in front of the cabin's fireplace. "I—yes, I do. How do you know that? Did your sister tell you that?"

"No. Your mother did."

Olivia's stomach dropped. "My mom? When—when did you see my mother?"

"A few months before she passed. I felt so sorry for you. It must have been hard with you being so young. We always need our mothers, don't we?"

Olivia's throat tightened, and her breaths turned shallow. She stretched her collar away from her neck and fanned the back of her shirt, scooting to the sofa's edge. "My mom, why was she here?"

"She brought my sister to visit."

Olivia leaned forward, flexing the fingers of her braced hand, and accepted the explanation, desperately wanting to avoid a minefield of implications from any other truth. The clipped papers stashed beneath her shirt scratched her skin, and she removed them, keeping them face down. She tried to picture her mother in this room, sitting where she was now, but neither a memory nor an image would come. She took a deep breath and unclipped the three items. She held up the five by seven print so Mary could see. "Do you recognize this woman and child?"

Mary glanced at the photo and then stared straight ahead. She looked again and reached out, taking the picture from Olivia and holding it in her lap. "Where did you get this?"

"From a friend. She left it for me. My friend—someone murdered her."

Mary gasped, drawing her hand to her heart. "I'm so sorry. That's terrible. But how does this involve me?"

Olivia tapped the photo, pointing to the child. "This baby—the police think Alexander killed my friend." She unfolded the newspaper article. "She left this behind, too. It's a story about Anna Jackson's accident."

Mary slid back, pushing her closed novel farther off to her side. "You remind me of your mother. You have the same eyes." She nodded slowly twice and then followed up with three quick head bobs as if she had conversed and agreed with herself. "Go—through the hallway. The second room on the right. In the closet, in the corner, there's a stack of boxes. Bring me the one on the bottom. It's blue."

Mary's bedroom was cozy and well kept. A patchwork quilted comforter covered the twin mattress, and several framed family photos decorated the dresser. Olivia pulled opened the closet's paired doors, revealing a tidy array of hanging clothes and a shoe shelving unit stocked with low wedge heels, white walking sneakers, and a pair of insulated ankle boots. She spied the pile of boxes and knelt on both knees to dislodge her target from the three-foot-tall tower. She piled the hodgepodge of storage cartons and plastic containers in reverse order and slid a navy photo box across the floor to her side, allowing her fingers to rest on a corner. She stared at the blank content label and then at the doorway, lifting the lid without taking her eyes off the room's entrance.

"Are you okay in there? Did you find it?"

"Yes. Coming." She closed the box, reordered the containers in the closet, and returned to the living room without further delay.

"Good, you found the right one." Mary removed the lid to reveal a jumbled assortment of pictures and papers. She picked up the photo on the top and showed it to Olivia. "See this. That's Martha and me all dressed up for Sunday services, standing by the town clock."

"My mom took one like that of me and A.J. when we were children. I was probably about six years old. That would have made him nine-ish."

"And this here, this was from James' and my fortieth wedding anniversary. Look at him. As handsome as the day I married him." Mary grabbed a stack of prints and set them aside. "I'll go through those later." She unfolded a sheet of paper, read it, and placed it on top of the pile. Then she unfolded a second sheet, read it, and handed it to Olivia.

There was a part of Olivia that wanted to be wrong, a part still praying for her suspicions to be mistaken. But she was right. It was a birth certificate issued for a baby boy. The mother, Anna J. Jackson. The father, unregistered. The baby, Alexander. "Who else knows?"

"It was my sister, myself, and your mother."

"My mom never told me."

"That's why Martha brought her that day. She

wanted someone else to know. We never imagined either of us would outlive her. She trusted your mother would protect him if needed. I trust you'll do the same."

Pressure billowed between Olivia's eyes as her shoulders rounded forward. The cloud that shadowed A.J. for over thirty years had lifted to reveal a disquieting reality. Orphaned by his mother. Abandoned, yet watched without acknowledgment by his grandfather. The heir to Grove Manor. She fought the impulse to think of her mother. The life—her story—she did not know. *Would she have ever told me?* Her mother brought her here as a child. *She led me back.*

"My sister was a nurse at the old Valley Hospital. They've renamed it since. She worked weekend nights in the ER, and one Saturday, somebody came rushing in to report a baby outside in a car seat. Martha carried Alexander in and examined him. He was fine, but she was certain of what had happened. They got abandonments every year. She watched after him through the night until social services took him the next day. There was something special about him. Martha loved him from then on. She did what she needed to do to adopt him."

Olivia held up the birth certificate. "How did she get this?"

"An agency in Winchester handled the adoption, but about ten months after my sister made everything legal, Jeremiah came into the ER one afternoon with stomach pain. Martha was there that day, not working. Alexander had a fever, and she took him to the hospital to have a doctor examine him. Now, when he was an infant, he had a round birthmark on his cheek, right below his ear. You could easily spot him in a room of a hundred babies. Jeremiah saw him that day, recognized him, and figured it all out. On Alexander's second birthday, he showed up at Martha's front door. Maybe it was guilt—who knows. He told her how his daughter lived in California during the pregnancy and planned to move back after she had the baby, but she was in that accident a few days after his birth. Jeremiah brought him back here, but a newborn was too much for someone like him. He gave my sister fifty-thousand dollars to help raise him—but nothing more. He didn't want his grandson in his life or to know the truth. She agreed on one condition—she wanted a copy of the birth certificate."

Olivia folded the paper the same as it had been all throughout the years and held it midway between them. "Jeremiah's property, Grove Manor—it's being sold tomorrow. A.J.'s in custody."

Mary gathered the photos she had set aside and placed them back in the box. Then she tapped the birth certificate. "That's yours now. You do with it as you will."

"What about his father?"

"Martha knew nothing of him except that he was from California. She always questioned whether she should've told Alexander about his family. My sister believed his past shouldn't burden him. He didn't choose it. He didn't have a say."

Hope walked out from the kitchen carrying a foil-covered plate. "You two still doing okay? I brought a dozen lemon drop cookies for you to take home if you'd like."

Olivia stood and leaned over, hugging Mary. Then she turned to Hope. "That's perfect, very kind of you." She inhaled a full breath, feeling as though she had been twice through a washer's spin cycle over the past hour. "Your mom has been helpful. I should go."

Mary grasped Olivia's hands. "Come to visit sometime and bring him back if you can."

"I will. With the help you've given me, I'll do whatever it takes. Thanks for seeing me. Take care, Mary."

Hope walked Olivia to her Escape. "Mom seems in good spirits. You're always welcome to call again. Here, don't forget your cookies. Careful driving now. A storm is heading your way soon, and that road taking you home turns treacherous when heavy rain falls."

CHAPTER 28

Olivia drove the winding route home, lost in how to navigate the uncharted territory ahead: A.J.'s lineage, Paige's murder, Grove Manor. She searched the sky for lines to connect the dots, but obsidian clouds charged with fatal strikes obscured guidance from the night's constellations. The evening smelled of ozone, and the forecasted storm struck halfway through the return drive. Violent updrafts competed with sinking air, and when the atmosphere could no longer support the weight of its contents, precipitation fell to the ground as hail. So much had changed since Monday. Her reluctant promise to probe Paige's death had led to revelations she never expected.

The hour was past eight when she arrived at her father's house. Cole's Defender was stationed toward the bottom of the driveway with its wipers slapping at a hurricane clip, though the rain had lightened to a lingering drizzle. The cruiser's headlamps illuminated every inch of ground from the mailbox to the scarecrow halfway into the field across the lane. She turned into the drive and abruptly halted, blinded by the high beams obscuring the distance between their opposing bumpers. Cole jumped out from behind the wheel and reached under his all-weather poncho, removing a flashlight while approaching her with one hand raised. He flipped the light a full turn, flubbing the catch and activating the strobe switch. Bert leisurely emerged from the passenger side sans monsoon gear, stretched his arms overhead, and moseyed around the rear of her vehicle. Cole tapped on the SUV's roof with the light's barrel end and ordered her to open the window, tracing loopy circles with his finger above her side mirror.

She squinted, shading her eyes. "Cole, turn that thing off."

"Ms. Olivia. I didn't realize it was you. Sorry."

She peered through the passenger window at Bert, who waved while speaking on his phone, answering only yes or no.

"You were expecting someone else?"

"We're under orders to watch your house and to question anyone who stops or tries to get in."

"Orders from?"

"Detective Hills."

"Right. Okay. Can I park in my driveway, please?"

Cole tipped his APP STAT PD ball cap, setting forth as though assigned a task of national security. With the cruiser transferred street side, Olivia parked at the upper end of the drive. Her phone buzzed as she slid out of the Escape. She glanced toward the house and then at the caller ID, staring at the screen until it silenced. Then the cell lit again, showing her wallpaper photo of Uluru along with the number of the recent contact she had not yet assigned a full profile. She painted on a Pan Am smile and dialed up a carefree tone.

"Hi, Preston." She peeked over her shoulder, sensing Bert on her heels.

Cole held his hand alongside his mouth as if sharing a secret she would have to pinky swear on. "We're escorting you to the door."

"Where have you been, Olivia?" Preston asked. "Why are you alone?"

She drew her phone away from her ear, pointing it at Bert. "Did you call Preston, just now, when I pulled in?"

"Sorry. He said I had to."

She kicked some loose gravel onto the grass and reanimated her cheeks, channeling her best Meryl Streep to speak to Preston again. "I'm fine. Thanks for sending the deputies. Have a pleasant evening."

"Olivia, where were you?"

She hesitated, attempting to assemble a believable explanation, but every second that passed provided evidence that she was hiding something. Angela's earlier admonition echoed—*You're hurting yourself. You're digging your own grave*—and she felt she was sinking in quicksand no matter which way she turned. "I went for a drive. And who says I was alone?"

"Were you alone? A drive, really? Where?"

"Around? Maybe."

An exasperated sigh graded her performance a failure. "Is there anything you want to share?" He paused for a breath, but cut the silence short. "Let me rephrase that for you, Olivia. Is there anything you should tell me?"

The preceding three hours replayed in fast forward. *I can't. Not now. Not him.* "No, we covered everything."

"Do I need to remind you what I said about you being careful until we figure this all out?"

"No. I understand. So, are we good here?"

"No, Olivia. We're not good here. Get in the house. Lock the doors. Cole and Bert will be outside tonight."

He hung up before she could wish him well again for the evening. She thanked her lookouts and invited them inside, but they would not abandon their post at the end of the driveway.

She entered through the front, finding her father lying on the sofa, watching a travel show on fishing for crabs in the Chesapeake Bay. He turned off the television and sat up, scooting to the edge of the couch. "I got to worrying. How's your wrist? Were you able to see Sophia's father?"

"No, but she gave me this brace. I'll see her again tomorrow. It's feeling much better than this afternoon."

"I planned on you being here for leftover meatloaf. I ate, but there's some left in foil in the convection oven. I kept it warm for you. The soup's in the refrigerator if you want that."

"Thanks, Dad, but I'm not too hungry. You might as well get comfortable—we need to talk."

Olivia settled on the sofa next to her father, and then she related all she had learned from her visit with Mary. When she finished, William slid back on the sofa with his arms folded, wearing the same inscrutable expression as on the day she told him she was moving to New York with Daniel.

"Dad—did you know any of this about A.J.? Martha and Jeremiah? Anna?"

"No, honey. I never asked your mother if she knew anything about his family history. Didn't have reason to. Why would I? She was closer to Martha than I was. And your mother wouldn't betray a confidence like that. When she got sick, well—if we needed to know, she would've told us."

"Why do you think she didn't?"

"Probably to protect him, and you. That's a load to carry. You two growing up together. I can't imagine she wanted you to wrestle with that if it weren't necessary. The decision to reveal that truth was Martha's. I don't blame her at all. She provided a home and a mother's love he never would have had."

Olivia picked up the birth certificate from the coffee table. "What do we do with this?"

"How that relates—your guess is better than mine. The police need to see it, though."

"A.J. warned me about them."

"Who?"

"Not sure. He wasn't all that specific, but he begged me to drop everything."

She handed the certificate to her father. He put his glasses on and read the details again, then looked at her.

"Listen to A.J. He always has your best interest at heart." He folded the paper and leaned into the corner of the couch. "That detective who was here today—you have his attention. He returned after you left, and I spoke with him for nearly an hour. The way he has those two sitting outside the house until you go." He grinned, shaking his head. "They're not here for my health, sweetie. As soon as you leave, I guarantee they'll be gone."

Though her head implored her not to exclude Preston from A.J.'s warning, her heart dismissed any case against him. "Paige learned the truth of A.J.'s past, but I'm sure she never got the chance to tell him. Someone found out she knew. Someone who had an interest in keeping the secret hidden." She slipped the photocopy out of her father's hand. "This should stop the auction, but it doesn't help him in the slightest with the charges."

"Honey, you're here for two more days. As much as you wanna help, it's not your fight. You can't do this alone. You shouldn't even be involved."

She swept her hair off her face and leaned forward, holding her splinted wrist in her lap. "There's something else that I've been wanting to talk to you about. I'm thinking of not going to New York."

"You mean on Sunday?"

She bowed her head, rubbing her eyes. "Ever."

"Sweetie, I'm not sure I understand. I thought that's what you wanted. You're all set to go. Don't let what's going on here affect your decision. You've been planning this for a long time. This is about your career, your life, your happiness. Are you feeling this way because of what happened with Daniel?"

"No, not because of him. I mean some, yes, but not entirely. The job—moving—is what I thought I wanted, but I'm not sure anymore. I've been having doubts for a while. It's not just about what happened to Paige, either. Being back here, seeing you—every time I think of New York now, I get knots in my stomach. I can't shake the feeling that I'm doubling down in the wrong direction. I don't want to disappoint you. You and Mom sacrificed so I could have these choices, and I didn't—"

"No, sweetie. Stop." He grabbed her hand. "First, you could never disappoint me. All I want is for you to follow your dreams and be happy. Live the life you want, the one that's best for you. No matter what, I'll always support you. Your mother would too. If you say moving there is going to make you unhappy, that's good enough for me. You've always made the right choices. I trust your decisions." He wrapped an arm around her shoulder. "If you don't go, where will you live? You already sold your condo. What about your job?"

"I'm not sure. I haven't thought through the details. I can't concentrate with all of this ..."

"Take one step at a time. Nothing needs deciding tonight. You've had quite a day and should get some rest. You're tired. Let this be for right now. We'll talk about it tomorrow."

She twirled his pencil on the coffee table, spinning it twice before the tip came to a stop, pointing at her.

"Why don't you get something to eat? You must be starving. Then go to bed, okay?" he told her. "Please. Those two outside will make sure it'll be quiet tonight."

"You're right, Dad. I'll be able to think better after some sleep."

"And after something to eat," he added. He kissed her cheek and pushed up from the sofa. "When you wake up, if that wrist is worse, we're calling a doctor. No arguments. Come get me tonight if you need anything."

"I will. I promise, Dad. I'll turn in soon. You head upstairs. I'll see you in the morning. Love you."

"Love you too, sweetie. Oh, and the detective needs a statement from you about what happened today. He said he'd come find you tomorrow when he could."

She watched as he climbed the stairs, and then spied Buddy asleep at his post by the kitchen door. The hour was near ten. She felt as though the day had yielded to its successor long ago. She tightened her wrist splint and lay on the couch. She opened the browser on her cell and fumbled typing with her left thumb. Her target—Benjamin Billingsley. She briefly thought of grabbing some leftovers from the refrigerator, but she was not that hungry. Her eyes were heavy, and her whole body felt drained. She abandoned her search and placed her phone on the table, hoping that a solid night of sleep would help her recover and be ready for what she had planned for tomorrow.

CHAPTER 29

Olivia woke Friday morning to the prods of two paws poking at her ribs. Buddy had apparently tired of waiting for her to wake and expedited the process. He jutted his nose toward her, ready to lap a slobbering sweep across her cheek, but she diverted his greeting before his tongue could swipe her face. She corralled him close, checking the cable box's LED. Five minutes till nine. The kitchen was silent, and she surmised her father was already outside, tending to the garden before the heat descended for the day.

Thoughts of the truths she unearthed yesterday buried any semblance of the morning's serenity. She removed her wrist splint, gauging the effects of her restful night. The swelling had decreased, but ample tenderness persisted at the base of her thumb and across the crease that bordered her palm. She curled her fingers to make a fist, pleased with at least that progress. Sophia texted her a summons for an eleven o'clock arrival at the clinic, and she replied with a yes, knowing that if she bailed on her pledge, Sophia would follow through on casting her as a card-carrying spinster. A modicum of pain was the price to pay to avoid further conflict with Josefina over the matter.

Olivia knew she would need to get to the bank before the close of the business day to stop the auction. She planned, though, to be there much earlier. The first item on her agenda was to talk with A.J. She hustled off the sofa and went upstairs to shower and change clothes. Within forty-five minutes, she was ready and out the door with a grab-and-go breakfast of an apple and two slices of Beverly's bread in hand. She said goodbye to her father and drove into town.

She parked the SUV three blocks from Sophia's clinic, toward the end of the square nearest to the police station. Preston's pickup was absent, and she made a mental note to include that stroke of luck in her nightly gratitude recap. Payne's cruiser, though, occupied its assigned space. She had no concerns about interference from Cole or Bert, but she had not devised a plan to grapple with further obstruction from Payne. She watched and waited, praying he would leave the head-quarters, allowing her to question A.J. uncontested. Fifteen minutes passed, but all remained still.

The mid-morning mini-heatwave already boasted a

breezeless eighty-three degrees, turning the Escape's interior into a sauna. She leaned forward, fanning the back of her shirt, and blasted the AC while aligning the vents to funnel the airflow full bore at her face. The relief was immediate, but another ten minutes passed, and all was quiet at the station's front. She ate her apple and slices of bread. Her phone buzzed with a text from Sophia: "See ya in 20." She drummed her thumbs on the steering wheel and killed the engine. With time running short, she exited the Escape and crossed the street, brainstorming strategies for stealing a few moments with A.J. to substantiate her suspicions.

She cracked the door, peeking inside, but the slivered view offered scant surveillance. A measured nudge revealed the reception desk again unoccupied, fueling her speculation there was no such staffing. Cole sat at his workstation, sussing out his approach to sandwich he held a few inches from his chin. She entered and glided over on tiptoes, speaking a pinch above a whisper. "Hey, Cole."

He welcomed her with a wide smile, liberating a glob of mayonnaise from the corner of his mouth. He had changed his uniform shirt to a dark-brown half-sleeve version after his all-nighter, but showed no weariness despite being short on sleep. "Ms. Olivia, I hope we weren't a bother to you last night."

"Not at all. Thanks so much again for being there."

"Serve and protect. That's what we do here. What brings you in this morning?"

She glanced at the remnants of the spread splattered on the file in front of him. "Is Payne around?"

"No. He went with Bert to Jillian's for a cup of her bold roast. I can help you with whatever you—"

"I want to speak with A.J."

Cole's toothy grin evaporated. "I'm not supposed to let you see him. I'm sorry. Chief said—"

"Please, Cole. Five minutes. If he comes back, I'll take the blame."

He gnawed at his thumbnail, and then flattened his matted, wavy hair with several passes from both hands. She sweetened the proposition. "Five minutes, Cole, and I'll guarantee you a date with Sophia on Saturday for the luncheon."

His face lit like the sky on the Fourth of July. He scooped his spillage from the manila folder and tossed it in the metal mesh bin next to the file cabinet behind his desk. He spread his fingers wide. "Five."

Then he ducked out of the station, leaving Olivia alone with A.J. for the precious few minutes. She had not fully prepared for this moment—seeing him, knowing more about his past than he did. Their eyes met, and she took a deep breath, blinking back tears. This was neither the time nor the place to convey all that needed to be shared.

"What are you doing here?" He peered past her toward the station's entrance. "Go away. You can't be here. You'll get arrested. What happened to your wrist?"

She reached through the bars for his hand. "Nothing.

You were meeting Paige at Grove Manor on Monday, weren't you?"

"Liv, let it alone."

"You listen to me. I only have five minutes. Did she ask you there because she told you she had information about your family?"

"How do you know that? And what do you mean, nothing? You're wearing a brace."

"It's fine. But you didn't meet her, right?"

He bowed his head. "I didn't have the chance. If it's fine, what's that doing on your wrist? How did you hurt it?"

She checked for movement at the door. "What were you doing in the woods then?" A.J. released her hand. She removed the copy of the distillery license from her pants pocket and held it up for him to view. "What do you know about this?"

He interlocked his fingers behind his neck, pacing within a three-step circle. "Liv, I swear, if you don't tell me what happened to you … Why won't you tell me?"

"This is a legal document. I found it in Paige's belongings." He ceased his back and forth, allowing his arms to rest by his sides. "A.J., the woods? If you were doing something with Billingsley, he had a permit."

He ran his hand from his brow to his chin. "Ben has a license, but Junior and I don't."

She tipped her head back as a trapdoor opened, swallowing her heart. "You and Junior—were doing what exactly?"

His shoulders slumped as his eyes drifted down. "We were distilling liquor."

She doubled over as if his words tunneled straight through her core. "Liquor? As in moonshine? You and Junior, together, were making moonshine in the woods?" He nodded. She straightened. Her voice escalated with each syllable. "What were you thinking? Junior?" She claimed her turn to pace. One hand shrouded her mouth as she holstered the other on her hip.

"I shouldn't have said anything. You'll just leave like the rest." His voice grew louder as he thrust his arm through the bars. "And tell me right now what happened to your wrist."

"What are you talking about? The rest?"

"Liv, I wasn't raised like you. I didn't have a family like yours. I never even had a father. Martha, you know I loved her, but I was given up on when I was born. I've always had to prove myself. No matter how hard I try, it's never enough. My mom, whoever she was, is gone. Martha is gone. Paige is gone. Can you see the pattern here?"

Olivia shook her head, allowing a deep breath to calm her tone. "No, A.J., you're not alone. Your birth mother, Martha, Paige ... them not being here has nothing to do with you. You don't have to prove anything to anyone. You're enough as you are. I'm not leaving you. I would never leave you."

"I needed money. I wanted to buy a home—move out of the inn. Someplace, maybe someday, Paige and I ...

Oh, I don't know. We weren't nearly at that stage, but I'm like you. I wanna be settled. Build a life with someone, have a family. Junior and I took equipment from Ben's plant near Hamilton's, and we built a still in the woods behind Grove Manor. We sold a couple cases in Culpepper the first go around. Turns out, moonshining is a lucrative business, so we kept at it."

Olivia stood, perplexed about where to even begin. Her thoughts crashed into one another like junkyard jalopies in a demolition derby. Cole's allotted five minutes had passed unenforced, and she was well aware she was on borrowed time. She softly closed her eyes, speaking as if every word pained her. "What do you know about a company called Materials Core Innovations?"

"Who? What are you talking about?"

The station door slammed open, and she swiveled, seeing Payne storming toward the cell. She reached for his hand. "You're not alone."

"Liv, watch yourself. Please, please be careful."

"Ms. Penn—"

"Chief. Any updates about who vandalized my dad's house? Have any leads?"

A.J. reached through the cell, placing his hand on her forearm. "Liv, wait. What happened to the house?"

"Ms. Penn, consider this your final warning. Next time, you'll be with your friend on the other side of those bars. Look around. Nobody's coming to rescue you. Am I clear?"

"Liv, what's going on?"

"Perfectly." She squeezed A.J.'s hand, then slowly backed away from the cell until her fingers slipped and fell from his grasp.

CHAPTER 30

Olivia hurried past a vacant suite half a block from the clinic, waving to Sophia, who paced on the sidewalk, emphatically tapping her watch. "Sorry, I'm a little late," she said as she arrived. "How's my favorite PT doing today? The one who wouldn't even think about causing me more pain. Because she's so caring and compassionate."

Sophia stretched her arm out, palm up, and took Olivia's hand without saying a word, lightly squeezing and curling her fingers one at a time.

"So, providing curbside assessments these days. I bet that's good for business. What, you just stand out here and wait for people wearing braces to walk by?"

A young'un sporting seersucker overalls tottered toward them with his mother, clutching a dripping mint chocolate chip ice-cream cone. He veered slightly in passing, staring at her splint. Olivia watched him watching her.

"How's the pain this morning?" Sophia asked. "I was wondering if you'd show."

She clenched her jaw, inhaling sharply as Sophia pressed into her palm between her thumb and index finger. "Usually, someone has to buy me a drink before they can hold my hand."

Sophia squeezed again, and Olivia flinched, closing her eyes and swallowing hard. The boy glanced back at her and stumbled, allowing his sweet treat to plummet to the sidewalk. She slipped her arm from Sophia's grasp.

"As if I had a choice. Your contraption helped during the night, so I suppose you know what you're doing."

"There you go again. Giving me the warm fuzzies. Get inside."

The clinic's cool air enveloped her as soon as she stepped across the welcome mat. She beelined for the sofa, preparing to pile into the coziness of the cushions.

"No, Liv. The table."

She wistfully eyed the five plump pillows decoratively aligned in desperate need of someone to prop, willing to volunteer herself for the service. "Really, I'm feeling much better. This could have waited until—"

"Tyler, no-no-no, don't touch." A crash boomed from the treatment room. "Tyler Wellington, I can't take you anywhere."

Giggles lofted into the foyer. "Pow! Pow!"

"You stop that right now, young man. You have some splaining to do to Ms. Sophia."

"Pow-pow!"

Sophia started toward the hallway. "Tori, what happened in there? Is everyone okay?"

"Soph, it's all good. Technically, it wasn't me. Did I hear Liv and her gimpy limb finally show up out there?"

"Hey, Tori," Olivia called. "Sounds like your demolition crew is working overtime today."

Tori popped into the doorway, carrying Tyler on her hip. "Soph, don't worry. Creepy skeleton dude in the corner took a spill, but he—or is it she—anyway, is once again standing tall, spooky, and kooky. There's a minor alignment issue with the feet, but you'll figure it out." She set Tyler on the ground where he immediately slipped out of his shoes and pulled off his socks. She tilted her head sideways, extending her arms toward Olivia. "Come here, you. Bring it in."

Olivia squatted instead and grasped Tyler's fingers, mimicking munching like the Cookie Monster as he flipped to his back, letting loose a rambunctious laugh. He covered his face with his hands and then lifted them as she tickled him on the side of his neck. "Peekaboo, I see you, Ty." He kicked his legs in delight and hid his eyes again, readying for another round. She ruffled his hair and stood, angling toward the table.

Tori scuttled forward and wrapped Olivia in her arms, pinning her elbows to her sides. "I bet Soph five bucks ya ditched her. You proved me wrong, you super-trooper."

She stiffened, sensing two little arms wrap around her leg. "Tori, please stop. You're hurting me." Tyler sat on her foot and encircled his legs around her calf, buddy hugging her while patting her knee. Tori stepped back and cradled Olivia's wrist, humming and hovering her hand over the brace. She inhaled to a count of four, exhaling over a count of eight. Olivia looked at Sophia, who just shrugged. "What are you doing, Tori?"

"Quiet, Liv. I'm directing healing energy to your wound."

She withdrew her forearm from Tori's grasp and swung her leg like a pendulum, much to Tyler's delight. "Okay then. Soph, can we get this over with? Tori, a little help down here with your kiddo."

Tori prompted Tyler to loosen his hold and then put her arm around Olivia's shoulders, guiding her to the table as if she was in danger of losing her way. She pulled out a chair, easing Olivia down like a teetering three-tier wedding cake. "There you go, hon. Let us take care of you, and don't forget, you owe Soph five dollars."

Olivia shook her head, scooting to the edge of her seat as Sophia removed the splint. Tyler crawled over to the table, and Tori bent forward, scooping him in her arms. Sophia moved Olivia's wrist every which way, pushing and poking, producing winces and cringes. When the exam was complete, she rose and went into the treatment room. Olivia massaged her palm, waiting until Sophia returned with an ice pack.

"Talk to me. Any news on A.J.?"

"I have some news all right. You're not going to believe it." Olivia leaned back, proceeding to relate what she had learned of his birth family. When she finished, Tori and Sophia wore twin expressions as if they had witnessed a grizzly cartwheel across the sidewalk.

Tori smoothed Tyler's hair, kissing him near his ear. "All these years, his grandfather lived up there at Grove Manor. Brutal. Goes to show that sharing DNA doesn't make you a family."

Sophia adjusted the ice pack on Olivia's wrist. "Did you tell him?"

"No. Not the right time. We need to keep this between the three of us right now. Once the police know and the auction is stopped, word will get out soon enough about his family. But nobody needs to know any sooner. The news doesn't stop there, though." Tyler pounded his fists on the table and grabbed Olivia's thumb, trying to lift her uninjured arm. She smiled at him, clasping and shaking his hand. "A.J. and Junior, together, have been operating a still in Grove Manor's backwoods."

Sophia's face blanked. "A what?"

Tori gasped and slapped the table. "A still? You mean like a moonshine still? He's making hooch? Fabricating firewater? Brewing bathtub gin? Running rotgut? Bottling the mountain dew?"

Sophia stared wide-eyed at Olivia, pointing at Tori. "Is that true? He told you that? Junior? How does that even ... do the police ... did Paige know?"

"He told me just before I came here. I'm not sure what Paige knew. Here's the thing, though. Billingsley has a legal distillery license."

Tori shifted Tyler in her lap. "Liv, this is way above my pay grade. Explain. That's his lawyer, right?"

"Billingsley operates a legal distillery out by Hamilton's under the regulations of the Virginia ABC. But A.J. and Junior were engaging in a side hustle outside the license limits."

Tyler snatched Olivia's brace from the table and flung it over his head. Sophia leaned down, retrieving the splint from where it fell on the floor, and secured it on Olivia's wrist. "How is that a thing? Is the lawyer in on it?"

"It's complex, but it's real. The lawyer ... I don't know. A.J. said it was him and Junior, but there's something unsettling about Payne."

Tori clapped Tyler's hands. "Hear that, baby boy? Momma has herself an idea for a start-up. You think the bank would approve a loan?"

"Liv, if this involves Billingsley, and he's representing A.J.—"

"I know, Soph. I had the same thought."

Tyler snickered, tapping Tori's nose. "How about it, the three of us," she said. "Wild Women Whiskey? Three Honeys Hooch? Bootlegging Buddy's Brew?"

"I'm calling Preston as soon as I leave here. I have to stop the auction." Olivia caught Tyler's hand as he reached out to pull on her splint's top strap. "I don't trust Payne. Soph, remember what your dad told you about him finding Paige? That when he called for the ambulance, she may have already been dead?"

Tori bounced Tyler on her knee and covered his ears. "You return to town, and all sorts of stuff hits the fan. You're a poor influence on my little angel."

Olivia tickled Tyler's toes. "Your mommy is incorrigible."

"I love you anyway, Liv, for the sake of keeping my chi balanced."

"And we're all the better if you keep your chi to yourself."

"If you'd tidy up your chi, Preston might—"

"Thanks, Tori. I'll handle my life from here."

"What do you think, Ty-Ty? Should Auntie write to herself for advice? There's a saying, Liv, the blind leading the blind."

She ignored the admonition. "Are we done here?"

Sophia reverted to therapist mode. "Your motion is better, and your pain has improved, right?"

"Improved enough."

"You still have swelling, but that's expected. Keep wearing the splint. Come tomorrow."

"But it's Saturday."

"Your point?"

"Liv, dear, don't fight it. Never upset the PT. Even my

cutie here knows that. Isn't that the truth, Ty-guy?" Tori swept his hair onto his forehead, eliciting a giggle. "Seriously, Liv. Watch yourself. My little pumpkin wants to see his auntie more—not locked up in jail, or worse. Besides, orange doesn't complement your complexion and stripes do you no justice either."

Sophia adjusted Olivia's brace. "Ditto that, Liv. If you need anything, I'm here. Call me. Don't do anything stupid."

"I won't. I'm going straight over to the bank once I get ahold of Preston and tell him about Anna. I don't know what to do about this moonshine business, but that has to be tabled right now. I'll let you know what happens." After exchanging a high-five with Tyler, she stood and exited the clinic.

Preston's F-150 remained absent. She stared at the green gooey splatter of melted ice cream on the sidewalk and pulled her phone from her pocket, opening her photos and reading the contact details for Materials Core Innovations.

"Good morning, Ms. Penn."

She turned as Billingsley and Steve strolled past the clinic, following on her heels. "Any developments with A.J.'s case?" she asked. "When's he being transferred?"

"Regretfully, I can't discuss legal matters with you," Billingsley said. "You understand, client-attorney privilege."

"Of course."

Steve gestured dismissively toward her brace. "New

fashion statement? Gosh, Ben, writers are dropping like flies around here. Who knew it was such a hazardous occupation? That must be some furious fiction you're into." He stepped closer, clasping his hands behind his back. "Very aggressive with your strokes. I bet you swing a mean hammer."

Billingsley checked the time. "We need to get moving, Steve."

"I can still pack a punch," Olivia said.

"How about that, Ben? A dual threat. A writer with a southpaw hook. She's a slugger, armed and ready to defend her featherweight title."

He grabbed Steve's elbow, pressing him forward. "Ms. Penn, have a pleasant day."

Steve shook off Ben's grip, and looked back over his shoulder as they walked away. "Get well soon. The world weeps when writers go silent."

The pair crossed the street, setting a course toward the bank. She scrolled to Preston's name in the call history and hovered her thumb above the dial icon, looking back and forth between the police station and the newspaper's office. A white cargo van neared from the end of the block, slowing as it passed her. Junior peered through his passenger side window, greeting her with a head nod and a two-finger salute. She relaxed her arm and slid into the Escape, starting the engine and blasting the AC. She expanded the photo of the business card for Materials Core Innovations, memorized the phone number, and dialed.

CHAPTER 31

"Good afternoon, Materials Core Innovations. How may I help you today?" Olivia hesitated, assuming the call would direct her first to an automated menu and not a bona fide living soul. "Hello, anyone there?"

"Hi, ma'am, I'm a reporter from the local newspaper in Apple Station, Virginia, and I'm following up on a call my colleague placed recently."

"Oh yeah, no, for sure. I remember you. You contacted us yesterday and talked to Grant."

Her animated demeanor stoked Olivia's courage. "Yes. That was me, Cassandra Collins. I spoke with Grant." She typed the company URL into her web browser search bar.

"Apple Station—can't forget that name. Like my hometown—Moosejaw." The "Who We Are" tab displayed on the mobile site, but the hyperlink was not clickable. Olivia reloaded the page and opened her settings, ensuring she was connecting through her carrier's network rather than Sophia's Wi-Fi. "I've been to Virginia before, several times. My aunt, on my mother's side, lives in Bentonville. Ever heard of it?"

Olivia flashed her broadest smile and gambled on fast-tracking the know-like-trust principle to sell her story. "Bentonville, sure. That's in Warren County—real close by. I go down that way to the Shenandoah Valley when the leaves change every fall."

"Lovely mountains. Reminds me of when I lived in Ontario and did much the same along the Niagara Parkway. Ever been up north leaf peeping?"

"Not to Ontario. Quebec, yes. I love traveling to Vermont when the colors peak, and right above the border, there's a small town I day-trip to whenever I get the chance. They have a bookstore and bistro I always stop by."

"I haven't been down to see my aunt for a couple years now, I bet. Last time I went, we spent an entire Saturday making apple butter outside with her neighbor. We stirred that stuff, taking turns for hours. It was a day-long party. Big copper kettle, open fire—we weren't done jarring it until nine at night. It was a ton of fun. I'll have to check into coming this fall, maybe drive through your neck of the woods. I'm so sorry, I'm bending your ear here. What can I help you with today, my dear?"

The company's webpage timed out during the reload, and Olivia refreshed the browser. "I called—back—to clarify some details I discussed with Grant."

"He had to travel north to a mining site. We're based in Saskatoon, so getting ahold of him will be hard until he gets to operations HQ by the lake. Is there something I can help you with? We're a family-owned business— Grant's my brother-in-law. I've done some work on the contract for the site there, so maybe I can fill in the blanks for you."

The homepage loaded but offered little information beyond contact numbers and stock photos of Saskatchewan. "The mining. I had questions about the mining."

"Okay. What about?"

"How about the process?"

"The process? Of what exactly?"

She felt like she was fishing at night with a day-old, half-eaten worm. "The process, when you—I guess I'm trying to—"

"Do you mean the sampling process? How we do it?"

"Yes. Exactly. The sampling process."

"Sure. It's very simple. We adhere to all the local and state regulations. Once the owner signs the lease and the Division of Mineral Mining approves the application, we'll come in and start the core drilling to determine the potential distribution."

A "What We Do" tab appeared in the menu bar, and she enlarged the window and clicked the link. "And then the samples of—"

"We'll analyze the samples for composition and purity."

An image-laden page loaded at a leisurely pace, revealing photos of heavy equipment, vast swaths of Canadian forestland, and an aerial panorama of a mining operation. "Can you tell me about the samples themselves? Are they more complex to extract than say some other type of deposit you may sample?"

"No. Core drilling for uranium is our primary business here."

Olivia froze. *Uranium?* Her cell's screen switched to display an incoming call from Angela.

"Ms. Collins, hello? Are you there?"

"I'm sorry. My cell cut out for a second. You were saying about uranium?"

"Yes. We operate primarily in the northern range of the province, but we consult on projects in your western states every so often. Your site there will be our first east coast venture. We'll get going on location when we receive the paperwork completing the contract."

"I see. This has been very helpful. I think I have what I need."

"It's been a pleasure. Please contact us if you have any more questions. Maybe I'll visit your town in the fall."

They ended the call, and Olivia launched a search for uranium mining in Virginia. Her cell rang again.

"Hi, Angela. I'm in the middle of something—"

"Olivia, we have our meeting with New York in five minutes. Did you forget? Please tell me you didn't forget. You forgot, didn't you?"

"No, of course not. It's on my calendar."

Angela grunted. "Clearly, you're lying. Never mind. Let's dial into the conference."

"No. I can't do this right now."

"What do you mean? We've had this scheduled for weeks."

Preston pulled his F-150 in front of the police station and hurried inside. She wasted no time, swiftly kicking her door wide. "Listen. I won't be up there on Monday."

"Olivia, look—that's fine. I'm sure, once you start, everything will get settled, but you should—"

"I'm not going to New York, period."

"What? What do you mean, period? What are you saying? Wait a second."

"Please, I can't talk right now."

"Are you telling me what I think you're telling me? You're not taking the job? Is that what you're saying here? Olivia, you're not thinking straight. That would be a monumental mistake. You'll lose your chance."

Olivia locked the Escape and hastened toward the end of the block. She had no desire to test Payne's resolve to jail her. Instead, she planned to call Preston once outside the bank. "Angela, I have to go. I'm sorry. I'll get in touch with you later and explain. Thanks for understanding."

She ended the conversation without waiting for a response and slipped between the bumpers of two parked cars, aiming to shortcut through the town square. Halfway across the street, her phone rang again.

"Angela, I can't——"

"Honey? It's me." William coughed, catching his breath. "I'm so sorry."

"Dad?" She stopped dead in front of an oncoming convertible. "What's wrong?"

"I couldn't stop him. He stole your bag, your laptop."

The driver of the jet black coupe braked short of kneecapping her, blaring at her with repeated bursts of his horn. "What? What are you talking about? Who is *he*? Are you okay?"

"I was upstairs, then there was a crash. The door was open and glass——"

"Dad, I can't understand you. Are you hurt?"

"I thought it was Buddy—I checked—I got pushed from behind, and then I knocked my head pretty good on the end table getting up."

Panic welled in her throat. The scene whirled around her like a merry-go-round gathering speed with each revolution. "Are you hurt? Did you call an ambulance? Are you okay? Did you call the police?"

"I'm all right, sweetie. I tried to catch him, but I felt dizzy when I got outside. The neighbor came over and helped me."

The driver blasted his horn again, adding a few choice words discernible by even novice lip readers. She jolted at the bumper trained inches from her legs, inhaling the acrid air of burning oil emanating from under the hood. She shuffled to her left, pivoted a half-turn, and stepped back from the convertible, blanking on where she had parked. She spun and looked toward the wrong end of the street. "The widow?"

"Yes. I'm so sorry. I tried to stop him."

She took two deep breaths, regained her focus, and bolted back in front of the irate driver. "I'm coming home right now." She hopped into the Escape and thumbed through her directory, scrolling to Preston's number. She peeled away from the curb and U-turned in the intersection amid oncoming traffic as her call jumped straight to his inbox. She hung up without leaving a message and veered around a blue subcompact crawling along on three tires and a spare, shouting at her phone's voice assist to dial Sophia.

"Hey, Liv. What's up?"

"Where's your dad?" Olivia explained twice what she knew of the scene at her father's house. She riddled her first attempt with so many missing clues that Sophia could not figure out if her father fell, had a stroke, or hit his head. Sophia promised to call her dad immediately. Then Olivia tried Preston's cell again, but she met with the same fate as before. Having no other choice, she called the station directly, trusting either Cole or Bert to get word to him.

"Apple Station Police. This is the chief."

She pounded the passenger seat, gritting her teeth and quick counting to three. A sharp pain stabbed at the base of her thumb, and her wrist throbbed against the constraint of the brace. She ripped both straps open to relieve the pressure, spreading pins and needles from her palm to her fingers. "This is Olivia Penn. Somebody broke into my dad's house and assaulted him."

A file cabinet drawer clamped shut, and a chair creaked rhythmically. "All right, Ms. Penn. As soon as I can free up an officer, I'll have someone come over to take a statement."

He hung up as she white-knuckled the phone, briefly glaring at the screen before tossing it across the passenger seat, straight into the door well.

CHAPTER 32

Olivia clipped the corner and accelerated into the driveway, nearly sentencing a bed of black-eyed Susans to an untimely demise. Buddy sprinted from his watch by the cucumber patch, yelping at her heels as she hurried to the porch. She ripped the screen door open, expecting to find all the hallmarks of a police procedural: forced entry, overturned furniture, scattered belongings. Instead, her father rested on the couch, pondering his daily crossword as if it was an ordinary, leisurely Friday afternoon. A tea-towel wrapped bag of ice lying next to the remotes on the coffee table offered the sole evidence of any hint of villainy. She rushed to the sofa and knelt by his side. "Dad, are you okay? What happened?"

He flashed his well-practiced, assured smile. "I'm okay, honey. I didn't mean to panic you." He gently squeezed her hand. "Don't worry. I just tapped my noggin a bit. Maybe it'll do me some good. I'm sorry I couldn't get your bag back. What did Sophia say about your wrist?"

"That doesn't matter. My bag doesn't matter." She stood and brushed his thinning gray hair aside, checking for injuries. "You shouldn't have chased after him. What were you thinking? Are you in pain? Are you dizzy? I called the police. This is my fault. It's all my fault."

"No, it's not. I'm all right, sweetie. Slow down. Calm down. This is not your fault."

"You have a bump and a bruise. There's blood here too. Sophia's dad is on his way. You're going to the hospital." She sensed sudden movement in her periphery and flinched as a woman about her age emerged from the kitchen carrying a glass.

"Here's your water, Mr. Penn." The stranger sported khaki cargos and an olive-green T-shirt with "Semper Fi" printed prominently across the front. She measured to Olivia's height and wore her hair in a low twisted bun. "You must be Olivia. I'm Samantha. You can call me Sam, though. I live next door."

He gestured toward Sam. "She's a marine."

"Thanks for helping my dad. It's good to meet you. I wish it was under better circumstances."

"I should've introduced myself to your family sooner. I'm Ready Reserve now—been that way since I moved here."

"Sure glad to have a marine as a neighbor." She

accepted the glass from Sam and passed it to her father. "Did you see who pushed you?"

Buddy barked, and Olivia spun toward the window, craning her neck for a view of the driveway. She rushed to the door, holding the screen open as Ernesto headed straight for William while Sophia wrangled Buddy back inside.

"Where is he?" Olivia asked. "He should've been here by now."

"Who are you talking about, Liv?" Sophia asked.

"Preston. Dad, do you remember any details? What the intruder was wearing?"

Sophia's father removed the tips of his stethoscope from his ears. "Could you please wait until I'm done?"

She nodded, and Sophia wrapped an arm around her shoulders, leading her away from the door to stand behind the couch. She bent forward, kissing William on his cheek as Ernesto released the valve of a blood pressure cuff.

"Looks good, Bill." He proceeded with his exam, assessing William's reflexes and strength while asking about pain, vertigo, and nausea.

Olivia went over to the window and looked out toward the road and then back at her father. "Dad, did you see which way the intruder ran?"

Ernesto glanced at Sophia, nodding subtly in Olivia's direction.

"Hey, Liv. Let's go into the kitchen while my dad finishes. Come on."

Olivia released the sheer, shaking her head. Sophia nudged and then tugged her elbow, refusing to release her hold until Olivia relented. Sam followed as they left the living room and pulled a chair away from the table, placing a hand on Olivia's shoulder, spurring her to sit.

She took two deep breaths, composing herself and remembering her manners. "Sophia, this is Sam, our neighbor who owns A.J.'s old house. She helped my dad when he thought it was a good idea to chase after the creep who pushed him down. I can't believe he tried to go after him. Sam—Sophia. That's her father in there. He's a doctor from the hospital."

Sophia slid onto a chair next to Olivia. "Did you reach Preston?"

"I tried twice but just got his voice mail. I had to call the station. Payne answered." She pushed back from the table and paced to the opening between the two rooms. "How is he?" she called. "He should go to the ER. Right?"

Ernesto was sitting beside her father on the couch. "Should he? Yes."

"But I'm not going to. I feel fine, honey. Really, I do."

"Your father is stubborn," Ernesto said.

Sophia sidled next to her. "Just like his daughter."

"Don't worry, Olivia. All his vitals look good. That thick skull of his has come in handy. He'll be okay. Bill, I want to make sure, though. I'm ordering a CT scan and X-rays." Her father frowned, raising his hands, but Ernesto shook his head. "It's not optional, Bill. Besides, if something happened to you on my watch, I would never hear the end of it from those two in there."

Sophia steered her back to the kitchen. "Liv, come on. My dad's taking good care of him." Sophia sat and angled a chair toward Olivia.

Olivia folded her arms and leaned against the counter, rocking back and forth. "Sam, did you see anything?"

She nodded, commandeering Olivia's abandoned chair. "Male, wearing a light gray hoodie and faded blue jeans. Ran behind the house with a dark navy briefcase slung across his body."

"You're positive it was a man?"

"Yes. Thin build. Early to mid-thirties. Camel work boots. I was fixing the fence between our yards, and I heard your beagle barking. Something sounded wrong— he was combative, aggressive. I walked across to make sure everything was okay. That's when I saw your dad having trouble on the steps. I ran over and lowered him to the ground. He briefed me on what happened, and I chased after the guy around the corner of the house where your garden is. He pulled away in a white compact before I could take him down. I tried to get your dad to call the police—"

"Was there anyone else in the car?"

"No. He was alone. Your dad insisted on contacting you first."

Olivia stilled and locked eyes with Sophia.

"Liv, are you thinking what I'm thinking?" Sophia asked.

Olivia dug the Escape's key from her pocket, stepping toward the back door. Sophia sprung from her seat, grabbing her elbow.

"Whoa, Liv. Where do you think you're going?"

"Let go."

Sophia tightened her grip and blocked the exit, placing her other hand on Olivia's shoulder. "You're not going anywhere. Preston will be here any minute."

"Or Payne. I can't wait. Get out of my way."

Sam rose and came to stand beside Sophia. Olivia glanced at her father in the living room. He held the ice compress on his head as he slumped, supported by the corner of the couch. The image of Paige leaving Grossman's office on Monday flashed and faded. *I should have gone with her.* She shook off Sophia's grasp and stepped sideways, parting the space between her and Sam. She managed to crack the door open, but Sophia slammed it shut.

"Liv, I'm not letting you go. You see what happened here? What happened to Paige?" She grabbed the splint. "What happened to you?"

Olivia gripped the knob, turning and withdrawing the latch. Light beamed through the door's narrow opening, shining along the ground between them. "Soph, I need you and Sam to stay here. Tell Preston everything. Tell him about A.J.'s mother and Junior. See that my dad goes to the hospital. Sam, please stand watch. Make sure nobody comes back until the police arrive. This needs to end now. It may be too late."

"Liv, please. Don't do this." Sophia reached out, but Olivia's hand slid from her grasp.

"I have to find Cassandra."

CHAPTER 33

Olivia sped to the newspaper's office via back roads, aiming to avoid passing police responders on the direct route between her father's house and the station. There was no time to negotiate with Payne or provide Preston with any explanations should their paths cross on the way to their conflicting destinations. Upon arriving into town, she found the street parking jammed bumper to bumper, block to block, with an influx of day trippers seeking first dibs on the pre-festival sidewalk sales. She unsuccessfully circled the square to locate a spot, then abruptly braked in front of the paper's suite, flipped on the hazards, and abandoned her vehicle in the middle of the road. She leapt the curb, halting a step shy of upending Dorothy, who stood on the walkway obscured by two closely parked minivans.

"Olivia! Oh, dear. You gave me a fright."

Floyd pointed at the misplaced Escape. "I don't think you can park there."

"I'm so sorry. I didn't see you. I'm in a hurry. It's an emergency."

She dashed toward the suite as Floyd shrugged, holding out his hand. "Dorothy, give me your whistle. I've got this."

Olivia barreled through the office's entrance, felling a coat stand that was serving as a fail-safe doorstop. Cooper rocketed from his swivel seat, spilling a tumbler of steaming coffee onto his lap. He double-timed a quick-step, separating his skin from the plastered gabardine of his trousers. "Hot-hot-hot. Liv, I wasn't expecting—oh, this burns where it shouldn't!"

"I'm sorry, Cooper. Where's Cassandra?"

"That's okay. It's only a pair of pants. I can wash—"

"Cooper, *Cassandra*."

"I don't know."

She hurried to Cassandra's desk, skimming the papers scattered across the surface. "When did you last see her?"

"Thirty minutes ago. That's when my meditation app chimed and I—"

"You're sure? She was here within the past half hour?"

"Yes." He took three deep breaths. "Okay, cooling down."

She ripped open the desk's top drawer and rifled through the contents, finding only office supplies, charging cords, and a cache of sugar substitute. The drawer underneath was deeper and weighted down with catalogs and cooking magazines. She grabbed half of the stack, tossed it onto the floor, and rummaged to the bottom, uncovering Cassandra's buried laptop. "Did she leave by herself?"

Cooper clutched a wad of moistened paper towels, dabbing at the stains on his slacks. "This isn't helping. No. Not by herself."

She flipped the laptop open, rousing the device from its slumber. A screensaver popped up of Cassandra with a Bengal cat snuggled to her cheek. "Who did she leave with?"

"Mr. Grossman's son."

She stared down the dialog box requesting a password and then honed her sight on Cooper. "What was he wearing?"

"That's a strange question. Do you always ask that if you are a journalist? I should note that." He retrieved his reporter's pad from his rear pocket.

"Cooper, focus. What did he have on?"

"I'm not sure. I wasn't paying attention. I should pay more attention to details like that." He squinted, stared at her shoes, and scribbled on page one of his pad.

She typed Cassandra's name. Denied. She tried again: 123456, QWERTY, admin, abc123, dragon. All failed. Her fingers hovered over the keyboard. "Do you know her password?"

He froze. He fiddled with his tie, folding the bottom

upward like a paper football. "No. Why would I know it?" He peered over his shoulder, studying the whiteboard behind him.

"Cooper, if you do, please. This is urgent."

He lifted a file and fanned himself. "The AC must be on the fritz. I should check into it. Now. Before Mom gets back."

She straightened, stalking toward him. "Cooper."

He curled his lips and wrapped his arms around himself, backing into his desk. "Okay, fine. Please don't tell her. I didn't read her personal writing. I swear. I wanted to see the pictures of her bakes. The almond sponge in her opera cake is divine."

"The what? No, never mind. Her password. What is it?"

"Sassy Cassy."

"Oh, good grief."

Olivia went back to the desk and typed it in, and the home screen unlocked to welcome her with a wallpaper of assorted tarts, pies, and patisseries. She scanned the names of the file folders on the desktop, but none hinted at relevance. She opened a browser, and her attention was caught by a bookmark task bar that housed a link to her "Penn's Pals" column. *Wow. Okay. Whatever.* She expanded the search history, and there it was. Lodged under a web address for a recipe for pan de muerto, the URL for Materials Core Innovations confirmed her suspicions.

"Were Cassandra and Junior in a hurry when they

left?"

"No. They were as casual as could be. I assumed they went to lunch. I guess I lost my chance with her. So, you think, maybe you and I sometime could—"

"Did she say when she'd be coming back?"

He shook his head. "Do you want me to call her? You won't tell her, will you?"

"No. I promise. Thanks, Cooper." She raced out of the office, leaving the laptop on the desk. Floyd stood behind her SUV, orchestrating traffic with his wife's whistle as Dorothy steered motorists from the opposite direction in coordination with his signals.

He opened the driver's side door. "Don't worry. We kept your Escape safe."

"Thanks so much. I'm sorry. I gotta go." She slid into the seat and shifted into drive within seconds.

Dorothy cupped her hand to her mouth, yelling with all the might she could muster. "Take care, my dear."

Olivia stuck her arm out the window and waved. Then she accelerated straight through the four-way stop at the end of the block, setting a course for Grove Manor.

CHAPTER 34

Olivia fast-tracked a mile from the town square within minutes of leaving the newspaper's office. Then she floored the Escape along the rural route, dispersing a debris trail into the narrow shoulder and scattering two turkey vultures tearing at the flesh of a freshly killed raccoon in the road ahead. The muted theme to *The Great British Baking Show* rang, and she shifted in her seat, slightly straightening her left hip. Her hand skimmed her thigh, shooting straight to the bottom of her pocket. She glanced first at the outline of her knuckles beneath the cotton canvas, and then at her right pocket lying flat. The ringtone sounded again. She traced the humming from the dampened vibrations and stretched across the passenger seat toward the door well, swerving into the oncoming lane. She straightened herself and the SUV, keeping her hands glued to the wheel while weighing another trial. A trio of texts begged for attention, but the distance was too wide to bridge, and the connection silenced.

She reined the Escape to a crawl as she turned into the lengthy driveway leading to the manor and inched along the slight incline to where it leveled off for the last quarter stretch of the lane. She pulled over onto the grass just shy of the peak, keeping concealed from both the upper window and porch sight lines. A red fox darted twenty yards ahead of her and froze, staring at the vehicle. She slowly opened her door, and the fox reversed course, sprinting back across the lower lawn and aiming for camouflage in the forest's underbrush. Its hasty retreat prompted a pair of cottontails to hop in the opposite direction toward the home, dispersing a trio of crows who protested with a raspy looped chorus: caw, caw, caw. She dashed for the cover of a dense tree line that bordered the right side of the drive forty feet from where she had parked, fearing the skittish critters may have broadcast her arrival to anyone in front of the property.

Once there, she raced forward in a semi-crouch, staying within the shadows. Within a minute, she advanced to where the trees curved away from the house, leaving a twenty-yard gap between her protected position and the entrance to the manor. Cassandra's Fiesta was parked parallel to the porch with both the driver and passenger side doors open, but no one was in sight. Olivia straightened in slow motion, but dropped immediately to a squat, peering back down the lane, unable to see the Escape. She clenched her jaw, surveying the home, and drove her fist into her thigh where her phone should be.

She schemed a route to the overgrown topiary lining the porch, and after double-checking, she bolted for the close-in cover, keeping low to the ground. The pair of rabbits that had fled the frightened fox watched her from behind the rear passenger tire of Cassandra's car with their ears alert and noses twitching. She scurried across the front of the home to the opposite corner to surveil the field between the manor and the backwoods. The expanse was empty except for two cardinals and a meandering monarch butterfly. She retraced her path, using the dense shrubs to avoid exposure, and ascended the steps with three strides.

A cut cable lock lay by her feet as she crouched against the entrance. She grasped the handle, released the latch, and cracked the door. The slit view afforded rapid reconnaissance of the empty staircase to her left. She expanded the gap six more inches to expose the foyer from the steps to the middle of the fireplace. With one more calculated effort, she scanned the entire second floor passageway that overlooked the grand vestibule below. The decrepit parlor that anchored the right wing remained in question. To widen the opening to scan the room, she had to reveal her position to anyone who may be inside.

A glance was all she needed. She slipped in and tiptoed to the empty parlor, hiding behind the doorframe to keep obscured from the vantage of the second-floor passage. Footsteps shuffled above her, and she traced the source as it moved toward the wall opposite of where she stood. She peeked around the corner of the entrance, strategizing the best route to the stairs. The movement above her ceased, replaced by two voices: one male, one muted.

She scampered into the foyer, hugging the interior perimeter below the passageway until she reached the staircase. Step by step, she ascended, with her focus locked on the darkened corridor leading to the room above the parlor. At the top of the landing, she hunched by the railing and tugged at several of the fractured posts, attempting to garner a weapon, but all the anchor points held without yielding a single pillar.

She glided to the hallway and stood with her back against the left side of the entrance, remaining inconspicuous to anyone who entered the corridor. The male yelled indistinctly, but his tone was both familiar and threatening. She slipped into the passage and eased sideways, adhering closely to the wall out of the direct line of sight from the door of the room where the couple were. Reaching into her pockets, she frantically fumbled for anything she could weaponize, but found only the Escape's key fob.

She now stood with her back against the wall just a few feet from the door. Had the assailant poked his head into the hall, she would have had nowhere to hide. A heavy thump vibrated through her back as the perpetrator leaned against the thin paneled wall. She seized the sudden, momentary opportunity to peek into the room. Cassandra sat in a wooden chair in the far corner, across from the dresser, restrained and gagged.

Olivia ducked back into the corridor, preparing to attack as soon as her opponent came into full view of the doorway. She chanced a second glance. She remained undetected by him, but not by Cassandra. As Olivia retreated to regain her cover, Cassandra's eyes widened in recognition. Olivia placed her index finger to her lips, imploring her to stay quiet, but the change in her countenance alerted the man to the hidden presence in the hallway. He stormed the door, arriving at the threshold at the same time as Olivia. She shifted her weight and drove her knee forward with full-on fury.

CHAPTER 35

Junior retracted his hips, downward blocking and deflecting Olivia's devastating strike. She pounced at him, closing the distance for a second shot, but he seized her arm, yanking her into the room before she could reload and launch. She tumbled to the ground to the right of the door, and as she planted to stand, her foot punched through the floorboard, jabbing her leg into the parlor. She wrangled her limb from the jagged hole, stumbling forward as her shoe caught in the gap. He stormed from behind and shoved her into the wall by the window. Her head hit hard. The impact disoriented her, and she staggered two steps back and doubled over. He charged toward her, and she uncoiled, swinging like a fierce heavyweight against the ropes in the twelfth round.

The strike stunned him, and he held his hands up, protecting himself from any repeated right hooks. The precious few seconds allowed Olivia to catch her breath and align her feet back under her. "Junior, stop. Nobody has to get hurt here." She extended her arm as a deterrent, keeping him at a distance to impede a second volley.

He glanced at Cassandra. "You don't understand."

"We can end this. We'll tell the police the truth."

"No. It's too late."

"It's not too late. Listen to me." She stood tall, moving away from the window to separate the fight from Cassandra's defenseless position. "I know you don't want anyone else to get hurt." Cassandra mumbled and cried as fresh streams of tears ran down her mascara-streaked face. "What do you say? Let her go. You and me—we'll talk this through. Okay?" He lunged forward, but she skipped out of his reach. "The police are on their way." She said it but did not believe it. No one knew she was here.

He lowered into a wrestler's crouch. "The cops won't find me. You're not supposed to be here. This doesn't involve you."

She countered his moves. "I don't care about your still in the woods. She doesn't care either." Cassandra nodded, stammering agreement as best she could. "I know you didn't kill Paige. Where are you gonna run? You'll look guilty. Don't let him get away with it. Don't take the fall for what he did to her."

"He made me bring her here. I didn't want to." His breaths turned quicker, deeper, and desperate. He leapt at Olivia, grabbing her right arm, and twisted it behind her the same way as her Krav Maga instructor had done to her during a two-day self-defense course she had attended last summer. She flexed at her waist, jutting her hips back, and rotated left, unleashing an elbow strike. The blow landed like a cruise missile with bull's-eye precision.

He released his grasp, cupping both hands over his face. Blood flowed from his palms, dripping in splatters from his forearms. He gasped for breath through his mouth. "You broke my nose!"

Olivia lunged forward. Junior stepped back. She set her right foot behind his, pushing him with everything she had. His slight frame and off-balance stance were no match for her rush. He landed on the floor like a felled lodgepole pine. But her momentum carried her too far, and she stumbled to a stop within inches of his hand. He grabbed her ankle and tugged her leg out from under her. She upended and lay on the ground next to him as she felt something streak from above her eye and down her cheek. She wiped her face with her fingers and saw them tinged with her blood. She spun a quarter turn, kicking at his stomach, but he deflected her blows, rolling out of reach.

The distance between the two of them allowed Olivia to thrust into a squat and pop up to stand. She squared her shoulders to face him. Spots flashed in front of her eyes as her periphery tunneled. The room spun, and her legs began to buckle. *Oh, no. Please no.* She hunched over, placing her hands above her knees, and took three quick, deep breaths, forcing oxygen to her lungs. He lurched forward, pushing her back, and she crumpled, landing on her side. He loomed over her and she tried to scoot out of reach, but he entrapped her within his stance. The scene stopped spinning, and her sight cleared as she bent her elbows to cover her head.

Cassandra screamed as loud as her gag permitted and rocked forward, jumping her chair inch by inch closer to them. Junior paused, distracted by the commotion, and leaned toward her, scowling as sweat and blood streaked down his face. The threat was enough for her to cease and silence. He looked back at Olivia and grabbed her shirt collar, lifting her shoulders from the ground. Then heavy footsteps pounded the length of the corridor. The three of them traced the sound along the wall that separated them from the hallway.

The late afternoon light filtered through the window, bathing the room in soft, golden tones. Two more steps and a shadow countered, eclipsing the doorway with darkness.

CHAPTER 36

Junior froze at the sight of his scowling father. With two strides, Frank seized his son's forearm, halting any further assault. Junior unfurled his fist, surrendering to the show of superior strength. Olivia rolled to her back and propped herself on her elbows as Cassandra eased her breathing and quieted her muffled cries. Her tears ceased and color crept into her cheeks. Olivia scooted away, distancing herself from the duo as Frank surveyed the scene, taking in the streak of blood that trickled from her forehead.

Then he turned back to Junior, glowering down at him. "Did you do that to her?"

Junior looked back and forth between the two of them without answering. His father lifted him by his collar and slammed him first against the wall and then to the ground. The percussion rattled the window and dispersed a dust cloud from the filthy floor. Frank stepped over and straddled his quivering body, thrusting a finger between his eyes.

"You don't hit a woman, boy!" He recoiled his fist as Junior curled into a ball, covering his head. Frank triggered his arm, but stopped shy of impact. Then he stood tall, unfettering his son from his stance, and kicked him from his side to his back with the sole of his boot.

Olivia rose rapidly, focusing on Frank as he drew his hand over his mouth several times while strolling to the dresser. He grabbed the glass shard from the fractured frame, examining the bite of the irregular edges. Then he returned the blade to the bureau and picked up both the fire truck and rattle. "You used to have a hook and ladder like this, son."

Frank eyed Olivia, tossing both toys toward the dresser. The rattle bounced off the corner and landed on the floor, while the fire truck fell upside down. He paced to where Junior lay petrified on the ground.

"Get up."

Junior rose cautiously, cowering a quarter-turn from his father. Blood splattered the front of his shirt, and sweat adhered the cotton to his chest.

"Get away from her."

Junior stepped back, and the pair stood side by side, dividing the distance between Olivia and Cassandra. Frank thrust his thumb toward the door as the frail floorboards creaked under his weight.

"Go outside. Wait in the van."

"But I—what are you going to do?"

"I said, go, now!"

Junior wiped a fresh flow of blood from his nose with his forearm and stepped around Frank. He snapped one last glance at Olivia and Cassandra and exited the room. Pallor washed over Cassandra's face as she whimpered with the crushing grasp of what she had witnessed. Olivia drew her shoulders back, steadying herself. She glared at Frank with the same intent as when he hid from her in the woods on her first visit to the manor the day after Paige's murder. He calmly placed his palm on the door, and with a gentle push, sealed off hope of escape.

CHAPTER 37

"I'm sorry, Olivia, that you got involved in this. I warned you. I really wish you would've stopped asking questions. Had you just listened to me, you wouldn't be here now. You made it to New York. That's where you should be. Why couldn't you let things be?"

She scanned the floor for sharp debris. "And allow you to pin Paige's murder on A.J.? You always said he was like a son to you."

Frank leaned back against the dresser. "Like a son, but not my son." He gestured to her wrist. "I never meant for you to get hurt. I didn't think the whole railing would come down like it did. Your dad was in the house working upstairs, and I just loosened the bracket. We had planned to take a break on the porch when I was finished with the lock on the front door. I knew he would lean against the railing at some point … like he always does. Him and his vitamin D."

"You wanted to hurt my dad?"

He straightened and stepped closer to Cassandra, inspecting her bindings. She inclined as far away as the ties permitted. "No. I just wanted the railing to loosen when he leaned against it. But the wood sheathing under the siding must've been rotten. I had planned to raise the suspicion that whoever slashed your tires also had tampered with the railing. That would have gotten him to call the police and given you more incentive to back off. If you thought that your little investigation was putting him in danger, maybe you would've stopped."

There was only filth on the floor. He meandered back toward the dresser, blocking access to the room's lone weapon. She stole a furtive glimpse at the door. There was no way. Two random bullets from long ago had weakened the window's pane to her right, and time had encouraged the splintering to spread in a pair of overlapping webs. She had never attempted to break a window. She had seen it done in the movies, and it all seemed so simple. But smashing the glass would inflict injury without a guarantee of yielding a weapon. *I might have to.* "You were my dad's best friend."

Frank slipped his fingers into his front pockets, standing casually, as if encouraging Olivia and Cassandra to savor their last breaths. "Bill and I go way back. Before he ever met your mother. I'm sorry it's come to this. Don't worry, I'll see him through his grief."

She shifted her weight onto her left foot, following through with a slight step to her right. Virtually undetectable, the maneuver inched her closer to an optimal striking stance for the brittle pane behind her. The realignment failed to improve her angle to either the dresser or the door. Cassandra's chest heaved with her efforts to both breathe deep and stifle her cries.

"How long have you known about A.J. and Anna?"

"Since I hired him when he was a teen." Frank propped his elbow on the dresser's edge, crossing his left boot over his right. "When I first started my company, I worked here for Jeremiah. One night over a bottle of bourbon, he told me all about his daughter and her baby. He gave me money to hire him once he got old enough, and train him. I just had to keep my mouth shut. He threw so many jobs my way between this place and what he owned in town, keeping it to myself wasn't a problem. When he died and the money stopped, it didn't matter. A.J. became an asset. Better worker than my boy."

"And Paige?"

He scratched his chin. "Yeah, well, she found out somehow."

Olivia's hand throbbed. Red and purple splotches spread across her palm, and her thumb felt like a dagger was jabbing at it beneath her brace. Frank reached behind his back, grasping the glass shard. Cassandra silenced her sobs, dropping and rounding her shoulders.

"The uranium," Olivia said. "You can't extract it."

He flashed a wry smile, laying the glass on the dresser, and folded his arms. "That, Olivia, could be worth millions. You're right, though. I can't legally get at it now. Maybe not even in my lifetime if the mining ban remains on the books. But someday, the boy may. It's my legacy."

"How do you figure?"

"Did you know my father left my mother when I was born? They were young, not married. He ran off with another woman. Forgot all about us. My mother raised me by herself. Grossman—that's her name." He scanned the room, silently ruminating, and then smirked. "Junior won't ever amount to much on his own. He could never run the business without me. He carries my name, though. My name—my legacy. This land, what lies underneath. Nobody will forget my name."

There was no path to the blade. There were no other means of attack. It would have to be the window. She inched closer. "Everyone will remember you for murdering Paige. That'll be your legacy."

Frank uncrossed his arms, standing square to her. "Olivia, our families aren't so different. Your mother, she was a writer. And you now? Her legacy lived through you. You became what she always wanted. See, my dear, had you gone to New York, others would remember your mother through you. My legacy will live through my son. I'm so sorry that it has to end here for your mother—and for you."

"You said I was like a daughter to you."

"Like a daughter, but not my daughter."

He stepped toward her. His deviation from the dresser opened a slim lane to the shard, offering the narrowest of odds if she was quick enough. She shifted away from the window, gambling he would track her trail. His echoed adjustment improved her angle to the dresser as he stood on the edge of the soiled, circular rug concealing the hole that had almost swallowed her on Tuesday. She projected his trajectory. With one more mirrored step, he would be in the dead center of the hole. His weight—over twice that of hers—would surely rupture the thin, decrepit particleboard guarding the breach. She withdrew fully from the window and paced backward, enticing him closer to the trap. A single stride more. She inched back. His weight transferred to his right foot, and he stepped upon the bullseye. The feeble board bent but did not break.

Olivia's breath abandoned her. The support had betrayed its promise. Her life drained from her limbs, pulling her shoulders down and fixing her feet to the floor. She breathed in. A scene flashed in her mind of a summer picnic when she was three. Her parents reclined on a blanket as Frank ran across the town square with her under his arm, giggling as she bounced about. She breathed out. She might still secure the glass shard, but not have the will to use it. She breathed in as a fly landed on her hand. She closed her eyes and heard it buzz. The field before her became like the darkest of night skies. She breathed out, glaring at him. He shifted his weight, and she closed her eyes to a memory of fireflies lighting a backyard sky. The child held in her mother's arms pointed. *There.* A flash to the right. *There.* A flash dead straight ahead. She opened her eyes, aiming them on Frank. *There.* Olivia charged and leapt at his core. He extended his arms, catching her in midair, and for a breath, the two of them were locked in an embrace. Frank's eyes widened, Olivia winked, and the board gave way. Together they plummeted and crashed into the parlor below.

CHAPTER 38

Frank's heels hammered into the floor a fraction before his legs crumpled, slamming him to his back and bouncing his head off a debris pile of fragmented gypsum, plaster, and rotted oak wood. Jarred and jolted, Olivia rolled off his chest, coughing and gasping for air. Her sight blurred and doubled as a bell tone shrilled ear to ear. "Olivia." She forced her eyes wide, looking up from the ground backward, spinning her head side to side to localize the muffled voice and determine where to direct her defense. "Olivia." She flipped to her stomach and pushed up onto her hands and knees, but her right arm collapsed, refusing to bear weight. "Olivia." She spun a quarter turn, angling her feet toward the incoming threat, and extended her left arm, preparing to strike. "Olivia, stop."

Her head thumped like taiko drums, pounding in double-time to keep pace with her racing pulse. A silhouette stood over her, and she squinted, leveling her hand above her brow as if shading her eyes from the midday sun. "Preston?"

"Yes, it's okay."

She stilled, letting two breaths ease the fight in her. "Preston. What—what are you doing here?" Full awareness of the scene suddenly seized her. She rolled, scrambling away from Frank, kicking with her heels to propel herself back as if he was ready to attack. "He did it … Cassandra … she's up … Junior … he's outside—"

"Olivia, stop. You're hurt." Preston anchored his palm on her shoulder, grounding her to prevent further injury. "We got Junior. It's okay."

She pinned her right arm to her stomach and tried to sit, wincing as she lifted her shoulders. He bolstered her back and propped her forward, stabilizing her until she was no longer threatening to topple. Frank lay motionless.

"Is he—is he dead?"

An illuminated column of dust wafted from above like snow in a globe in no hurry to coat the ground. Preston gazed at the hole in the ceiling, where the light shined through.

He looked back at her. "No. You knocked him out pretty good, though." A soft smile brightened his face. "Neither of his feet are pointing in the right direction."

Cole raced into the parlor. "Ms. Collins is upstairs," Preston told him. "Call for three ambulances from dispatch. Go now."

Cole backpedaled and scurried toward the steps, passing Bert as he sidestepped through the entrance. Bert joined Preston by Olivia's side, helping to keep her upright. "Geez, Olivia. What happened? Are you all right? Did he hurt you?"

"No, I'll be okay. We had ourselves a falling-out." Bert glanced at Preston, who subtly shook his head. "What?" she said. "Was that too soon?"

"Bert, secure him. When EMS gets here, you stay with him. Understand?"

"Got it, Preston."

"Really, you two. I'm A-OK peachy keen." She tried for a double thumbs-up, perplexed why her right one would not move. "I don't need an ambulance. Let me get up." She labored to roll over to her knees, swaying as she shook off Preston's efforts to keep her still.

Preston grasped both of her shoulders. "Olivia, stop. I'm pretty sure you hit your head. Let me help you." He swept her hair out of her eyes, examining the cut above her brow. "How does that bump feel?"

She traced the outline of the swollen lump with two fingers. "That can't be good. Stings a bit."

"I bet it does. What else hurts?"

She cringed as she lifted her wrist.

"How about those fingers and toes, can you wiggle those?"

She smiled slightly and then tried to wipe the blurriness from her eyes. "Your medical prowess continues to astonish me. But, yes. I can wiggle them—well, most of them anyway."

"I'll take that as a complement." He gently brushed her cheek with his thumb. "You had some dirt there. You think you're okay to get up?"

"Yeah."

"Let's get you out of here." He wrapped his arm around her waist, lifting her before she could rally any of her own strength to help with the transition. "Doing okay?"

"A little woozy."

"Don't worry. I've gotcha. I won't let go." He steadied her, walking her into the foyer and out of the manor.

He waited with her on the porch, only safeguarding her down the steps once the sirens and flashing lights of the first ambulance on scene crested the peak of the driveway. A paramedic popped out of the passenger side, holding her hand up to keep them in place until she opened the rear doors. A second paramedic guided a stretcher out of the rig and joined his co-worker in rolling it over to Olivia at the bottom step. Preston balanced her as she leaned on the edge and swung her legs onto the cot. The paramedics raised the back rest and began their triage, dividing their efforts between her wound and wrist.

Cole emerged from the manor, swaddling Cassandra with his APP STAT PD lightweight duty jacket. The second and third ambulance silently arrived in tandem and parked, allowing for ample operating space between each unit. Olivia saw Cassandra speak to Preston, and he turned, pointing toward the three responders huddled around her.

She closed her eyes, resting back against the stretcher, while one paramedic removed a blood pressure cuff as the other cleaned dirt from her wound.

"Olivia."

She turned her head toward Preston's voice. Cassandra stood beside him with tears rolling down her cheeks. She embraced Olivia, managing only a few whispered words of gratitude between her relieved cries. The paramedics debated the merits of cutting away Olivia's splint, deciding merely to loosen the brace to ease pressure and ensure circulation.

"Cole, take Ms. Collins over to the ambulance," one of the paramedics said. "Ma'am, let's get you checked out, okay?" Cassandra nodded and wiped her eyes, leaning into Cole's arms, and walked with him to the second transport.

Preston waited by Olivia's side as the EMT applied a dressing over her cut. Then the paramedics packed up their gear and called in an ETA to the ER along with their preliminary assessment of her injuries.

"How did you know I was here?" she asked Preston.

He tipped his Stetson slightly back. "It made sense to me you'd go exactly where I asked you not to."

She grimaced, gingerly touching her bandage. "Oh! Please, don't make me laugh."

He grinned and leaned closer, resting a hand on the

stretcher's backrest near her shoulder. "Truth is, when I got to your father's house, your friends told me you went to find Cassandra. I followed your trail."

"Did they tell you about A.J.?"

"They did."

"Did they tell you—everything?"

He nodded. "We'll get it figured out. You concentrate on you right now," he said as the EMT covered her with a blanket. "Looks like they're ready to take you in. I'll call your father and let him know you're safe. I'm going to follow behind."

"You don't have to come."

"I need your statement."

"Right. Of course."

"And I want to make sure you're okay."

He aligned his hat and stepped back, allowing the crew to load her into the ambulance. She reached for his hand, and they enfolded each other's grasp on instinct. "Thanks for finding me. If you hadn't come, I don't know what—"

"You seemed to handle things okay on your own, but don't go making a habit of it. One thing I know now for sure—" He released her hold as the paramedics lifted and pushed the stretcher back. "I never want to end up on your bad side, Gunny."

CHAPTER 39

Olivia groaned, venting five days' worth of exhaustion. "Stay overnight? I don't think that's necessary."

The attending physician removed a stack of folded lab printouts from her coat pocket and scribbled three bulleted notes on the back of the bottom sheet. "That's my recommendation, and those are my orders. You sustained a significant blow to your head. Your scans look good, but we want to observe you overnight."

Sophia positioned a pillow under Olivia's right arm. "You should retest her. It's hard to get things through her thick skull sometimes."

"As long as you don't prescribe any PT."

Sophia tapped the cast on Olivia's broken wrist. "We'll be seeing plenty of each other."

"You two can decide on that. For now, rest and relax. I'll be back in the morning to check in after rounds and discharge you if your tests are normal." The doctor exited, and Maria joined her daughter and William in the hospital room.

Maria hugged Olivia, taking care in avoiding her cast. "Mija, my dear. I'm so sorry." She brushed Olivia's hair away from her bandage. "Mamá wanted to come, but I told her to stay home. You'll see her soon enough. William, how are you holding up?"

"I'm okay. Your husband gave me a thorough going over and said everything came back normal. It's her I'm worried about." He rose from a chair by her bed.

"Dad, you heard the doctor. I'm fine." He tried his best to smile, but his eyes moistened, and he choked up when trying to speak. She squeezed his hand with as much strength as she could muster. "Really, don't worry. I'm going to be okay. Hey, how about checking with Jed about my tires? Could you do that for me? He said he may call today, and he might need an okay to go ahead with the work. What about Cassandra? Have they released her?"

He pulled a tissue from his front pocket and dabbed his nose. "Sure, honey. I'll call him. I'll make sure he gets a good set put on. Cassandra was filling out forms by the nurses' station, talking to the detective. She seemed about ready to leave."

Beverly burst into the room bearing a bouquet of red roses and a basket teeming with bits and bobs of comforts and treats. "Olivia! Oh, dear. How are you? You're so brave. My Preston must think you're the bravest."

"I don't know about that. I'm lucky—grateful that he came when he did. Those are stunning. You didn't need to do that. Thank you. That's very kind."

"Nonsense. We're practically family." Beverly embraced Olivia as Sophia and her mother glanced at one another, suppressing mutual amusement at the budding addition to the Styles family tree. "There's more." She scoured the basket's interior and removed a pint-size teddy bear uniformed like a Texas Ranger. She coaxed a wave from the plush cub and then choreographed the furry fellow to dance a jig.

Olivia's cheeks warmed. "Bev, you shouldn't have gone to such trouble. How cute—badge, hat, and boots. What about that, Soph? Really something, huh?"

Beverly beamed. "He's bona fide and justified."

Sophia grabbed the cuddly companion. "Really something indeed, Liv. You know who this reminds me of?"

Olivia shoved the pillow under her arm off the edge of the bed. "Soph, dear friend, please—some help here?"

"Just saying, Liv. That's all." She retrieved the jettisoned diversion and repositioned Olivia's arm, dispatching a teasing smile. Then she snatched the bear back and had it steal a peck from Olivia's cheek. "All yours. A special buddy by your side to support you while you heal."

Beverly giggled, gleaming with a twinkle in her eyes. "Will you and your dad be able to come tomorrow? If you're well enough, that is."

"Of course. We'll be there. The doctor plans to discharge me in the morning."

Her father tenderly placed his fingers on her cast. "Only if you're up to it."

"I will be."

Beverly clapped. "Splendid. Preston is so looking forward to it. As am I. How lovely to have the heroes of the day sitting at our table—together. Now, if you'll excuse me, I saw that son of mine at the end of the hall-way, and I want to have a few words with him before he disappears on me again. You take care, Olivia."

Maria rose. "William, why don't we walk outside and get some fresh air."

"Go ahead, Dad. Get yourself some coffee. Soph will stay with me. I'm not going anywhere."

"All right. We won't be far. I have my cell. Call me if you need me."

Sophia grabbed the snuggly trooper, stuffing him between Olivia's arm and her side. "Here. You should keep this guy near you. For protection. All night."

Olivia denned the bear next to the bed's rail, gauging the enormity of her gift basket. "It was nice of Bev to bring all—and I do mean *all*—of that."

"And so quick. Apparently, you're like family."

Olivia leaned her head back, turning her neck from side to side. "Don't even go there."

Sophia sat in the chair next to the bed, micro-adjusting the pillow under Olivia's arm. "Hear anything about A.J. yet? And what's going to happen with Junior?

If he wasn't involved in Paige's murder, why did he even break in to your dad's house and take your laptop?"

"Before I went for my X-ray, I spoke with Preston, and he told me Junior confessed right away that Frank put him up to it. He must have thought I found evidence, or maybe he thought Paige had sent me something about A.J.'s family. My dad surprised Junior and just ended up in the wrong place at the wrong time. The prosecutor will drop A.J.'s charges. Cole searched the woods when we left, but he didn't find evidence of a still."

"What do you think happened to it?"

Tori poked her head into the room. "Well, ladies, don't point fingers at me. My moonshine enterprise proposes to be one hundred percent legit and at least ninety proof." She strolled in, her cheeky smile fading as Olivia's injuries came into full light. "Liv, wow. You're a frightful sight."

"You warm my heart."

"Because I love you, Liv, I will always tell you the brutal truth. Tyler sends his best raspberries your way."

"I appreciate you coming. You didn't have to. Or maybe you shouldn't have."

Tori whipped out her cell and snapped a photo. "And miss the opportunity to share on the socials you decked out in this gorgeous gown?"

"Hey, what was that for? You better not post that anywhere."

"It's all about leverage, my dear. Now, I have it. Remember, if you fancy any walkabouts while you're here, make sure you're tied together in the back. Keep yourself classy."

Olivia grinned, grabbing an empty medicine cup from her tray table and throwing it southpaw at Tori. "Classy enough?"

"More sassy than classy. Soph, is Preston around? He should see this side of her. Or perhaps, the other side."

Sophia pursed her lips, silently laughing as Olivia stared at her, shaking her head. "Oh, what a friend I have in you. Anyway. Back to A.J. I'll talk to him tomorrow after I'm discharged and he has had some time to rest. The bank stopped the auction."

Tori sat on the edge of the bed. "Soph told me about the uranium. What was Grossman going to do? Build a bomb?"

"Why am I not surprised that's your first theory? No to the bomb. Extracted uranium undergoes enrichment, and then it's used primarily as fuel in nuclear power plants. But here in Virginia, state law regulates extraction, and there's currently a ban on mining uranium. You can explore for it, but not remove it. Someday, though, you may be able to."

Tori leaned forward, aiming her phone again. "So, Frank intended to buy the manor and wait until the ban gets lifted? See, I'm following you here, Liv. How about one with a flash?"

Olivia grabbed the cell and handed it to Sophia. "If it's ever lifted."

Sophia viewed the photo Tori had captured, setting it

as the home and lock screen wallpaper. "What about Payne? Remember what my dad said about him finding Paige?"

"I don't know, Soph. I want this all to be over. Frank killed Paige once he knew she had evidence that A.J. is the legal heir of the property. I'm just glad June will see justice for her loss. Small compensation, but at least she'll have that. How or if Payne's involved in any of this? That's a mystery for another day. Here's hoping our paths never have to cross again."

The three friends reminisced about Paige, laughing and shedding a few tears along the way. They made plans to attend her services on Monday and visit regularly with June over the coming weeks. Then Maria and William returned, each carrying a cup of coffee.

Tori rose as Sophia handed her phone back. "I'll take my leave. I had to make sure for my Tyler's sake that his auntie is still in one piece." She unlocked the screen, displaying her wallpaper like a trophy. "Get well soon, Liv. And remember, leverage."

"Mija, we should go, too, and let Olivia rest," Maria said.

"Okay. Liv, you call me in the morning. First thing." Sophia hugged her, and the three left together.

William slid his chair closer to the bed and fluffed the pillow under her head. "How are you feeling, honey?"

"I'm fine. It's unnecessary for me to be here—"

"Sweetie, don't start that again."

Preston stepped into view outside the room and

tapped on the open door with his knuckles. "Is this a bad time? I can wait if you two are busy."

Olivia waved him in. "No, you're good."

He removed his Stetson and stood at the foot of her bed. "I wanted to let you know A.J.'s been released. Frank and Junior are in custody." He spotted the flower arrangement on the counter below the supply cabinets. "Is that from my mother?"

"You above all would recognize her style." She grabbed the teddy bear, adjusting his rancher hat and straightening his silver badge. "This fellow has officially relieved Cole and Bert of their guard duties."

His dimple flashed. "What about you? How's the head and wrist?"

"Completely fine and broken. I want to go home, sleep in my bed tonight. I don't want to be in this hospital."

A nurse entered the room and checked her vitals. "Sir, will you be staying the evening?" she asked William.

"Dad, no. You go home. There's no sense in us both having to stay."

"Yes, if she's here, I'm here."

"Sure. I'll find a reclining chair and bring you a pillow and blanket for the night." The RN charted her findings and left to gather what he needed.

When the three of them were alone again, Preston asked, "Can I get either of you anything?"

"No, thanks." Olivia glanced at her father. "We're good."

Preston nodded, scanning the room as if searching for clues. "All right, then." He put his hat on, took it off, fumbled with the brim, and shifted it from one hand to the other. He pulled his phone out of his shirt pocket, but it slipped from his grip and fell to the floor. Bending forward, he picked it up and bumped his head on the corner of the bed as he stood.

Olivia cringed and waved her call button. "Detective Hills, do you need a doctor?"

He clenched his jaw as he rubbed his temple. "No, Ms. Penn. I believe you've been through worse today. Besides, somebody once told me my true talents were being wasted in law enforcement. So, as they say—heal thyself." He shoved the cell into his jeans pocket and checked his watch. "Okay. Well, I guess that's it for now. I'll be in touch. I'll need to follow up on some details with you, but it can wait until you're feeling better. I'll give you a call. So, anyway. Okay. I'll let you two go. If you need anything, you've got my number. You take care now." He turned to leave.

"Preston," she called, and he looked back, meeting her eyes. "Thanks again for being there. We'll see you tomorrow."

He smiled, tipping his Stetson. "Sleep well, Olivia. I'll see you tomorrow. Good night, Mr. Penn."

William remained by Olivia's side so she would not be alone. The nursing staff checked in on her twice every hour. She broached the matter of Frank's betrayal, but her father put her off, saying there would be time for that discussion later. The coming weeks were to be about healing and moving forward, not about pain and looking back. As the evening advanced, he dimmed the room's lights when she dozed on and off while watching a documentary on Scotland. She fell asleep with his hand holding hers.

CHAPTER 40

William handed Olivia a glass of ice tea and popped off the top of a prescription vial. "Are you sure about this?" He funneled two tiny, round pills into her waiting palm.

She relaxed, leaning back on the living room couch with Buddy's head in her lap and one paw resting on her cast. She slipped the pain medication between her lips, swallowing the tablets with a sip of the sweet tea. "Positive. I want to get out. It's a beautiful day. Besides, we'll disappoint Bev if we don't show."

"I meant you wanting to stay here, in Apple Station."

She rubbed Buddy's neck below his collar and guided him to the ground. "I'm tired of the city life anyhow." She lay her forearm on a double stack of down pillows as Buddy climbed back onto the couch, nuzzling his nose next to her wrist. "This is what I need."

"And work? They're okay with everything?"

"I'm taking a few weeks off." She tried to pinch her

thumb to her index finger, but the cast prevented the connection. "Writing will be difficult until I get this removed and replaced by a more flexible splint. I spoke with Angela, and she insisted I take as much time as I need. We'll sort through everything. As an astute elder once advised me, it's not a decision I have to make today."

He rose from the sofa. "Wise words from a Jedi. You'll find your way, young grasshopper."

"Completely mashing genres there, Dad."

"When you reach my age, you get to say anything you want. This is the way. I hope you understand this means no home gym. But I'll make the sacrifice, for your sake. Remember, vegetables aren't a daily requirement. Everyone knows that."

"Don't worry too much about either. I won't impose long."

He leaned forward, kissing her cheek. "As long as you need. I'm so glad you're okay, honey. I'll be ready to go when you are."

"Give me twenty minutes."

William went to recline in a rocker on the porch while he waited. She stroked Buddy's head and lifted his chin from her lap. He followed her first into the study, where she retrieved her recovered work bag, and then through the kitchen and out the back door. He snatched his ball from the base of the steps, scampered in front of her, and dropped it at her feet. "Sure thing, little guy." She threw the ball toward Sam's house, and he bounded across the yard and through the fence's open gate.

Then she unlocked the cottage and slung her work bag on the desk. She stood by the bookcase of her mother's writings, skimming her fingers along the spines of the binders, and lingered on the volume labeled *Memories, Olivia*. She sat in the desk chair and removed her mother's blue-lacquer fountain pen from the bag's panel pocket, placing it next to her writing journal and reading glasses. Buddy barked, lying on the welcome mat with his ball by his side and tail wagging with a snappy, spirited beat. She smiled, adjusting the height of the seat so her feet were flat, and her back was well supported. "Perfect." She finished arranging the desk as her workspace, plugging in her laptop but leaving it closed. Then she stashed her bag on the floor, leaning it against the wall.

After she locked the cottage, she walked back to the house to join her father on the porch. He grabbed a hat from inside, and then they looked over the garden before leaving for the festival. All the seedlings had grown. The tomato plants' leaves were a healthy dark green, and their stalks stood straight, thickened and strong.

William drove them to town, insisting she held passenger status until she no longer required pain medication. The heat wave from earlier in the week had lifted, ushering in a refreshing late-spring seventy-degree day. Festival revelers covered the square, toe-tapping to the tunes of The Pickle Barrels under a bluebird sky. The aroma from the smokers promised savory, hearty mounds of barbecue beef, pork, and chicken for all who came ready to feast.

William parked the Escape in a secret spot in an alley behind the inn, and they strolled together past the newspaper's office on their way to meet Beverly.

"Liv!" Sophia waved, jogging across the street. "We're a few tables in, near the stage."

"Honey, I'll walk ahead and find our seats."

"Okay, Dad. I'll be right over."

Sophia pointed to her cast. "How's the wrist this morning?"

"It doesn't tickle."

"I still can't understand what you were thinking, going out there alone. Never do something like that again. But, perhaps, you're not so bad to have around in a jam."

"There you go again. Giving me the warm fuzzies. One thing I may have neglected to mention last night before you left the hospital—your date will be joining you for lunch, so have an extra seat available."

"Excuse me? My what? Liv, dearest friend—for now —what did you do?"

"Good luck and good hunting."

Sophia shook her head, smiling. "We're not done here. We'll continue this conversation when you stop by our table. My mom wants to speak with you too. But it looks like your new bestie is coming this way, so I'll let you two chat. We aren't finished with this, though." She stepped back, playfully jabbing a scolding finger at Olivia, and turned to rejoin her family on the square.

Cassandra passed Carol's Comforts at a relaxed clip, sporting a purple festival T-shirt with her hair pulled back in a loose ponytail. Olivia raised her hand to wave, scrunching her fingers as much as her cast allowed. "How are you feeling today?" she asked when Cassandra reached her.

"Since I'm not the one who fell through a ceiling, not too bad—all things considered. You?"

"I'm okay. It looks worse than it feels."

"Olivia—"

"How about just Liv?"

Cassandra grinned and nodded. "I didn't get to thank you properly. Last night … he would have killed me if you hadn't come."

"We took them down together. You picked up right where Paige left off, didn't you?"

"I may have peeked at her laptop before the police took it, but that's off the record."

"Understood. Just for my sanity—you and Junior never were a couple, were you?"

"No. I used him for access to Grossman's office to gather information. My natural charm makes men melt."

"Well played."

"So, Liv. Unconfirmed rumors report that you're hanging around Apple Station. Is that true?"

She glanced toward Beverly's inn. "I'm not sure

about your source, but it's true. You're stuck with me—for a little while."

Cassandra scanned across the square. "I was wondering ... without Paige, there's space that needs filling in the paper until we can hire someone full time. We could have Cooper contribute, but his mother asked me to vet other options. We agreed readers would be interested in having a hometown 'Penn's Pals' column. Maybe once a week, you could answer a few questions?"

"You're offering me a position?"

"Not a job per se because there's no pay involved. We could budget for lunches."

"That makes it so much more appealing." She peered through the newspaper's window, glimpsing Cooper darting toward the entrance. "I can't write another 'Penn's Pals' column, though. That's an actual paying gig."

"No, I get it. I just thought I would ask."

The office door swung open and Cooper emerged decked out in a khaki safari vest pinned with a DIY "Press Pass" ID. "Liv, I was so scared, the police came, and I told them, and then I didn't hear anything, and—"

"Cooper, I may not be here if it wasn't for you. You're my hero." He wiped his eyes as she embraced him. "Looks like you're ready to do some shooting in that outfit."

He stepped back, straightening his badge. "Mom promoted me to official photographer. Well, it's just for the festival, but she said we'll see how it goes. Keep your fingers crossed for me."

"Cooper, that's fantastic. Congratulations. And I will, fingers and toes."

"Will you still help me with my writing?"

"Of course."

He leaned in, brushing her cheek with a soft kiss. "I'm sorry, I had to." He turned, smiling as wide as the sky, and ducked back into the office.

"Well, Liv, or is it Mrs. Robinson now?"

"No, I don't think so. Apparently, he's weirded out by the age gap. Although, rumor has it that you may want to watch out for that cub." Cassandra shot a stumped double take through the window. "Back to what you asked me about writing. We'll have to sort out some terms, but how about we all get together on Tuesday and talk about developing—we'll call it 'The Cozy Column'—for a limited run until you find your replacement."

"Serious? You'll do it? Cooper's mom will be over the moon happy. Thanks, Liv."

"I'll let you be the one who tells Cooper, and I suggest you change your password."

"Deal and done. I have to talk to him now anyway. Gary's rabbits are at it again. Let's catch up later."

"Sounds great."

Cassandra removed her aviator glasses, hanging them from her shirt's collar. "Okay, Liv. I'll see ya around."

CHAPTER 41

Olivia weaved her way through the maze of folding tables to greet Sophia's family. Ernesto inspected her cast and the fingers of her right hand. "How is your head this morning? Any pain?"

She traced the length of the bandage covering her cut. "No. Feels fine. The medication is handling the wrist."

"Okay. Nothing strenuous this week. Got it? Once that cast comes off, you see my daughter. Understand?"

Olivia dared a peek at Sophia, who balanced on the corner of her seat, as distant from Cole as possible. She agreed without objection to Ernesto's prescription and pulled out a chair next to her unamused friend.

Sophia poked Olivia's leg. "Liv, we so need to chat about this. You owe me big. Anytime—anywhere. I'm calling this in on you."

Olivia drew deep from her well of willpower, pursing

her lips to keep from laughing. "I don't understand. Is there a problem?"

Josefina reached between the two of them, grasping Olivia's left hand. "You get married soon and stop worrying us."

"I second that, Liv. I have a candidate for you."

Josefina shook her head as Cole attacked a rack of baby back ribs. "Ay-ay-ay." She lifted the platter of her tres leches entry for the baking competition and headed for the judge's tent.

Sophia jumped to her feet. "I better help her with that. If you'll excuse me, Cole. It may be a while, so if you have policing duties, I understand if you need to leave—soon."

He grinned with a mouthful of meat. "I'm off the clock until five, Ms. Sophia. I'm yours for the entire afternoon." He winked, wiping his mouth with a wad of napkins.

"Super." She faced Olivia, speaking through gritted teeth. "Anytime—anywhere."

Olivia offered a mischievous thumbs-up. "I should go too."

As Sophia left, Maria stood and beckoned to her. "Mija, can I talk to you for a second?" She led her a few feet from the table. "Sophia tells me you'll be staying around for a while."

"I've decided that's best right now. I want to be here. Spend time with my dad. I need to be here. For him, for me."

"As long as you're deciding what's best for you, right? We all love you. You're a part of our family. If you need to go, your family will always support you. When you need to come home, you always have our open arms and hearts." Maria cradled Olivia's cheek in her hand and embraced her.

"Olivia! Over here." They turned as Beverly waved from her table two rows over. Preston caught her eye and prepped a place for her, pulling out a chair.

Maria nodded, slipping an arm around her shoulders. "You go on now. Looks like someone's ready for you."

Olivia smiled, stepping forward with an open heart, finally feeling she had made it home.

The End

SHEDDING SOME LIGHT

Is moonshine legal in Virginia?

Firewater, rotgut, white lightning. Whatever term is used, all typically refer to illegally distilled alcohol. Moonshine in the United States originated in the Revolution's aftermath when the Federal government instituted a tax on liquor to help pay for the expense of the war. Many ignored this regulation and continued to manufacture and sell spirits without payment of the excise. The practice persisted and proliferated during the Prohibition Era from 1920 to 1933. Franklin County in the foothills of the Blue Ridge Mountains of Virginia became known as the "Moonshine Capital of the World."

"Moonshiners" refers to those who manufactured the spirits, whereas the term "bootleggers" applies to those who sold and transported the product. Bootleggers used "stock" cars for distribution. These vehicles appeared ordinary (i.e., stock) from the outside; however, their interiors were altered to conceal the illicit goods. Skilled drivers were in demand, and often, bootleggers staged races for bragging rights and building résumés. After the repeal of Prohibition, the need for this unique skill declined. The former leadfoots organized their events, and the sport now known as NASCAR was born.

In the most basic iteration, moonshine is corn (although any grain or combination of grains will do), sugar, yeast, and water (a mixture referred to as "mash") that undergoes a two-step process. The first stage is fermentation. Yeast breaks down sugar, resulting in alcohol. During distillation, evaporated alcohol cools and turns back to a liquid. The product gets collected, jarred, and sold as moonshine. "Firewater" is clear and possesses a strong "bite." Other distilled liquors, such as whiskey, differ in that they undergo an aging process that imparts distinctive hues and mellows the harsh taste. Moonshine typically has a high "proof." Alcohol content is half of the stated proof (e.g., a 100 proof moonshine is 50 percent alcohol). In Virginia, permitted licensees can sell distilled liquor up to 151 proof. Retailers can sell higher proof alcohol only to those who possess a grain alcohol permit. Even slight amounts of spirits at such proofs may lead to rapid alcohol poisoning.

Today, "moonshine" remains illegal in Virginia because unpermitted manufacturers and sellers distribute the distilled liquor without collecting taxes. However, individuals may produce distilled liquor branded as "moonshine" with approval from two permitting agencies. To comply, one requires both a distillery license from the Virginia Alcoholic Beverage Control Authority (ABC) and a Beverage Distilled Spirits Plant permit from the Alcohol and Tobacco Tax and Trade Bureau (TTB). A distillery license allows one to manufacture and sell spirits only to authorized outlets. The TTB permit requires that production of the distilled liquor occurs in a qualified spirits plant. Possession of stills or components to make stills without the proper permit is illegal.

What are the penalties? Violation of the manufacturing terms is a Class 6 felony with penalties of up to five years in prison and/or a fine of up to $10,000 for each offense. Violations may include (but are not limited to) possession of a still, distilling from a residence or a shed, yard, or enclosure attached to a residence, and unlawful manufacturing of materials used to produce distilled spirits. Also illegal is the purchase, receipt, and production of distilled spirits where one knows or should reasonably know the Federal tax has not been paid. Anyone who removes or conceals distilled spirits on which the tax has not been paid is in violation of the statutes.

In our story, Benjamin Billingsley had both permits necessary to manufacture and sell "moonshine." A.J. and Junior did not. Allegedly, they possessed equipment, manufactured, and sold distilled liquor without the required permits and without collecting taxes. Yikes. But where's the evidence? What happened to the still and why did Chief Payne not pursue any further investigation against A.J.? Continue to follow the story throughout *The Olivia Penn Mystery Series.*

None of this represents legal advice and is intended only for entertainment use as an overview of laws regulating distilled spirits in Virginia at the time of this writing. Laws vary by state. Please don't manufacture or sell illegal moonshine. Please don't end up in the pokey.

Uranium in Virginia

A little-known fact about the Commonwealth: one of the largest recoverable, single-site uranium deposits in the United States is on private land close to the border with North Carolina in Pittsylvania County, Virginia. Estimates gauge the deposit to contain 119 million pounds of uranium valued between $6–7 billion.

Development of uranium for commercial use involves three processes: mining, milling, and storage. Mining refers to the extraction of deposits from the ground. Individual states, the Office of Surface Mining Reclamation and Enforcement, and the U.S. Department of the Interior regulate these procedures. The Nuclear Regulatory Commission, as prescribed by the Atomic Energy Act (AEA), oversees the milling (i.e., the operations to produce yellowcake) and storage of waste (i.e., tailings).

In the aftermath of the Three Mile Island accident on March 28, 1979, in Pennsylvania, Virginia lawmakers in 1982 instituted a one-year moratorium on mining uranium. The legislature extended the ban indefinitely the following year. The owners of the private deposit in southern Virginia have sought to overturn this prohibition through the years, but opponents have countered their efforts with each challenge. Those against development of the resource argue that the specific extraction technique required by this site may have significant environmental and health impacts.

The Supreme Court addressed Virginia's moratorium on uranium mining in June 2019 (Supreme Court Case 16-1275). Ownership claimed that environmental and health concerns related to the milling and storage of uranium had motivated the ban. Neither process, though, is under the purview of state lawmakers. Those who sought repeal argued Virginia's moratorium preempted the AEA. The Supreme Court disagreed, ruling the AEA only regulated the activities after the extraction process. The ruling rejected the questions regarding the moratorium's motivation. The ban on extraction remains.

Geographical surveys suggest uranium deposits may exist in smaller quantities throughout the state. In the early 1980s, a uranium corporation acquired leasing rights of 16,000 acres of potentially rich grounds in Fauquier, Orange, Madison, and Culpepper counties. Exploration highlighted portions of the northern and central Piedmont and the Blueridge as areas of interest as well. At this time, only the Pittsylvania site is commercially viable.

In our story, Apple Station is proximal to potential

deposits. If lawmakers repeal the moratorium on mining, the ramifications would extend beyond the Pittsylvania site. Frank was right in his estimation that he would never see a dime from his attempted acquisition of Grove Manor, but the land itself someday may be worth millions. Permits for exploration of uranium remain legal and are subject to application. Thus, the role of Materials Core Innovations in sampling the distribution of uranium at Grove Manor was above board and within the state's requirements for exploration of natural resources.

Another story-related fun fact: Canada has one of the world's largest reserves of recoverable uranium. The McArthur River Mine in Saskatchewan, Canada, is the most extensive and contains some of the highest-grade uranium in the world.

ACKNOWLEDGMENTS

I'm deeply grateful for all those who have supported me in the writing of this book.

Thank you to my brilliant editor Serena Clarke. Your encouragement, guidance, and instruction are appreciated beyond words. Thank you to my wonderful proofreader LaVerne Clark for having my back and being my last line of defense. Thank you to Robin Vuchnich for your exquisite cover art. Your design brings a smile to my heart.

Thank you to the welcoming and supportive communities of Sisters in Crime and the James River Writers.

In memory of my parents ... with much gratitude ... to my mom, who always made sure I had plenty of pens and paper to write my stories, and to my dad, who always encouraged me and whose biggest hope was that someday I would be writing books. *I did it Dad!*

ACKNOWLEDGMENTS

Thank you to my husband ... for all the years, for all the laughter, for all the support—my love always.